THE IMPORTANCE
OF HAVING
SPUNK

Cover design by Leif Sodergren

ISBN 978-91-979188-2-4

LEMONGULCHBOOKS
www.lemongulchbooks.com

Also by
Donovan O'Malley

LEMON GULCH
NEW EDITION

A darkly comic moral tale --
12-year-old over-grown precocious misfit Danny
narrates his surprising adventures in his search
for acceptance in "a uncaring world".

OUR YANK

A Comic Novel --
An American student comes of age in Oxford
during the Cuban Missile Crisis of 1962.

THE JIMMY JONES SKANDAL

The five-year-old with a secret!

A humorous bedtime story for grown-ups.
Illustrations by the author.

Coming soon --

MY DARLING PROSOPOPOEIA

The Rise and Fall of Ritterhouse Fay.

DONOVAN O'MALLEY

THE IMPORTANCE OF HAVING SPUNK

LEMONGULCHBOOKS
www.lemongulchbooks.com

1

"Am I being punished?!" sobs petite yet formidable Christine from the window of a speeding car. "Do the gods punish someone who desires something too much?! Am I the very stuff of legend?!"

"Turn left, Dexter!" cries Violet, Christine's devoted lover of five years, also formidable but not petite -- not even polite -- as she thumps this poor, addled man at the wheel.

"Ouch!" squeals Dexter and makes a hard left. Their car skids, plunges from a splendid Swedish highway down a narrow dirt road into thick pine forest aglow in midsummer twilight.

"Why do my fertile windows come and go like ducks on a dirty great pond?!" sobs Christine, twenty-something and counting. We're late! Perhaps too late!" Then, catching Violet's surreptitious grin from the corner of a flooding eye, adds "What is so sodding funny, Violet?!"

"I was only thinking of our little tiny Isabella Victoria Gloria," replies Violet, lying through her teeth. Duplicitous thirty-something Violet. It was she who made them late. It was she who had secretly held the roadmap upside down in Norway and issued false instructions to the poor Dexter. It was she, horrid Violet who shuddering with guilt had perpetrated this first instalment of a soon to be vile series of underhanded yet benevolent acts. It was she, it was she, it was she! These, my own horrid thoughts, thinks Violet, condemn me!

But guilty Violet also knows that her subterfuge is necessary for the derailment of Christine's madly impetuous and destructive new scheme. A scheme initiated by a single photograph! One sodding photograph born of a chance meeting with this poor addled man at the wheel who had proffered it. This American clown, forty-something Dexter who with his bimbo boyfriend, nineteen-year-old Brad, were spectators at that Judo tournament in Trondheim, Norway.

1

The photograph in question, when subjected to the frantic machinations of Christine's current reproductive hysteria, had coalesced into a nuclear event for her bewildered but utterly devoted and now guilt-ridden Violet.

To wit: Dexter showed Christine a photograph of his best friend, Dennis, who had lived for years with his younger Afro-Swedish lover, Lars, in a secluded cabin in Sweden miles from the taint of corrupting mankind. Christine had instantly fallen for Dennis's 'Viking' colouring, as well as his securely bucolic address. He was, Christine decided on the spot, to be the sperm donor for the child she ached...and ached...and ached to produce: Christine and Violet's long-sought Isabella Victoria Gloria. My God! and they were ready now! Their Judo School was flourishing, though they had even more grandiose ideas for it, and they'd just bought a house with a lovely garden in which their golden child could play.

But now Christine had unilaterally jettisoned their plan! The plan they two had perfected together, the sperm bank in Earls Court. And Christine alone had chosen a sperm donor whose name would forever attach itself to their lives and that of their child to be. I will prevent it, thinks suffering Violet, even if I must become a dirty, rotten rat to do it, Viking colouring or not! So Violet, burning with searing guilt, snaps, "You aimed us at the North Pole, Dexter, and drove for six hours Due North and made her late!"

Then, deceitful Violet, lying Violet, volatile Violet, thumps poor innocent Dexter decisively yet again on his aching shoulder.

Oh what a tangled web we weave when first we practise to deceive thinks Christine's forlorn lover. Violet thumps people only when she's totally upset then instantly regrets it. She is normally, ask her, she'll tell you, an even-tempered, delightfully mellow woman. This new, sharp tone she has abruptly under duress adopted, this unpleasant demeanour, is simply not her -- though others might in the past have taken exception. This newly acquired churlishness is but the result of the unbear- able stress that her mercurial darling, Christine, has thrust roughly upon her and forced her to bear. So she will, bearing the unbearable, appear to reluctantly acquiesce to Christine's crazy new scheme but secretly to undermine it. Chrissie, thinks Violet, must be made to realise that we must go back to our plan: London, and the Earls Court sperm bank and that personable Icelandic sperm technician, Gunilla Harridansdottir!

Violet gazes unhappily out the car window staring at the miserable greenish blur of a billion passing pines -- in any case, she thinks, we are late and the later the better! I am the keeper of the books. And they are cooked. Burnt to a crisp! This personalised Fertile Windows Schedule is in my hands alone. By making us late I have thrown at least one of Christine's fertile windows out the window! Then the guilt. That awful so very uncharacteristic guilt.

2

The two women, clad in identical red tartan hunting vests and crammed between their two gigantic backpacks perch tragically at the edge of the rear seat, mutually discontent, and pumping hot, wet breath into the back of poor addled Dexter's neck.

"I did not," mutters Dexter, unconsciously depressing the gas pedal in an extremely irritating and car-shuddering way, "I did not aim us at the North Pole."

"Yes you did, Dexter," says Christine, "We drove and drove and sodding drove."

"And drove," adds Violet, "Due sodding North."

"It was like the surface of the moon," moans Christine through drying tears.

"The surface of the moon, Dexter," adds Violet. Oh, this painful treachery! But it seems the sideshow must go on.

"We were meant," continues Dexter, rubbing his throbbing shoulder -- it's not the first time Violet has thumped him and had he not been a gentleman he'd have thumped her right back -- "We were meant to drive Due South from Trondheim, Norway, ladies, why would I aim us Due North?"

"Need I remind you that we are sharing expenses for this rented car? We have known you for three, gruelling days. You are not improving," replies Christine in a more normal yet ear-penetrating tone, further annoyed that they cannot communicate with their hosts-to-be just now because their mobile telephones are useless in this...this wilderness! There was so much groundwork to be done too! She might even have informed their prospective sperm donor of her intentions. On second thoughts...

Christine had always seen to most things and Violet had liked it that way. Until recently Violet found herself up against a brick wall, needed a change, as often happens after five years of a partnership. So she enrolled, with her equally brick-walled Chrissie, for evening-courses in Assorted Foreign Languages, Domestic Psychology, Humane Reproduction and last, but assuredly not least, Instinctual Knowledge, and had become almost thoroughly enlightened. But! "A lot of knowledge," almost-thoroughly-enlightened-Christine was constantly telling Violet, "is a dangerous thing. N'est ce-pas?"

This had proved to be disastrously true. Especially now that Humane Reproduction had unexpectedly merged with Instinctual Knowledge and hammered the last nail in the coffin of their mutual Earls Court Sperm Bank plans for Isabella Victoria Gloria.

Violet fumes a bit and plucks at a zipper in her tartan hunting vest -- they'd had no intention whatever to hunt! -- hunting was hateful! -- killing all though cuddly little birds and other desperately endangered species, but Christine had insisted upon the hunting vests just in case they were invited to a Hunt Breakfast somewhere in this alien Far North. Christine had read about Nordic Hunt Breakfasts in a travel brochure and insisted they experience one and Violet had protested and told her in that case she should hunt one down and Christine said she would hunt one down as she certainly had just the hunting vest for it and Violet said good for you and Christine said no, she had two sodding hunting vests and if it were too cold she would wear them both simultaneously and Violet, exhausted, had as usual backed down. It was futile to oppose Christine when she was on heat. Now, here they are, at the top of the sodding world nearly, in this frantic search for Nordic spunk and Violet is fed up. So she frowns and says, carefully, "I have but one word to say to you, Christine. But one word."

"Do not say that word, Violet!"

"I shall say it! One word!"

"All right! Say it if you must!"

"One word," snaps Violet, "Earls Court."

"That's two words," says Dexter.

"Shut up, Dexter," says Violet.

"Shut up, Dexter," says Christine, who continues, "Earls Court has been settled, well and truly settled!"

"By you, Christine!" says Violet. That's it, thinks Violet, just the right balance -- resist too much and Christine might demand the last remaining reproductive responsibility allowed me, the Fertile Windows Notebook. Then all would be lost.

"Where in God's name is Brad?" moans Dexter.

"Can't you be silent for five minutes about that moronic bimbo?" snaps Violet, well aware that poor Dexter had sulked nearly silently for the last million miles.

This absurd loss of valuable time, worries Christine, could put an abrupt end to all, well, most of hers and Violet's, hopes and dreams -- at least for another month. But it would then be too late for this desirable, colourful though problematic, spunk of the North. She wasn't getting any younger and an opportunity like this could not, Violet's violent objections aside, be missed. But Dexter had made them late, jeopardising the time needed for the vital persuasion of the Donor-to-be. "Oh, why must it always be 'cherchez el hombre'?!" thinks Christine, making expert use of two of her evening-class Assorted Languages at once and wondering how she can, in the immediate future, use guilty Dexter's culpability creatively. All, even ethical behaviour, will be willingly slaughtered on the bloody alter of hers and Violet's present need. Whether Violet likes it or not. N'est ce-pas?

5

Dexter, anxious and heartbreakingly eager at the very same time because he hopes soon to see Brad, the recent light of his life, twitches violently -- as he always does when thinking of Brad -- and twists the steering wheel just in time. The car veers sharply.

"What was that?!" screams Christine.

"An animal!" cries Dexter, "We nearly ran down a wild animal!"

"An animal?!" cries Christine.

"What is this place?" snaps Violet, "A sodding zoo?"

"What kind of animal?!" cries Christine.

"How should I know what kind of animal?!" yells Dexter, "I'm not an Eskimo!"

"That's a new one on me, Dexter," snaps Violet, "I thought we were on our way to visit your two frigging Eskimo friends."

"Language," says Christine, "Shame on you, Vi, you should know better. And why, Violet Heather Rose, should you know better?"

Violet hangs her head, "Because I was reared in a convent," she says, pointedly ignoring Dexter's ironical smile in the rear-view mirror.

"That's right, love. And Dexter's dear friend, Dennis, is not an Eskimo. There are no Eskimos in Sweden, darling. Eskimos live at the South Pole tending their penguin flocks. That's what Mummy always said when I was a wee girl and I have never had reason then or now to doubt her. Dexter's friend, Dennis, is a Viking. A Viking with a capital 'V'.

"Perhaps not with a capital 'V', darling," says Dexter who, fully emerged from his million-mile sulk, must abruptly twist the wheel once again. The car veers again.

"Another animal," mutters Dexter, cursing the day before yesterday when he'd met these two women whose combined hot breath currently flambés the back of his neck. But it had saved money and allowed him to buy a bargain pair of lederhosen plus new designer briefs for Brad. When and if Brad ever turns up.

3

Back-packed, lederhosened Brad, drop-dead gorgeous, built, and as dim as a guy can be without actually being called dim to his face, pulls berries from a bush a mere ten yards from the winding forest road that Dexter and Christine and Violet in a billowing cloud of dust and mutual recrimination, have yet to come careening down. Brad had set out on his own to hitchhike, to find himself.

He had earlier in the day thanked an equally thankful, lederhosen-loving German motorist for the ride from Trondheim with multiple stops along the way to admire the beauty of the landscape -- and other things -- and had been dropped off by the side of the highway with a large fistful of Euros and a profusion of stray pine-needles sticking to his bottom.

People of both sexes were constantly poking money -- and other things -- into Brad's face, and other places. He just never could turn down money, or other things, in other places. "If it feels good, do it!" Brad often says -- a hangover, thought Dexter, from Brad's die-hard hippie grandparents. Though Dexter hadn't a clue that Brad often acted upon this simple inherited thesis. Brad, to Dexter, was an innocent. The last of the criminal innocents.

So, with his minutely detailed map of Swedish trails and tiny forest roads tucked under his arm, Brad mashes those newly plucked berries between his fingers and rolls them into cigarette paper and sits on a rock in the clear, clean air. He lights up. Do not ask him what he is thinking. For he does not know. A perfect vacuum is better left unexplored. Better, ignorance, than the abyss.

As Brad sucks at his berry ciggie, a rudimentary thought splashes about deep within his head but soon gurgles, chokes and drowns. "Geez" he says, certain something enlightening has flashed close by, "Geez."

And, agreeably baffled, he pulls his MP3 earphones closer over his faultlessly formed ears and clicks. Mother Nature's miscellaneous murmurings will now be accompanied.

"Oh, Isabella Victoria Gloria, where are you, little tiny one?" moans Christine.

"Isabella is twinkling, Chrissie, in the heavenly firmament. That's where our wee Isabella is. Directly over Earls Court."

"We are sharing expenses with a rat, whispers Christine. A rat who has made us seriously, perhaps tragically late."

I'm the true rat, thinks Violet and hides her face and winces.

"A rat," continues Christine, with a tiny, vindictive tug over the back of the car seat at poor Dexter's thinning hair. She reflects for a moment, drops her head into Violet's comforting cleavage, "Is it a crime to want?" she moans, then sits up with a jolt, her watery eyes aflame with hurt, "Why must my fertile windows come and go, without reason, like ducks on a dirty great pond!"

"Chrissie, you've got to be strong. You've got to have spunk!"

"Of course we've got to have spunk! That's the whole sodding point! We've come for spunk! But it could be too late to matter!" sobs Christine, pounding on the car-seat directly behind Dexter's head.

"Now look what you've done, Dexter," growls Violet. You've made her cry. You men are all alike."

"Wonderful, isn't it?" mutters Dexter, rubbing his still throbbing shoulder and rather liking poor Violet who is almost as miserable and needy as he is. Anyway, he's finally sussed she held the map upside down. He may be blameless. But he's no stool pigeon.

Christine's sobs suddenly cease. Her eyes widen with wonder. "Violet! Why isn't it getting dark?! It is eleven pm! Am I going mad?! Why isn't it getting dark?!"

"Don't you remember in Norway, Chrissie? It never got dark in Norway either."

"So it didn't. I thought it was just me."

"We're in Sweden, girlies, the land of the midnight sun,"

mutters Dexter attempting to keep their car centred on this tiny, twisting, excuse for a road.

"We knew that! And do not refer to us as girlies," says Violet ominously, "We are women."

"And we're late," moans Christine, whose new, precious plan awry, is lovingly embraced and rocked by perpetrator Violet, her formidable, even rude, though devoted, plethorically worried and only recently deceptive, lover of five years.

"We're so very late," mews Christine into the harsh linen of Violet's identical tartan hunting vest, "and soon it will be too late. Dexter has made us late."

4

"Dexter is late," sighs Lars and pours a large bowl of creamy batter into two cake tins. Lars will use this time efficiently making even more cake. With guests, he reckons, you got to have plen-ty cake. In this case, butter cream tortes -- a veritable host of butter cream tortes. He likes that word: "veritable". It has four lovely syllables. He loves English and all its syllables. English is so wonderfully eclectic, has a veritable treasure-chest of words. Far more words, it seems, than his native Swedish.

"Dexter is undoubtedly late through no fault of his own," replies Dennis, "He just tumbles into these situations."

"If Dexter is too much late he will be struck down by Hell Storm," says Lars, "It is foreseen. The telephones will explode in all likelihood. Like last time. It is good I bake now. Later I maybe cannot. In all likelihood."

Lars likes that word, "likelihood" too. It sounds friendly, flexible though secure. He squats and places the cake tins carefully into the oven. "One hundred seventy five degrees Celsius."

"My film is a catastrophe!" moans Dennis. He thumps a DVD case against his sweating forehead.

"Dexter is six hours and twenty-five minutes late."

"They're driving from Trondheim," says Dennis, still

9

thumping his forehead, "Their arrival time was only approximate. Anything can happen on the road from Trondheim."

As indeed it had nine years ago -- he'd met Lars on that road from Trondheim, measuring in precisely metered footsteps the exact walking distance between Trondheim and Bergen for his Master's Degree in Physio-Topography. Or something. For which Lars has yet to find practical use, although he derives immense satisfaction from just knowing what he knows. Which Lars himself reckons, during endless hours in the kitchen, is the beginning of wisdom.

Lars taps the temperature gauge on the cooker. "Celsius. Not Fahrenheit. You never remember, Dennis, you live in Sweden ten years and you never remember this vital difference. Who are these bloomin' people Dexter brings?"

"Two English lesbians from London. That's all I know. I hope to God they're quiet. I need my peace, particularly now. Lars, love, what shall we do about my worthless, my vile DVD film?!"

Lars sets his mixing bowl in the sink, turns on the tap. "Vimmin? Dexter is driving vimmen to us?"

" Yes, Vimmen. In a car."

"Vhy vimmen?"

"Stop that! Your English is better than mine. I know it has always amused you to do that but you do it to get a rise out of me."

"It's the only way to get a rise out of you. You never rise anymore."

Lars didn't really mean this. What he means is that Dennis doesn't rise as often as he had in the past. But they had been together almost ten years -- legally married (in Sweden) for eight -- and Dennis rose an astonishing amount considering his age. No. That wasn't truthful of you, Lars, that 'never'. I'll be more careful, thinks Lars, in the future, in all likelihood. I am the logical one. Dennis is the creative one. Dennis is the sensitive soul. Dennis tries so hard to please. Too hard.

So Lars feels a little guilty. Is good to feel guilty. Sometimes. Better to feel a little guilty sometimes than to be pompous as he is on occasion. He would be the first to admit it. Why? Because it's the bloomin' truth, isn't it? Lars is nothing if not matter-of-fact.

"I've got a lot on my mind, love, besides this bloody film and our bloomless tomatoes, and The Mob," says Dennis. "I believe I am going half-mad."

"You are already half-mad. All geniuses are."

"How do we pay Biff and Bart? They'll sue."

"They will not sue. This is not America. We will give these vimmen cake. Ja. With lady guests we got to have plen-ty cake."

"By all means. Let 'em eat cake."

"And beer," Says Lars, "lesbians love beer. With lesbians we got to have plen-ty beer. Ja. Plen-ty beer, plen-ty cake."

Dennis taps his DVD-battered forehead repeatedly with a bitten-to-the-nail thumb, gazes hopelessly at Lars who looks up, grins encouragingly.

"The English like cake, Denny. You like cake. Yum-yum!"

"But Biff and Bart still want their money. Five hundred pounds ain't hay."

"Pooh on Biff and Bart! We could have done that DVD ourselves!"

"No we couldn't, love. I'm too fat and you're too old."

Dennis lays his hand gently on Lars's neck, counts himself lucky to have that neck to lay his hand on -- to have any neck, at his age, to lay his hand on. But most particularly, this neck, his coffee-coloured Swede's neck. Lars turns his cheek, nuzzles, thinks, My dear old Denny. All is right in the world.

Dennis the worrier glows, thinks: Almost all is right in the world, For the next five minutes. God I hope these women are quiet.

The car flies down the road -- suddenly veers.

"Another animal?!" screams Violet.

"A blow-out! Hold onto your sombreros, girls, screams Dexter, "we've got a blow-out!"

"A puncture!" screams Christine, clinging to Violet, "Vi! We've got a sodding puncture!"

"I am not too old. I am thir-ty-one," says Lars and opens

the fridge. At least three dozen butter packets tumble from an over-packed shelf to the floor. He stoops, places one carefully beside another mixing bowl, sets the others back in the fridge. "I am glad we got plen-ty butter. With lady guests we got to have plen-ty butter. I am thir-ty-one. You are not so bloomin' fat."

Lars believes everything he says. If he didn't believe everything he said, he'd force himself to. Inconsistency can find no perch in the head of this determined Swede. Not if he can help it. And he can. And he does. He has two Master's degrees and a pending Ph.D to prove it.

5

"Do you think it's a bear, Vi?" asks Christine, joining Dexter tight behind the formidable and recently often rude Violet who gestures towards the rustling pines holding aloft their only weapon, the tire wrench, "Do bears rustle like that?"

"Possibly," replies Violet.

But of course it's not a bear. It is only hiking Brad, light of Dexter's life who, safe under his boisterous earphones and just out of sight, pauses, takes out a hunting knife and scrapes off a bit of odd mushroom growing from the side of a mighty pine he has only a moment before with ineffable gratitude, hugged. He drops this foreign fungi into his lederhosen pocket beside his ciggie-kit.

Only yards away, Christine and Violet, now on their hands and knees, scratch through the shrubbery. "Why did you do this to us, Violet? Why did you chuck our wheel nuts at Dexter and strand us in this desolate place?"

"Because I felt like it."

"I knew there was an excellent reason. I forgive you darling."

"Oh good," says Violet, biting her tongue and ruing, yes, that is the proper word, ruing the evening a few days before, that they'd met poor, addled Dexter who now ferries them into this horrid, terrifying forest primeval to meet two utter strangers and appropriate the spunk of one.

"With lady guests we got to have plen-ty wood," grunts Lars and splits a small log with an axe. "Lady guests like it cosy. Even in the summer days. (Chop) There is Hell Storm coming. With bloomin' storms we got to have plenty bloomin' wood." (Chop)

Lars fondly remembers a woman guest from California who had stayed with him and his mother when he was a child. She constantly used that fascinating word, 'bloomin', for everything but flowers, and she needed an electric heater in the guestroom all that summer to foil the bracing northern air.

"It's no good making safe-sex propaganda pornography if the pornography is no good as pornography," whines Dennis, "Nobody'll buy it, love. And a shrinking audience -- pardon the pun."

(Chop) "What is pun?"

Lars knows perfectly well 'what is pun' but it's fun to needle Dennis -- keeps him from being too serious.

"I lose my libido instantly when I watch it. Out the window! Kaput! Do you lose yours?"

But Lars is not to be deterred from the task at hand, "Where is Dexter and his vimmen? Have you (Chop) melted the butter?"

"Nope."

"Go melt butter. Who is this Brad-man?"

Beating time to his MP3 player with an inappropriately sandaled foot, considering the terrain, Brad rolls his crushed tree-fungus into a cigarette paper, licks it and seals it, sticks it between his lips and lights up. He takes a deep puff, pulls a goony face, drops himself on a mossy fallen tree trunk, beats time for a moment that seems like an hour but isn't, pulls himself up and, taking an uncanny interest in everything he passes -- trees, plants, insects, toads, birds, elk dung (some behemoth rabbit?!), he disappears into the thickening, darkening yet beckoning forest.

"Brad was meant to come with Dexter, share expenses," says

Dennis, "He cancelled. Wants to hitch rides, travel on his own to 'find himself'."

Brad, staring at the glowing sunset sky, walks into a tree, falls over a small, mossy hillock, finds himself sprawled on his stomach. Giggles. Rolls his eyes. Giggles again. Then bursts into tears at the sheer beauty of it all.

"A friend of Dexter who does not desire to travel with Dexter?" asks Lars who seriously considers the very deepest responsibilities of friendship as he whips a delicious sauce in a large bowl while Dennis melts butter in a pot on the cooker. "Pooh! He is no bloomin' friend."
"I'm only telling you what Dexter told me over the telephone from Trondheim. Through bitterest tears."
Dennis wishes he could cry more. It would be such a relief. Crying over sad movies simply doesn't count. He must be more able to cry over personal crises and/or literary and deeply cultural events. He knows he would cry if Lars left him. Dreadfully! Why am I so morbidly thoughtful just now? thinks Dennis. Yes! Biff and Bart mentioned Sicily in their last phone call. I was too nervy to get what it was about. Is it a sign? Is my life about to come to an abrupt Italianate end? Will Biff and Bart set The Mob on me? Are they more than just extraordinarily handsome-hunk janitors in a funfair? Do they own the funfair?! Are they not what they seem? This has lately been one of the horrors of Dennis's last harrowing thoughts before merciful sleep claims him each night -- something, anything, being not what it seems! Love, friendship, a seemingly harmless snake! How ridiculous! He must not take himself so seriously. Must not allow fantastical thoughts to master him! His exceedingly fruitful imagination was always his strongest and weakest trait -- his Achilles heel in a shining boot. A boot that has kicked him too often in his well-formed, only slightly overweight bottom.
The butter begins to smoke, Lars grabs the pot from Dennis, begins expertly to fold the melted butter into that delicious sauce, says: "This sauce will lounge betwixt the cake's three

layers."

"Maybe my failure lies with Biff and Bart," moans Dennis, "their accents are atrocious! I should have coached them more. Jesus! Where do Swedes learn their English?"

"Sicily?" quips Lars, "We need more butter. Melt, please. Females love butter. With lady guests we got to have plen-ty butter."

Lars continues to whip the sauce as Dennis frowns -- he must have Lars's attention somehow! He desperately needs Lars's attention while under stress and Lars is impossible when he's cooking! I'm such a baby! thinks Dennis, I'm hysterical! If I hadn't lost my unfinished epic novel I'd have some gravitas to lean on.

Dennis fetches another packet of butter, drops it in the pot. "Biff and Bart looked the part. If only they could act. God! I dream of making a socially conscious safe-sex film rippling with muscles and responsible sexual attitudes but it's always... you know, love, always..."

"Ja. I know about your dream. I righteously concur. But why does Dexter bring us vimmen?"

"It was convenient."

"Vimmen is convenient?"

#

Christine, Violet and Dexter, their six eyes peeled for those recently jettisoned wheel-nuts, crawl wearily through flesh-tearing shrubbery over knee-bruising pebbles unwittingly discarded by long-gone glaciers.

"You've been here before. Do they really have bears out here, Dexter?" asks Violet, jumping from her knees and colliding with a low but luckily flexible limb. Dexter stands too, stretches, wipes his brow. "Yes, love, they do really have bears out here. But you must promise to leave the hairy beasts alone."

"Get back on those knees, Dexter!" snaps Violet, "You've had

15

plenty of practice there! Help us find our nuts! "

There! She's done it again, regrets it instantly but cannot apologise. She must attempt to be a better person in spite of all these recent tribulations. A better person for Isabella Victoria Gloria's sake -- a perfect mother for their child to be. But good God! If she began apologising now she'd be hoarse by dinner. And dinner, when is that to be? She's starving. Why is she here? They needn't be here at all! It's just that Chrissie...

"You've got all the nuts you'll ever need, Violet," replies Dexter who nevertheless drops to his knees, roots under a bush for the foolishly jettisoned wheel nuts.

Christine titters, Violet chuckles, Dexter giggles. They laugh together, big stress-releasing guffaws, aware for a mutual moment of the absurdity of their pine-treed predicament. It will be their last collective laugh for some time.

In their chicken yard, Lars pours grain into a feeder. Dennis follows, anxiously stirring a large bowl of butter cream icing. Several hens cluster round, peck at the grain and a large rooster approaches menacingly. Dennis rubs a shallow scratch on the back of his hand, thinks "All I need is another rooster attack," backs away, says: "Biff and Bart want their money or they'll sue. Or maybe something...worse. Like The Mob."

"You do go on about The Mob, Dennis!"

Dennis had read recent Online newspaper articles about the New Crime Syndicates sweeping up from the south over Northern Europe. He's even jumpier than usual.

"It is 22.30. Where is Dexter and his vimmen?"

Dennis leans against the henhouse, stirs his bowl, contemplating a contract on his head, cries "Oh, love, my miserable safe-sex film is a flop! And I'm a flop!"

The menacing rooster misconstrues Dennis's futile cry for a taunt, leaps at him. Dennis topples backwards, a scratch on the back of his other hand. Lars handily catches the mixing bowl, looks into it. "With guests we got to have plen-ty butter cream icing!"

Dennis sprawls in the muck, gazes up at Lars in admiration.

Let the Mob take me and spare him. Oh, but he'd miss me so, this devoted lad of mine. Maybe they should just take the both of us?

Dennis doesn't really believe this. Fantasy is simply his salvation, that Achilles heel in a shining boot. "Yes, he thinks, 'my salvation', grasping this newly lodged quasi-comfort snatched in extremis from his fervid and swelling fantasy library. Imagination and Lars. He has them both! What a lucky man I am, he repeats in his head several times till that throng of threatening thoughts diminishes. What an extremely lucky man I am!

In the lingering twilight the women, under their massive backpacks, and Dexter, toting his fine, fake-alligator suitcase, make their weary way down this endless rut of a road.

"Where in God's name is Brad?!" moans Dexter.

"A bear ate him," snaps Violet.

"It's getting dark," whimpers Christine, "It's finally getting dark."

"Wouldn't it just?!" snaps Violet, "Just when we needed it not to! I hate the sodding wilderness!"

"It *is* uncooperative." moans Christine.

"And so far from Earls Court," adds Violet, drooping.

If dispirited Violet, or any of them, had looked anywhere but in the dust of the rutty road at their feet, they would have seen at this moment through a densely leaf-framed space, sprawled on a mossy hillock about ten yards away, Brad, another homemade ciggie clinging from his lip. He thumps to the secret rhythm of his earphones and simultaneously pulls a sleeping-bag from his backpack.

"Hoooot! Hoooot!" hoots a wise old owl staring curiously down from a pine-needled limb. Two sleek white-tailed deer graze nearby and a fat brown toad huddles on a rock a few inches from Brad's sandaled foot. None of these innocent creatures feel threatened by Brad for he himself is a child of Nature. And if he'd bothered to lift those lush-lashed lids on his baby blue eyes he could have just made out his worried friend, Dexter, plus alligator suitcase plus Christine and Violet under their massive backpacks as, hungry and plotting in their desperate ways for disparate things, they trudge into this now darkening, still dazzling, dilatory sunset.

Brad, yawning, hangs his much-admired lederhosen on a nearby limb, carefully arranges his sleeping bag on a bed of moss, climbs into it, all the while beating time to his very personal music. Lying on his back, he lights another fungi ciggie, takes a deep drag and gazes, awestruck, up at the miraculous purpling sky in which a handful of twinkling stars have begun to embed themselves. He takes another deep drag and wipes a tear from his eye. A sob catches at the back of his throat. "I am so insignificant" he whispers, uncharacteristically reflective, to the purpling twilight.

'Oh, Brad. You are so right,' pipes a tiny sweet voice in his head. Brad grins. It is good to be right. He closes his eyes and a tear trickles off his cheek, tumbles, douses a tiny beetle at its evening meal of greenest moss.

7

"I vant to be alone," gasps Greta Garbo from the upstairs bedroom's television screen.

Dennis slouches, misting, on the bed as Garbo speaks her last words to her very last lover. It's so easy to cry over this, isn't it? thinks Dennis, I must grow up! Grown men don't cry when consumptive courtesans die.

But there is a certain painful joy in the contemplation of it. For Dennis, Painful Joy is a given.

"The strawberries need veeding," calls Lars up the stairs, "They von't vait. I go now. I veed them. Hell Storm is coming."

"Yes, love," replies Dennis as he dabs tissues at his welling eyes "Veed avay. With lady guests we got to have plen-ty strawberries."

"We got plen-ty butter, plen-ty cake, plen-ty wood, plen-ty strawberries, plen-ty beer and no bloomin' guests," calls Lars, "Where is Dexter with his vimmen!?"

A sudden hammering at the cabin door!

"On our doorstep, apparently. I'll be right down, love."

Dennis clicks off the telly, dabs his tears away before the basin mirror -- he must learn to control himself! He is a solidly masculine man. This, he has been assured by many, is universally agreed. These poignant lapses, well, serve only to define his humanity, his vulnerability to the errr...the vicissitudes of others. He dabs his eyes again, makes a sad face, makes a happy face, thrusts a comb through his perfectly lovely, curly, golden hair, pinches pink his somewhat chubby cheeks, wonders if Mum will ring again tonight and berate him for not providing a grandchild or two. Or three. Or four.

Still smarting from Greta's mannered demise -- Dennis feels artifice so deeply -- he shoots out of the bedroom and down the stairs, comes immediately face to face with his dear old friend, Dexter.

"Jesus H. Christ!" hisses Dexter and slams his fake alligator suitcase to the floor and waves his meticulously manicured fingers in tight little circles in the air ala Bette Davis in Beyond the Forest, his all-time favourite film ("Yes! Yes! I am Rosa Moline and I've got peritonitis!").

"You are late, Dexter," grunts Lars and passes out the front door, calling after "I like your new nose. The strawberries need veeding. They von't vait. Hell Storm approaches in all likelihood."

"You don't know the half of it!" moans Dexter, glowing from Lars's apt compliment on his pricey nose job.

Dennis hugs Dexter, says "Love your new nose! Pricey?"

Dexter, doubly pleased, nods and says "Jesus H. Christ!" again and motions through the door with a thumb at Christine and Violet who stand wildly gesticulating at the centre of Lars's neatly clipped lawn. "Jesus H. Christ!" gasps Dexter yet again and drops himself on a large leather sofa. "Sorry, Dennis, "But I'm just a wee bit tense after the journey from Hell with the dildo duo," he adds, accepting with a thankful nod, Dennis's hastily presented glass of whisky.

"Violet!" shrieks Christine from the garden, "What a gorgeous setting!"

"Chrissie! I've had enough! I've lost my nerve! I will not let you go through with this!" cries Violet the rat, temporarily throwing caution and even deceit to the winds.

"But I must, Violet! I must!"

"You can't!"

"But I must! For our little tiny Isabella Victoria Gloria's sake!"

Violet flails her arms and shakes her head, crying "No! No! No!"

"Yes! Yes! Yes!" replies Christine at a similar decibel.

"Hello," says Lars and passes on his way to the strawberry patch, "Strawberries von't vait."

"No! No! No!" cries Violet.

"Yes! Yes! Yes!" cries Christine who sinks to her knees and pulls flailing Violet down beside her. "Look, love!" whispers Christine close into Violet's ear, urgently gesturing at the dubiously darkening Nordic sky, "Up there! It's little tiny Isabella!"

"Where?!" cries Violet, scrubbing at her wet eyes with her rough tartan sleeve.

"There! That little tiny star in the middle!"

"Oh, God! It is! Our little tiny Isabella!" screams Violet, guilt momentarily jettisoned by joy.

"She's waiting for us, love!" cries Christine, "All I've got to do is get knocked-up!"

"Oh, my!" whispers Dennis from the cabin porch where he and Dexter now gaze with disquietude: Dennis's puzzled, Dexter's almost palpable. "What are they going on about?"

"Don't ask," replies Dexter, splashing his whisky, "Do not ask," and jerkily splashing it again.

Dennis shrugs, decides it's time he's greeted his crazy guests so he switches on the porch lamp and plunges with open arms towards Christine and Violet who have yet to notice anyone, though both have a hazy recollection of veeding strawberries and some transient handsome black man with a heavy accent.

As Dennis passes beneath the porch lamp, Christine squints up and here, through need-driven eyes, sees his blond, curly hair aflame in a golden aura; his pink, freshly pinched cheeks; his tall, strong and only moderately seedy physique; his, well, Viking demeanour.

"Violet!" cries Christine almost reverently, "This, indeed, is our Viking!" and instantly superimposed over the approaching Dennis is the pullulating vision of an ecstatic little girl in the purest white, canvas judo clothing. "Mummy! Mummy!" she squeals, "Mummy, Mummy!"

Christine grabs Violet's hand and drags her, kicking, across Lars's nicely clipped lawn to scoop up and swing their imaginary golden child between them.

"Isabella!" cries Christine, "Little tiny Isabella Victoria Gloria!"

Dennis pauses and watches, mesmerised by the mad game these two woman play. He lowers his welcoming arms but retains his smile and admittedly masculine stance, though his handsome but only marginally seedy jaw sags.

"Hello?!" he calls, "Hello and welcome?!"

Violet's joy vanishes. She sobers and lambasted by guilt and dire discontent explodes into tears and flees to seclude herself behind a nearby too easily found pine. Christine, still immersed in her phantom-child reverie, pivots and gazes dreamily at Dennis who has at last begun to return to his own human form.

"Welcome," says Dennis, "I'm Dennis."

"Oh, I know!" cries Christine and snatches his photo from her hunting vest pocket, thrusts it in his face, "I know!"

Where did she get my photo? wonders Dennis for a moment but is soon distracted, nay terrified, by the gimlet gaze Christine has fixed upon him.

Violet, sobbing softly, watches from behind that pine tree, despises trees -- especially pines, especially so many pines, loathes cabins in the woods, impeccably clipped lawns, interminable twilights, Scandinavia, and this new menace, Dennis. Though not necessarily in that order.

8

"I didn't like the way Christine stared at me at dinner," splutters Dennis through his late evening toothpaste. Lars lounges in their bed happily thumbing through a massive cookbook. "She looks at me," sighs Dennis, "as though I am a leg of lamb and she is a shark."

He gargles, spits in the bedroom basin.

"I got leg of lamb in freezer. We will have lamb roast tomorrow," replies Lars, flipping to a page of his well-worn cookbook, "Hell Storm is coming. I roast if electricity is in function. If not, I use wood stove. I hope they enjoyed their fish dinner. They said nothing. The little whining one just stared at you while the big mean one glared at her."

"And they refused the beer every time you offered it. They've got something up their sleeves, Lars. These are not your average lesbians."

"I will accoutre decorative sleeve on this lamb leg."

"Accoutre?" asks Dennis.

Lars holds up the cookbook. "Like this."

Dennis, gazes absently at the illustration Lars has thrust at him, repeats "These are not your average lesbians. They've got something up their sleeves."

Violet, pouting in the little guestroom directly below Dennis and Lars's bedroom, yanks a sodden hanky from her sleeve, swabs her eyes, blows her nose, and flops herself on one of the two narrow but extremely comfortable -- Lars saw to that -- beds. She sniffles and watches Christine take from her own backpack an identical tartan hunting vest to the one she wears and lay it on the bed beside Violet's. This makes, thinks Violet -- including the two they presently wear -- four identical tartan hunting vests and the hunting season is months away though Christine hasn't the slightest intention to hunt anything,

22

with the possible exception of that Hunt Breakfast but... Violet simply can't finish the thought and whimpers, eyes downcast, nose a-dribble: "Chrissie? Chrissie, baby, whistle to me. Whistle to Vi-Vi. Whistle 'Melancholy Baby' to your melancholy baby. It calms Vi-Vi down." Though Violet knows she doesn't deserve that soothing whistle, considering the darkest evil that presently lurks in her rat-like heart.

"No!" snaps Christine and empties onto her bed the entire contents of her backpack, carefully lays each item side by side and looks up suspiciously at Violet. "All right, Violet, where is it?"

"Where is what?" sniffs Violet and guiltily dabs her eyes with the sodden hanky, seriously wondering if her deceitful ruse is worth the awful cost of such suffering.

"My turkey-baster. Where is it?!"

Christine moves in quickly, pushes Violet aside, up-ends Violet's backpack and out falls an enormous eye-dropper-like turkey-baster.

"Thief!" cries Christine, "Do you realise what I paid for this turkey-baster in Norway?! You'd think they'd never heard of turkey-basters in Norway!" She thrusts out her hand. "And great grandmother Nana's petite demitasse, Violet, I'll have it! I perpetually carry it with me. It's my major good luck talisman as you very well know. Where, Violet, is my Nana's petite demitasse?!"

Violet rises, reluctantly pulls a tiny porcelain cup from one of the huge wool stockings in the jumble of clothes on the bed, hands it to Christine who spits on it and polishes it against her hunting vest.

"This petite demitasse is ancient. It is appropriately ornate. It is vital."

Violet grabs Christine's hand, holds tight. "Chrissie? Do you really mean to go through with this?"

"How much time have we got?"

Violet lets go Christine's hand, looks away.

"How much time, Vi-Vi-? Until my next sodding window? According to you, we've missed the sodding first one!"

Violet takes the small pad from her pocket, turns the pages back and forth, turns deviously back to Christine and lies: "You peak tomorrow afternoon. At...errr... (that horrid guilt now floods in) precisely four-thirty, give or take a few seconds."

"Leaving almost no preparation time! It's extraordinarily lucky for Dexter I haven't ovulated yet or he'd be minus one withered gonad! We'd better get some sleep, Violet. Tomorrow is a busy day and I don't like the way Dennis looks at me as though I were a man-eating shark. He might be excessively difficult to persuade."

Christine pauses, ponders for a moment, nearly forlorn but not quite, "Am I really that frightening, Violet?"

Violet hesitates, looks away guiltily -- why must she feel constantly guilty?! -- Christine herself has caused this untenable situation! Why must I, her devoted Violet, shoulder all the blame and self-imposed guilt?! In a flash she knows -- compliments of evening-class Domestic Psychology. Because I've got a sodding Guilt-Complex. That's why! Relieved, Violet begins to contemplate deceitful deeds not yet committed and the enlightened ease with which she will now commit them.

"Am I frightening?" repeats Christine almost poignantly.

"Sometimes," replies Violet, subtly pushing thoughts of major deception temporarily aside, "But I do love you, Chrissie, darling. I believe I loved you even before I met you and, of course, even more, now, after I've met you. You are simply my cuppa." But not served in that flaming petite demitasse! Thinks wicked Violet who continues "I will always love you because there is something about you that is totally wunderbar" -- might as well throw in her evening-class German too -- "And though I am terrified of this whole precipitous and tragic change of plans, I shall... cooperate -- has deception no limits? -- to the best of my..."

"Violet."

"Yes, Chrissie, my very own dearest darling?"

"Do not hide my turkey-baster again."

"No, Chrissie."

"Or my sodding petite demitasse."

"No, Chrissie."

9

"I'll answer it, Lars. It's two AM, it'll be Mummy. She can't sleep and intends to make very certain I can't either."

Dennis flicks on the bed-lamp, takes up the phone, "Hello, Mummy."

Diagonally across the North Sea -- though many miles farther south in London, Dennis's mother sits before her dressing table scooping great gobs of face cream from a large jar and slapping it on with nervous little gestures. Her telephone is fortunately cradled in a most convenient device on her shoulder.

"Mummy, darling, is that you?"

"I want a grandchild, Dennis," says Lars sleepily.

"I want a grandchild, Dennis," says Dennis's Mum, many miles farther south, "Deborah Cramer was presented with grandchild number five, a bouncing baby girl..."

"Oh, I'm so glad the infant didn't shatter when they dropped her!" replies Dennis with mock alarm.

"...promptly at four-forty-five yesterday afternoon," says Mum adroitly ignoring her son's little jest. "It's her sixth grandchild. Her daughter just shoots them out year after year like clockwork. Doesn't bat an eye! I want a grandchild, Dennis. If your father were around, he would agree with me."

"That would be the first time," murmurs Dennis.

"What did you say, dear?"

"I said I'm sure he would, Mummy darling."

"Don't be snide to your mother, Dennis. It's much too late at night for that."

"It's morning, Mummy. It's the very next day."

"Really? Then I'm sorry for calling so late --"

"So early."

"-- but I'm lonely and I lose all track of time."

"Look, Mummy, I'm sorry I'm so irritable, but I'm being harassed by The Mob, dear."

"The Mob?"

"Possibly."

"Do you mean the May-fia, darling?"

"The Southern Lion is at the Northern gates, Mummykins. The new Crime Syndicates are swooping up from the Mediterranean and making a bee-line for dear old Sweden. Surf the Net, darling. See for yourself."

"I gave up surfing, darling, years ago. After I had you I was never the same. My physiognomy was irretrievably altered. Besides I hated those dreadful sunburns -- but Dennis darling, how life-threatening! Have the May-fia stuck a contract on your head?!"

"I hope not," says Dennis, worriedly running his fingers through his curly golden locks.

"Are you being swindled, dear, threatened with erasing? No kisses of death?"

"I hope not."

"Extorted?"

"Not to my immediate knowledge, Mummy. Although I have been not so subtly harassed by telephone."

"Stay away from that Mob, Dennis, and that Mob will stay away from you."

"Sound advice. Look, Mummy, I'll ring you in the morning -- I mean later today."

"I want a grandchild, Dennis. By whatever means. You are forty and I can bear it no longer."

"But Mummy --"

"They're doing miraculous things with lesbians these days. There are thousands of lesbians about, dear. You'd be flabbergasted."

"Would I?"

"Find yourself a qualified international lesbian on that worldwide internet thingy of yours, darling. Make Mummy happy."

"Look, Mummy, I'll ring you in the morning -- I mean later today."

"No you won't," mumbles Lars sleepily, "You say you will but you never do."

Mum wipes the face cream off with great upward strokes -- keeps her still firm, and meltingly lovely, sixty-something face from sagging -- pauses, takes up a silver-framed photo from her dressing table and gazes fondly for a moment first at the prepubescent Dennis, then at her young self and her preternaturally handsome young ex-husband, suddenly remembers she's on the telephone, "No you won't," she repeats, "You say you'll ring but you never do."

"I promise, Mummy."

"Pwomise?"

"Pwomise."

"Pwomise," mumbles Lars sleepily from the far corner of the bed, "I bloomin' pwomise."

"Goodnight then, Denny-Dens," says Mum, "and remember, I want a grandchild. Somehow. Hugs to Larsy."

Mum hangs up the telephone and wipes a tear from a cream-clogged though still elegantly long eyelash -- she's kept her looks and knows it, wishes she could have kept her husband, and would have. If he hadn't...she drops this unproductive late night dialogue with herself -- she's so much like Dennis. Or rather, vice versa.

She pads to her kitchen, sets a saucepan of milk on the cooker, sits to wait. She will have her grandchild regardless of her stubborn son's resistance. It would be such an easy thing for Dennis -- a moment or two of agreeable self-manipulation -- they do enjoy it -- and voila, the raw material in the palm of her hand. Err, his hand, as it were. Then all she has to do is find a proper vehicle -- a severely unoccupied lesbian perhaps, though these she has heard are extremely difficult to find. But almost any female vehicle will do to bring this precious cargo to the ramp and, nine months hence, without further delay, to cheerfully off-load. She will have her grandchild!

She sighs. A lot to consider. But first she'll have her warm milk and a biscuit. And, perhaps, a bit later, a box of choccies. Specials. Like Dennis's daddy used to buy her -- when he felt like it. Which wasn't often. Sod him. The sod. But she wishes she hadn't thought that.

"I can't sleep," moans Dennis, I shall never sleep again," as he tucks himself in beside his beloved Lars who has already begun to snore lightly and in an orderly fashion.

Christine and Violet, however, lie sleeping restlessly directly below the boys in the little guestroom on their two narrow beds. Visions of motherhood frolic happily across Christine's somnolent face; canvas-clad, teeny-bopper Isabella is being presented with her black belt amidst the motherly tears of similarly garbed Chrissie and Vi.

Violet, unfortunately, poor dear, writhes on her bed, is twitching with nightmares of duplicity and penultimate abandonment. She's twitching rather more than Dexter twitches when he ponders his absent, in many more ways than one, Brad.

Dexter snores on the living-room floor beside a large stone hearth, his fake alligator suitcase tight beside him, his weary, forty-something frame flopped onto a semi-inflated rubber mattress -- he had run out of pumping breath, unusual for Dexter who has always made such a point of physical fitness. He's encased in his sleeping bag, twitching too, though not so violently as Violet at this particular moment in the wee hours. He is beset by visions of Brad's broken though agreeably naked body, buttocks up, naturally, lying at the bottom of some... some, well, Nordic crag and being torn into small portions by an ill-defined Grendel-like creature with extra-large claws. Poor semi-comatose Dexter, drenched in sweat, suddenly wakes, bolts upright.

"Brad?!" he calls pitifully into the summer semi-darkness, "Brad?!"

Brad, of course, protected by major gods of the North, lies warm and snug in his sleeping bag, watched over by his Disney ensemble of new animal pals: the hooting owl, the two smiling deer, the toad who croaks affectionately from one of Brad's inappropriate hiking sandals.

Brad is dreaming of that wealthy German motorist's sincere suggestion to meet him next Thursday in Barlin. Or was it Bercelona? Well, it was Europe anyways.

Even the silvery moon, 'walking the night in her silver shoon', as Dexter often puts it, seems to favour Brad who rests serene as that nakedly recumbent statue of the very long deceased Percy Bysshe Shelly. But there the resemblance to comely Percy Bysshe abruptly ends. As Dexter might say. Has said.

The deer continue contentedly to graze. The owl hoots once again and the toad slumbers, with one eye open and peeled on sleeping Brad from whom even the goodly creatures of the forest cannot tear their affectionate gaze.

Dexter can't sleep. He wipes his sweating forehead with a nicely initialled hanky and fumbles out of his sleeping bag. He finds his fake alligator night-kit in his fake alligator suitcase and waddles in his lovely yellow silk pyjamas through the kitchen to the tiny bathroom and extracts a bottle of sleeping pills from his night-kit. He gulps one down with a glass of refreshing well-water and cannot help exulting in his sleek newly-engineered nose's reflection in the basin mirror. Ah, but then why did Brad not travel with me instead of leaving me and my beauteous new honker to the mercy of les belles dames sans merci? But Wotan! What have I done?! What will Dennis say when he knows why I've brung 'um? Thinks Dexter, though not nearly so lucidly.

He pops another sleeping pill, swallows, chokes, trickles with nervy sweat and wipes his brow again with that nice silk hanky and clamps it to his shiny new, shapely nose, sniffs. "Brad gave me this," says Dexter aloud, shaking the lovely, fragrant hanky in the air, "But Jesus H. Christ! Where is he?!"

He then twitches violently and takes four deep breaths to calm down. "Brad," he mutters, Brad-Brad-Brad. Wherefore art thou, mon petit?"

Christine and Violet's serendipitous disgorging of

29

evening-class fragments of Shakespeare and French is catching. Especially for Dexter who once, for an excessively short time, himself taught evening-class French and even a smattering of The Bard. But let's not go there -- thinks Dexter with a shiver.

10

"They are quite perfect, Dennis," murmurs Christine in some awe. "Are they not quite, quite perfect, Violet?"

"In their perfect, perfect sodding way," snaps Violet, simply as a sop to soothe her simpering Christine. Violet again runs all those sibilant S's through her head, decides to ditch her aching, alliterative alienation for the time being. But of course will say aloud anything that comes to mind to placate Christine, who is not herself at all. When Christine is not herself, thinks Violet, then I, also, am not myself. A fair trade! N'est-ce-pas?

Christine had been referring just now to Dennis's teeth, glittering under the morning sun between pink, glowing-with-health-lips which he is at last allowed to relax in order to sip Lars's fresh-brewed morning coffee which stands at his right elbow on the sun-drenched garden table.

"Your choppers, Dennis, are they in their natural state?" inquires Christine affectionately.

Dennis nods, his lips ache but he manages: "I am as Dame Nature made me."

"They just grew in that way? Every one of them?" inquires Christine.

"Ja," replies Lars, "I vatched them."

"Crikey! You two have been together a long time! Did you hear that, Violet? They just grew in that way. He 'vatched' them. Think of the money we'll save on Isabella's braces!"

"Hurrah," says Violet more sullen than the gods had meant to make her.

"Where is Brad?!" cries Dexter.

"A bear ate him," snaps Violet and of course she's sorry to be so, well, churlish, but, you see... it's Chrissie...and...

Brad wakes, sits up in his warm, unimaginably comfy sleeping bag and rubs his eyes. Miniscule diamonds of dew tumble from ridiculously thick lashes. A tom-tit alights on a nearby delightfully fragile branch and celebrates morning with an arpeggio trill, a sleeping hare awakens, leaps over Brad's feet and a family of tiny hedgehogs parades proudly by. Brad grins engagingly at it all, murmurs "I am so insignificant" and is again instantly and fervently seconded by that teeny tiny sweet voice in his head.

Now the dear boy finds a huge German chocolate bar in his backpack and eagerly unwraps it, all the while observing his forest friends with as much focus as he can muster this early -- or indeed at any other time in the day. He munches happily, his mind a soothing blank, then carefully folds the chocolate bar's foil wrapper, plants it in his ciggie kit and springs from his cosy sleeping bag.

He strips off his designer shorts and designer T-shirt and makes his way gloriously naked -- a state in which a multi-discomfited Dexter often imagines him -- to a perfectly ideal little lake into which he dives and paddles and splashes and giggles. And giggles. And giggles!

"Golden curls," sighs Christine, "Golden curls hath Dennis the Viking" Then: "Your golden curls, Dennis, are they au-natural?"

"Only his hairdresser knows," replies Lars with a wink, "that'd be me."

Christine's gimlet eye swivels instantly to Lars. "Odd, that you, Lars the Swede who, according to all the laws of geography should be blond, has black hair," says Christine with more squinching of her brow than it can attractively sustain.

"It would be odder still," replies Dexter, "if he hadn't."

"The hair?" asks Christine, "Does Dennis's hair look natural to you, Violet?"

"In its sodding way."

31

"But have you ever seen such colouring?! Vi?! Look at the man's sodding cheeks! Roses in high sodding summer! Aren't they sodding singular?!"

"He pinches them," mutters Violet, "Often. I have caught him at it twice."

Christine stares intently at the increasingly discomfited Dennis as he attempts to chew a breakfast scone. "Mmmmmm," she murmurs, "Mmmmmm," and his adam's apple flushes from pink to purple and back.

Lars serves more scones and studiously observes Christine who under Violet's watchful eye, takes up a very large, very full glass of water, grasps it in both hands, drains it and sets it down, staring all the while at Dennis who has given up chewing, gone dry in the mouth, and can only rasp, in a last attempt to swallow the parched remains of his scone.

"I vatch you, Christine," intones Lars at his most sententious, coming to Dennis's rescue. "I vatch you now and yesterday, in dinner. You drink too much vater."

"It is totally impossible to drink too much 'vater', is it not, Violet?"

"Totally impossible," replies Violet, "the body simply excretes what it cannot use. It is a simple matter of excretion, pure and simple."

"With body, nothing are pure and simple," says Lars, employing now, his best faux-pidgin English. Body functions is complex."

"Are complex, Lars," says Christine.

"Not that complex," mutters Violet.

"To whom it may concern:" sniffs Christine, "I never drink less than seven glasses of 'vater' a day."

"Our dearly departed Katherine Hepburn drank eight! God rest her steely soul," adds Violet plaintively.

"Who is Katja Hepburn?" asks Lars.

"Well, really, how can one argue with that?!" replies Christine.

"You have flushed avay all vater-soluble witamins of your body," insists Lars.

"I haven't flushed 'avay' anything!"

"She hasn't flushed avay anything!" cries Violet, "Leave her alone, you cad!"

Violet is not quite sure just where cad came from -- it just popped out -- though Christine had been recently reading aloud from a Victorian thriller, their evening-class homework. Violet loves it when Chrissie reads aloud to her. When she whistles too. Nobody in the whole world can whistle like her Christine can whistle.

But Christine is worried. Her total geographical paradigm is violently shifting. Evening-class Congenial Geography was quite categorical about Swedish hair, indeed, about world hair. Who is this coffee-coloured Swede?! He can't even be genuine Swedish! Everyone knows Swedes are, well, blond, like Dennis. Who is, well, English, but then... There is nothing for it! I shall have to speak to our Congenial Geography instructor upon our return.

"I do not flush things away!" cries Christine, dragging herself kicking and screaming back to the matter at hand.

"But darling," smirks Dexter, "darling, you must flush something away. Think, precious, think. There you are this morning squatting delicately in the loo. Your hand, having just flung the used tissue into the commode, reaches upward for the chain..."

"Shut up, Dexter," snaps Violet, "You, like many, many men, are vile!" -- that Victorian thriller again -- but how satisfying to have so many arcane words at ones 'behest', Violet, careful to conceal it, smiles to herself. She is cunning, though congenial and will win in the end. It's in the stars. Perhaps not these stars but those other stars directly over you-know-where. And gifts of gold, frankincense and myrrh would not be inappropriate nine months hence if all goes according to intrigue. A smug smile is called for. Here it is!

"What are you smiling at, Violet," asks Christine.

"Nothing Chrissie, nothing at all."

"My dear, dear Lars," says Christine, now somewhat shaken, "Lars is your name?"

"Ja. Lars Viktor Trappsteg. I took Mama's name."

"My dear Lars Viktor Trap-door, what is all this about flushing away?"

"How big is these seven glasses of vater?"

"About this size," peeps Christine, now trembling, holding up her newly empty glass.

"Of that size you must imbibe only two. Else flush-flush!"

"Hey mister!" cries Violet, bounding in and thumping Lars soundly -- though not nearly so soundly nor so serially as she has Dexter, "Now just you wait a damned minute!"

"My dear Lars Viktor Trap-door," manages Christine in a tiny quaking voice, "though I have fallen in love with you in record time, especially your transcendent cuisine, you are speaking absolute rubbish."

Violet thumps Lars (gently) again, moans: "Please leave her alone."

"Where in God's name is Brad?!" shrieks Dexter, who springs up from the garden table and darts, in his mauve, gold embroidered bedroom slippers, into the very dense, nearby woods.

"A bear'll eat him," quips Violet who, really, *actually*, didn't completely mean it. Then the guilt.

11

"Have you ever thought, Dennis," asks Christine, "of fathering a child?"

Violet casts a sorrowing look at Christine, slams down a half-eaten scone and bolts into the cabin as Lars pours another coffee for Dennis who has just splashed his own over his freshly-laundered-by-Lars linen summer-ensemble shorts.

"You have the wisitors, Dennis!" hollers the little Troll-like man from atop his clattering bicycle as he sails over the lawn stopping abruptly just behind Christine who screams bloody murder. But Violet, wits about her and fully recovered from her two-hour sulk, instantly assumes a defensive judo position beside her beloved damsel-in-distress.

"Christine, Violet, Dexter?" says Dennis, moving in quickly to separate Violet from the threatened little Troll, "May I present our neighbour, Sven? He lives under a bridge down the road. Not exactly under a bridge, but very near a bridge."

Sven the Troll dismounts problematically from his bicycle and shakes hands with everyone. "Where be you from?" he asks warily, wondering why two of these three strange men wear identical hunting vests though they are not, by a long chalk, twins. Neither is it the hunting season.

"London," say Christine and Violet in unison, "We be from London."

"I be from California," says Dexter at his jovial best.

"Ah! California!" says Sven, "A wery long vay!"

"Ja," replies Dexter, "A wery long vay!"

"So is London," interjects Violet, "Everywhere is a very long way from here!"

"I be to Singapore!" replies Sven with an emphatic belch.

"Jolly good!" says Christine, attempting, as her mother continually implores, to never be revolted by bad manners but 'show her best side'.

"Oh ja!" replies Sven, belching again.

Violet frowns and turns away in disgust.

"You surf?" asks Sven between two more lightly leek-scented belches.

"Every day! We've got a top-of-the-line computer and all the latest software!" says Christine.

Sven is puzzled. "You surf the ocean vah-vehs?"

"Ocean 'vah-vehs'?" whispers Violet into Christine's ear, "What the fuck is he talking about?"

"Language, Violet!" hisses Christine.

"Ocean 'waves,'" says Dennis, "as in California beaches."

"Oh! I see! I see!" cries Christine, delighted that she seems suddenly, somehow, to understand Swedish.

"I be to Singapore!" shouts Sven, "I am eight-ty-five! Farewell!"

Old Sven, with difficulty, mounts his bicycle, sways wildly from side to side as his wheels gain a grip in the beautifully clipped lawn, and pedals away.

Christine pulls Violet to her side, whispers: "How much time have we got? Scrutinise our Fertile Windows immediately!"

Violet could cry! Just sit right down and cry! But she whispers "You know, Chrissie. I told you last night, darling. Four-thirty this afternoon give or take a few seconds." Violet could bite her tongue!

"Four-thirty this afternoon give or take a few seconds," whispers Christine, "Sunday. Our fateful day, Vi. Oestrus Sunday. Dennis's reaction to my comment about fatherhood this morning was not promising. So here's the plan: We'll take in some sights, wear him down, put him off his guard. Then, when he is suitably fatigued and suspects nothing, we'll strike! But we've got to work fast and I mean fast!"

What are they up to? thinks Dexter, though he knows full well.

What are they up to? thinks Dennis who hasn't a clue.

What are they up to? thinks Lars, referring to the bloomless tomato plants in their moderately sized hothouse, toward which he now veritably ambles. In all reasonable likelihood.

About a kilometre away amidst a thicket of seedling pine, the cheerily naked Brad, his MP3 player belted about his slim, taut waist, sways to his silent music and squats to pluck a luscious wild strawberry as a brightly coloured woodpecker nods approvingly from a contiguous, picturesquely hollow though still verdant tree.

Several gruelling, sight-seeing hours later Christine declares, "What a perfectly lovely castle! You are very fortunate, Dennis, to have a whole castle right in your own backyard."

Her mum had forced the young Christine to balance simultaneously, nearly a whole library shelf on her head -- to attain poise. It never stuck. Not unless Christine really concentrated. But Christine never concentrated unless she had a specific goal in mind -- as now. Then anything was possible. Like the first time she clamped her eyes on Violet on Clapham Common and had her for tea within the hour. It is very nearly impossible to thwart me, thinks Christine who smiles with pleasure at her own self assurance. An indefatigable self assurance that will proceed, she has not the slightest doubt, undiluted to tiny Isabella Victoria Gloria's glistening little genome.

"We do not own this castle," replies Lars, sensibly, if dogmatically after some consideration, "And it is not in our backyard which is precisely eight kilometres from where you stand upon that..."

"Parapet," coaches Dennis.

"Parapet," repeats Lars who knows very well the ancient architectural feature upon which Christine stands. But it is always good to draw in Dennis, especially when he's jumpy. It momentarily takes Dennis's ultra-sensitive mind off his chronic anxiety and allows him to get on with his more creative machinations. Which, Lars is certain, will one day result in fabulous riches as well as the saving of many innocent lives, possibly through enlightened, though well-produced pornography. This could even result in the repayment of their perpetually massive debt to Lars's ever-generous mum -- not that the lovely munificent lady expects it. Perhaps Dennis's unfinished epic novel will be the keys to the kingdom of their success?! If Dennis can only remember where he has left it. It was either left on a floppy disc at his mum's in Belsize Park or in the cloakroom at Victoria station. Thus, in either case, sadly untraceable. Particularly in Belsize Park.

After a suitably charming laugh apropos her delightfully didactic mum, Christine adds, "I was metaphorically speaking, of course," and gazes out from the old castle's 'parapet' (so that's what its called) at a picturesque lake 'peppered' -- she almost continues -- with swans.

"Meta-vhat?" asks Lars, ever the tease.

"Never mind, love, it's much too complicated to explain to a foreigner."

"Good," replies Lars, "I be not so swimmingly with similes and bloomin' abstruse imagery."

Christine gives him a blank look and mentally thumbs

through page after page of evening-class course work for a clue to abstruse imagery, as Violet continues with "Where are these famous sodding Viking Rune Stones that everyone's always blabbing about?"

"There ain't none here," says Lars.

"Ain't any here, dear," corrects Christine and immediately licks her little finger, wags it in the air, cries "Joke, everyone, joke!".

"Where in God's name is Brad!" cries Dexter who has been sitting by himself on a cold, hard stone step and moping in a hard-to-miss way.

Had Brad, at last fully clothed, turned his head from his well-mapped forest trail he would have seen, nestling among manicured bushes set in that immaculately clipped lawn, Lars and Dennis's charming cabin, compliments of Lars's mum. But life is brimming with missed opportunities and Brad did not turn his currently wreathed with wild-ivy head, but continued through the happy, ever-so-friendly-to-Brad woods.

"But wait!" a little bird seems to twitter "Be careful! Watch where you are going!"

Ah! It is too late! Brad falls squealing over a mossy mini-hillock and splashes into a babbling brook. A good-natured squirrel laughs and chatters from a lichened ledge, a hare twitches its whiskers in the cutest way and a giant toad lands with a great liquid plop into the babbling brook beside the giggling Brad. What has Brad been smoking now?! A question often asked by all.

Brad pulls himself from the babbling brook, finds a patch of gloriously sunny, mossy hillock, removes his wet lederhosen and tank top and designer shorts and hangs them and his sodden backpack across a limb to dry. He dons his fortunately waterproof music paraphernalia from a waterproof pouch in his backpack takes his ciggie-kit and rolls something experimental into it and lights up, thumping, as usual, to the thrumming beat in his ears.

Now he's supine, all comfy and naked, snoozing on the

moss in his sunny mini-clearing. Dexter, no doubt, would have traded his left ball for a glimpse of this fabulous forest idyll.

But idylls always end, or at least are impaired, or they wouldn't be 'idylls', and an elephantine though well-disposed elk approaches, trots beneath Brad's makeshift clothes-line limb, scoops up the lot -- unintentionally of course -- and carries it away on his broad elk's antlers.

12

Meanwhile, back at the castle:

"Violet, I am dying for an ice-cream. Can you fetch me one, love, from that pleasant little peasant in the palace foyer? There's a love."

Violet, as though shot from a crossbow, sails out of the cluttered Hall of Ancient Armoury and obediently darts to the foyer for a lolly for her lover.

"You and Lars are err... loyal, Dennis?" ventures Christine after a pregnant moment (would that it were!) in her most Mum-pleasing, charm-mode.

"Loyal?" parries perplexed Dennis.

"No musical beds?"

"What do you mean?"

"I mean," replies Christine, brows arched meaningfully, "I mean you don't err... sit where you oughtn't?"

"I have always been extremely fastidious about where I rest my bottom, Christine. As though it were any of your business."

Lars and Dexter have meanwhile shuffled within comfortable eavesdropping range; Lars because Dennis's bottom does deeply concern him, and Dexter, because, well, he's simply a gossip, and would tell all at the drop of a condom and an après-bonk cigarette, though his very own story is actually much too sad to be told. Still...

"Is this true?" asks Christine, gyrating abruptly in Dexter's direction. "Is this blissful tale of fanatical sexual loyalty a true fact?

"Indeed it is, Christine," replies Dexter, personal anguish momentarily vanquished, harmless envy rising, "Dennis and Lars are paired for life. Like lovely white Canadian snow geese. Their butts are as loyal as butts can be in a largely imperfect world."

"Meaning?"

"Meaning," says Dexter, hands clasped to the heavens, "they are as faithful as the day is long. That, my dear, is saying a lot. Particularly at this utterly ridiculous latitude."

"Damn!" cries Christine, "Violet, isn't that sodding touching?!"

Christine, twists round, looks about and in a mild panic exclaims "Violet? Violet, love?!" Then, panic growing exponentially, "Where is Violet?! Violet?! Where on earth are you, love?!"

"You sent her off for your ice-cream," says Dennis.

"Oh. So I did."

Violet, however, has made a habit of disappearing these days, thinks Christine, you'd have thought I was to blame for her incessant disappearances and non-stop...err...angst (yes, that's it, with a 't'). She runs to hide behind trees or to seclude herself in our guestroom over God only knows what trivial incident. But she'll soon see how right I am. How right this whole Viking caper is for the both of us. Meanwhile, she makes me sodding edgy.

Violet puffs back into The Hall of Ancient Armoury, thrusts a dripping raspberry ice-cream into Christine's hand and drops herself sulkily onto a nearby stone step, slurps noisily at her own ice-cream. Let the boys fend for themselves!

"Thank you, darling," says Christine, not quite soon enough nor quite sweet enough to appease Violet who puffs and glowers. "But do inform me, Violet, love, when you decide to trot off somewhere -- even if it's under orders. N'est ce-pas?"

"Lars love, do you think Brad is forever lost in these ubiquitous woods?" asks Dexter, no longer able to contain himself, "In this...colossal confusion of conifers? It does happen, doesn't it?"

"A bear just spat out his left arm," slurps Violet from her

cold, stone step.

"Then it's settled, Dennis," chirps Christine.

"What is settled?" asks Lars , "just the facts, please."

"What's settled?" asks Dennis.

"It. You'll be daddy, of course."

"I'll be what?!"

"I'm in oestrus."

"You're what?!"

"She's fee-cund as a ferret," snaps Violet with a hideously resigned frown though comfortably aware that the next stated fertile window is a myth of mendacious Violet's making.

"I am preparing," adds Christine, flushed with womanly pride, "to drop eggs into my pleasantly engorged uterine lining."

"Let's hope they aren't all in one basket," says Dexter with a good-natured leer.

"Drop your eggs?" asks Lars.

"Eggs?!" asks Dennis.

"She means egg," hisses Violet, her raspberry ice-cream dribbling from her chin, "One egg only, as is most usual fallopian-wise," adds Christine's deceitful lover.

"I and my Violet want a baby, Dennis. You shall be our Viking daddy."

"Not bloody Viking likely!" exclaims Dennis, leaping away and moving off at speed to peer longingly at a massive display of medieval chain-mail -- then, frantically over his shoulder: "I'm no Viking, Christine! Not even of any kind! I'm not even Swedish. I...I...dye my hair!"

Dennis rockets away, to nervously peruse a series of potentially lethal, portable armour-piercers. Christine follows, "You do not dye your hair! Does he, Lars?! You've marvellous colouring, Dennis! Hasn't he, Violet?! Pink and gold! Pink skin does not lie, Dennis!"

"He pinches his cheeks!" shouts Violet close over Christine's shoulder, "I have caught him at it! He pinches them in a deeply masochistic manner! Hard. It is a practice to be frowned upon!"

Dennis bounds away ever faster, scurrying down a spiral stone staircase. Christine swoops after, Violet at her heels, their shouts echoing in the dungeon, seventy, if not more, terrifying feet below.

"Through these holes in the walls, upon their enemies," calls Lars as he and Dexter rush after the others, "they poured variegated boiling oils!"

"Variegated boiling oils!" puffs Dexter, "My word!"

"I'll have to speak to Lars about this matter!" bleats Dennis, over his shoulder as he descends, four at time, the ancient stone steps of this heretofore peaceful, even comforting, castle where he and Lars had spent so much restful time. What has initiated this attack on my creative solitude?! thinks Dennis, it most certainly could not be my own gorgeous...errr...persona. Or could it?

"Lars is right behind us, Dennis! Ask him, if you require his permission to ejaculate!" cries Christine as she too descends by leaps and bounds this ancient, once peaceful -- notwithstanding those endless cauldrons of 'variegated' boiling oils -- stone staircase.

"Not now!" cries Dennis.

"But you must, honeybuns! We haven't much time!"

"Please do not call me 'honeybuns'!" cries Dennis over his shoulder, "I am nobody's honeybuns! Not even for ready money!"

"Does a woman's body revolt you or something?!" shouts Christine at Dennis's back. "Revolt you or something?!" echoes Violet, directly behind Christine, hoping against hope that this is indeed the case, and will preclude further dangerous interference with Christine's chronologically anomalous reproductive regalia (compliments of Humane Reproduction 2B).

"My God!" screams Christine, "You don't think I wanted you to touch me, do you?! You poor mad fool! We've got a turkey-baster!"

"A turkey bloody what?" puffs Dennis, sailing down, down, down.

"A huge syringe, honeybuns," cries Christine, still at Dennis's heels, "Purchased in Trondheim at great expense for this very occasion! It looks like a giant eye-dropper!"

Violet makes a large, obscene squeezing motion to illustrate

Christine's point. "A giant eye-dropper!" she adds, simultaneously abhorring the madness that has brought about this fecund fiasco.

Dennis, irritated and baffled, leaps down seemingly endless stone steps, fervently wishing he were anywhere else.

"I've got a petite demitasse too!" shouts Christine, "For your spunk! It was my great grandmother Nana's. It's an antique!"

"A petite demitasse?!" cries Dennis, jumping another four steps at once.

"A demitasse is a small porcelain cup!" cries Christine, jumping four more.

"I know what a bloody demitasse is! But I don't know what the hell you're talking about!" cries Dennis, his definitively blue Viking eyes red-ringed and close to tears more real than those he'll ever shed for a movie.

"Well, stop and I'll tell you!"

Dennis must stop! He has reached the bottom of the steps and finds himself breathless and imprisoned behind a high iron gate in a small, walled, and horrifyingly claustrophobic courtyard beside a "NO EXIT!" sign. He suddenly feels like a character in some long existentialist play. Why hadn't he read more Sartre? He adored Sartre!

"My petite demitasse is to contain the spermatozoans which you shall agreeably release by your own hand," says Christine who rushes beside him with a friendly grin and pets Dennis's shoulder, very much like but not quite like the way she and Violet pet their enormous, black bitch, Messalina, "The turkey-baster" adds Christine, "is for the act of insemination."

"Christine, darling, do you actually expect Dennis to form an alliance with a demitasse, no matter how old, and procreate with a syringe?!" puffs Dexter who now lands beside her with a great plop at the bottom of the stairs.

"That petite demitasse belonged to my great grandmother Nana! It is antique porcelain!" cries Christine.

"Darling!" puffs Dexter, "The substance is immaterial!"

13

Here is Christine's cherished 'petite' demitasse. It was great grandmother Nana's. It is an antique. It is Christine's constantly carried, good luck charm. And a perfectly lovely, delicately hand-painted petite demitasse it is. Exquisite. But what is Christine's exquisitely hand-painted petite demitasse doing on the shining top of Dennis and Lars's little bedroom telly? And what is Dennis doing here? On the bed at four-eighteen in the afternoon on Sunday? He must be mad! These are Dennis's exact thoughts as he fumbles with his fly and clicks on the DVD player:

"What do you think of this, big fella?" asks Biff, muscular, gorgeous and spectacularly naked, from the telly screen.

"Vow! Vhat is that, Biff?!" says Bart, Biff's equal in every way, also naked, muscular and spectacular.

"Vhat does it look like, partner?" asks Biff.

"A...a wi-brator?!" says Bart.

Click and buzz.

"Uh!" grunts Dennis, "Uh-Uh-Uh" his weary though definitively blue eyes glued to the telly screen, his golden curls matted on his sweating, frowning forehead as he feverishly attempts to manipulate life into his malingering member, "Uh! Uh! Uh!"

Christine, directly below in the little guest room lies flat on her back, blankets up to her chin, a thermometer stuck at the corner of her mouth, sweat beading on her frowning forehead too. Her eyes flick towards the ceiling, drawn by an extremely irritating buzz. "For God's sake, Dennis!" she cries at the buzzing ceiling, "I'm peaking! What on earth is going on up there?!"

Dennis's flushed face skews anxiously in the glare of the telly screen.

"You ain't never tried nothin' like this before, have you,

Bart?" says wooden, though naked and spectacular Biff.

"No I ain't," replies Bart, "Vhat do you call it?"

"Safe-sex, partner!" says Biff with a grin as broad and blank and nearly as bewitching as Brad's.

"Safe sex?!" asks Bart.

"Ja! Safe-sex!" says Biff, the 'wi-brator' buzzing quickly up to cover Bart's simulated stimulation.

"Vow! Yee-sus!" moans Bart over the increasingly loud buzz.

"Is good?" asks Biff.

"Is not good!" moans Dennis, his right arm gravely fatigued, his right hand cripplingly cramped, his brain critically close to overload.

How does he get himself into these panicking predicaments? Why must he pander his life away simply to be loved and accepted by one and all?! Even people he doesn't like! Even strangers! Thank God for Lars -- his ship in a storm -- or is it 'rock' in a storm? Rock to cling to? Why am I forever trapped in the bloodshot eye of this hectic hurricane?! Buffeted by forces I am forever striving to please?!

These thoughts, however, do not contribute to the task in hand (as it were) and neither does: "For God's sake, Dennis!" screams Christine from below, having just snatched the thermometer from her mouth and squinted at it then added, "I've just peaked! I'm optimum-oestrus! It's time, for God's sake! I am optimum sodding oestrus!"

Dennis's head flops back on his sodden pillow. This seminal debacle has only enhanced his already dangerously depressing sense of failure. My God! my film is rubbish! Hopeless! And Biff and Bart, Mob molls to the core who...

"Now you try it with me, big fella," grunts Biff from the TV screen with a smile that might more easily denote a pleasant bowel movement.

"Yee-sus, Biff! I am not -- I mean -- I ain't sure I can do that!"

"Sure you can, big fella! And it is absolutely safe! With a sterilized wi-brator, by yimminy!"

The DVD vibrator now buzzes in a much enhanced way, a way Dennis was proud to have painstakingly engineered...until now.

"For God's sake, Dennis!" screams Christine from below, "What are you doing up there?! Drying your hair?!"

But now! Now! Dennis, driven by humiliation, concentrating harder than he has ever concentrated before, his tortured arm and hand a blur, his sagging member twitching to sluggish life, his left foot in spasm kicking over a lamp, his perfect teeth clenched in a death mask, his pink cheeks scarlet, his mind a harrowing miscellany of failure -- succeeds!

"I knew you could do it, partner," sighs naked Biff who lies back, pulls on his tight black briefs and gives naked Bart a chaste peck on the cheek. "Think safe-sex, partner!"

"Right on, Biff! S-S for safe-sex. You can turn off that sterilized wi-brator for now, partner!"

Dennis switches off the DVD with his toe, grabs Nana's 'petite' demitasse from the immaculate telly top, scoops up at least a quarter demitasse of Sisyphean effort from his stomach (he'd loved Camus too, why hadn't he read his 'Myth of' ?!). jumps from the bed, pulls his shorts and trousers up and leaps down the stairs to an unknown fate.

Could all failure be erased with...no! He refuses to think of it! But...could all life's false starts, his all too real defeats be put right with a...with a perfect heir?!

"Dennis!" screams Christine, "I've peaked and am rapidly declining!"

"I'm coming!" cries Dennis.

"At last!" calls Christine to the ceiling, "Oh at last!"

"What were you doing up there?!" snaps Christine, wagging her turkey-baster at him as Dennis bursts through the guestroom door.

"This!" declares Dennis with a certain crazy pride, and thrusts the demitasse at Christine who snatches it and waves him from the room.

"Goodo!" she cries, "Nothing can stop us now! Isabella Victoria Gloria, here we come!"

Dennis slams out the door and drops himself into a chair in the living-room. He wrings his sweating fingers, feels irretrievably responsible for the disaster he is certain will follow. They coerced him! Yes! Coerced! Lars was no help at all -- said he: "Dennis, you must do this on his own." And Mummy! Well! Mummy will be ecstatic. And...in a way, a rather nice way, it just may get him off the hook with her. No more telephone calls in the wee hours. No more...But God! Oh God! At what cost?! Can his 'perfect heir' pay the price? "Christine!" he calls through the door, "Christine, are you all right?!"

No answer.

Dennis panics. "Christine?!"

He hammers on the door. "Christine?!"

"Come in, Denny, dear."

Dennis, hesitant, quivering and terrified that she's just called him 'Denny', inches the guestroom door open and tiptoes to the bed where Christine, flat on her back and mysteriously glowing, lies beneath a great pile of blankets still as stone. Not moving her head or body, or even the muscles of her face, she swivels her eyes up at Dennis.

"Christine? Are you all right?" repeats Dennis, so softly, so deferentially but so anxious and still quivering. Has she somehow snapped her spine with that enormous turkey-baster?

"Ummm" sighs Christine," inert as a pillar of salt, only "Ummmm."

Dennis tiptoes closer. "Are you errr, sure?"

"Ummmm."

"Then why aren't you moving?"

"Insertion," purrs immobile Christine through her teeth, "went 'A-Okay'. Got to lie here for a moment. Let it stew."

"Of course," replies Dennis, fascinated in an eerie way, a very particularly eerie way, "How unconscionably stupid of me."

"Wouldn't want to shake anything loose, would I?" purrs Christine.

"Oh, God no."

Christine manages a tight tiny smile, says: "My eggs apparently shake out quite easily."

Why is he so fascinated with this bizarre situation? He simply can't make it out, just stands here, like an...an expectant father? So interested. So indulgent. So...proud? Has he suddenly been struck with some awful prehistoric predilection lodged unknown deep in his genes?

"Oh? Your eggs shake out quite easily, do they?"

"Uh-huh. Research, conclusively substantiated by, and exhaustive reading of, our evening-class Humane Reproduction brochures, reveals that I apparently possess an exquisitely fragile internal arrangement subject to anomalies too numerous to number and identify."

"Ummm." says Dennis, whose trembling has subsided but not disappeared.

"My gynaecologist calls it "The Perilous Perch Syndrome. My eggs could bolt at any moment. Without a trace. Like a thief in the night. And my fertile windows? My God! Even worse! I am, in fact, a walking anomaly."

Dennis regards this woman he has so recently inseminated with some wonder, some... tenderness? She is after all, a woman, and completely unfathomable to Dennis and his ilk. My 'ilk?' thinks Dennis, never having quite determined just what his ilk is -- other than, of course, his all-consuming passion for his super-systematic Lars which goes without saying. His black Swede. Yes. He is defined by Lars. Lars is his meaning, his raison -- if you will -- d'etre. He must, one day, tell him so. If he can only tear Lars away from his butter cream icing or straw-berry tending or wood chopping or his bloomin' greenhouse tomatoes that won't bloom but...

"I do appreciate this, Dennis," whispers Christine.

"My pleasure, I'm sure...I mean..." he blushes outrageously.

"Isn't it exciting?" sings Christine, "Billions of little you's doing battle over just one little me?! We're precious, Dennis, both of us. Priceless in this weary, wacky world."

Dennis begins to shiver with a vengeance, backs away, his mind awash with alarming possibilities manifest in this mad act of impregnation.

"Sit down, honeybuns, before you fall down." murmurs Christine. Dennis sits stiffly on the bed opposite, aiming as always to please, his perfect manners at last at parade rest.

"Only one little you will win, Denny," whispers Christine.

"Quite," murmurs Dennis, wishing she'd ditch the 'Denny'.

"One little you plus one little me equals little tiny Isabella Victoria Gloria!"

14

"Gentlemen! Gentlemen!" thunders Violet to Lars and Dexter as they mosey through a fetching forest glade, "Today, unfortunately today, the only effective political leader must also be an effective liar. In other words, gentlemen, a con-man..."

"Don't you mean 'con-person'?" asks Dexter.

"No," says Violet with finality, "man is the correct operative noun here. And don't interrupt. Because," she sonorously continues, "given the present global mess, there is not one government in the so-called western world that has the wherewithal to implement truly innovative, effective and sane socioeconomic policy. Since nothing truly innovative, effective and sane is possible, the masses must be seduced into believing in the Myth of Progress even as they are shunted into the gutters to starve. Gentlemen, we are being conned."

"I beg your pardon, dearest Miss," says Dexter, "I am not being conned."

Violet stops dead in the glade. "Dexter, my evening-class instructor will, for a reasonable fee I am certain, be happy to provide you with a book on political thought in the early twenty-first century. Do us all a favour and read it and I'll speak to you one day at some length!"

"I'll look forward to that," says Dexter, backing subtly out of Violet's thumping range.

Violet gives Dexter a damning look, anxiously checks her watch, gazes hopelessly in the direction of the cabin hoping against hope that her dastardly Fertile-Windows juggling has put the kibosh on Christine's famously fickle fecundity.

Only yards away, ear-phoned Brad, naked thanks to that kit-snatching elk, water-proof MP3 player and money belt secure about his waist, traipses groovily, his hippie grandparents might say, amongst the flourishing plenitude of conifers, wildest of berries and fascinating, smoke-worthy fungi agreeably stalked by a host of tiny, curious creatures.

"Did you hear a bear rustling?" asks Violet as the three step out of their verdant glade onto the narrow road just as that ancient Troll, Sven by name, comes cycling by at speed and hollers "Hello, boys!" and disappears around yet another redundantly forested bend.

"Jesus! Must he always sneak up like that?" cries Violet, loathing, for a moment, the very flora from which frightening old Sven had sprung. It must be her allergies playing up and making her so churlish; that, and Christine, of course, who this very minute turkey-baster in hand is -- No. It is impossible! My juggled Fertile Window Tables prevent it! But Violet, shaken to her hiking boots, frowns and sneaks another nervous look at her watch and searching recklessly for even alien succour, snaps "Do you think Christine and Dennis have conceived yet?"

"It's conceivable," replies Dexter.

No comfort there.

Back in the guestroom: "I and Violet had a nice long talk about you last night, Dennis. We feel -- at least I feel -- that you are our correct Viking."

"But I have assured you, Christine, I am not a Viking. Not even of any kind."

"Violet insists you're too fat but I told Violet that beggars cannot be choosers and she acquiesced -- in a way. Or seems to have acquiesced -- in a way. You never know with our Violet, do you?"

Christine, from her pillow, peers impishly at Dennis, waits for an answer. It comes: "Errr...apparently not. But you obviously know her heaps better than I do."

Christine sighs and stretches, pointing her blanket-covered

unpainted toenails sharply at the ceiling. "Did you and Lars have a nice long talk too? About us and my fecund needs?"

"Actually, no."

"Dennis! Why ever not?"

"Violet thinks I'm too fat?"

"Let's face it, honeybuns, you are not the ideal weight for a male-person of your height and bone structure. You are somewhat plumper than your little piccie."

Christine snatches Dennis's photo from beneath the blankets, pokes it in his face. "Dexter gave this to us. Isn't it exciting? That's the whole reason we're here!"

"I must thank Dexter." -- How could he?! thinks Dennis.

"Dennis. We are prepared to accept your weight problem as your colouring is top-notch."

"How nice." What perfectly pompous women, thinks Dennis.

Violet, trailed by Lars and Dexter, plods along the dusty forest road kicking at pebbles and stomping squirrel-sized black slugs to goo.

"She hates the 'fucking wilderness'," confides Dexter to Lars, "Those were her exact words."

Violet attacks a large tree fungus with a vicious swipe of her walking stick and covertly wipes a tear from her cheek. It isn't that she's really seriously worried about the remote possibility of procreation at this particular moment -- she saw to that earlier immersed in her newly adopted rat-like cunning. It's mostly that she fears even the tiniest sign of affection for Dennis -- given his sticky little gift -- could flower into a Frankenstein that might destroy them all. Lars and Dexter, gently but silently noting a tear or two, pass her by and continue up the road.

"Hates the fucking wilderness?" whispers Lars, "It's understandable. So would I if I were in her boots."

"You are in her boots, sweetie," says Dexter with a naughty grin.

"Why didn't you and Lars have a nice long talk? This is a matter of some import, honeybuns."

Dennis twisting his clenched fingers, shifts uncomfortably at the edge of the other bed, secretly horrified -- he seems to have absolutely no feelings in these fingers. "Didn't need to. Lars said 'Why not?'"

"Not very sentimental, these Nordic types."

"However," says Dennis with an explosive sigh that surprises even him, "I have always wanted a child, I suppose. Somewhere deep inside. God knows Mum wants a grandchild."

He sighs again, just as volubly. "Yes, deep inside -- I've never verbalized this to anyone, Christine -- perhaps I'm vain. Perhaps it's something more... a primeval, though contrary-to-my-nature genetically embedded need to father a..."

"He's not a neo-Nazi, Lars?!" gasps Christine, with some alarm.

"A black neo-Nazi?! God, no! Lars is just logical to his fingertips."

Yet another sigh. "Lars saw this, this need in me. The prospect of a child conjures up in a man a vision of the future. When a man..."

"Lars does strike me as just a bit over-organized."

"...When a man..."

"I prefer a little adventure myself," chuckles Christine, folding both arms carefully behind her head, "There was this Norwegian on a bicycle -- your colouring, of course, or I shouldn't have given him a second look. Maybe he was a bit more reddish than you but I don't mind reddish though curly golden blond gets my vote every time. He was cycling along, whistling happily and I forced Dexter to pull up beside him and I yelled out the car window that I wanted him to father my child -- you've got to say these things straight out or you just frighten people away. N'est ce-pas?"

Christine grins, recalls the Norwegian's open-mouthed stare at the precise second he stopped whistling and lost his balance, chuckles to herself.

"What happened?"

"He fell off his bike and we drove on. I wasn't really serious. I didn't know a thing about him."

"You just left him there? He might have been injured."

"Or septic. I felt so guilty."

"Christine, I do think that was a bit cold-blooded."

"I told you I felt guilty! It was cheeky but I had no idea of his health history and it was obvious he had a faulty sense of balance. He wouldn't have done at all. What if little tiny Isabella dreams of becoming a great dancer? And can't."

"She wouldn't have been the first."

"Be serious, honeybuns. He might have passed his vertigo on to her."

"Maybe it wasn't vertigo. Maybe you just drove the poor Norwegian bastard into a ditch!"

"Maybe this, maybe that! You're awfully tentative for a man!"

"Your behaviour was disgraceful!"

"Goodo! Our first quarrel!"

15

Lars lazily contemplates "being in Violet's boots" as he weeds a singularly weedless row of strawberries in his meticulously maintained vegetable garden. Not far beyond, Dexter lies quivering -- an open book over his face, dreaming his nightmares in a newly-repaired-by-Lars deck chair at the very centre of Lars's surgically edged and clipped lawn.

On his knees in this superbly weeded row of strawberries Lars happily surveys the other fruits of his labours, from the scientifically designed hen-house, with fourteen technically superb egg-laying levels (for five hens and the possibility of a laying-annex for twenty more!), to the solar-heated, super-fermenting mulch/garbage box, to the hothouse's gravity-watering system, to the strawberry patch in which he now squats. He is content. He and Dennis, happily lack only a mobile telephone. They reside, by choice, in this beautifully isolated, peaceful patch, mid-forest, on the face of this 'tumultuous world' -- according to Dennis (excerpted from a near forgotten phrase in his epic novel -- if only he could find it!).

Lars, and Lars's prosperous mother, of course, have provided a stable, comfortable, culturally conducive environment for Dennis, the "artistic" one of this long-standing and fanatically devoted union. Yes. Lars, notwithstanding 'being in Violet's boots' -- and being cuckolded by one and the same over-age, over-decorated petite demitasse, doesn't actually care a fig. After all, what's a little semen under the bridge? Which brings to mind a certain bridge. And semen. And his lovely Dennis. Is good, thinks Lars. Then, suddenly, here she is, dusty-booted, in all her disenchantment, hovering above him, a dark silhouette against the so recently smiling summer sun, her shadow smudging his perfect contentment. A veritable bloomin' killjoy!

"Hello, Violet," says Lars at his amiable best.

"You don't look Swedish to me."

"Don't I?"

"No."

"Well I am."

"Well you don't look it."

"I was born here. My Papa was an American draft-dodger."

"What happened to him?"

"He went back to California under a nom d'plume."

"He was a writer?"

"No. A milliner."

Lars wets his little finger, sticks it in the air ala Christine, "Joke!"

He'd used this well-constructed little jest before with far greater success. But Violet, so fiercely intent on man's inhumanity to women, completely ignores it, says: "Your poor, dear mum."

"Not at all. Mama was bloomin' happy."

Violet ponders a moment, exceedingly moved, eyes clouding with sentiment, adds "God bless her then!"

She swipes at her eyes before he has time to notice, squints at Lars as he delicately removes a tiny snail from a strawberry stem and pulls up a nearly invisible etiolated weed-root. "What are you doing then?"

"Veeding. This, as we say in Sweden, is the 'period of ecstasy'. In very early summer, everything grows crazy- frenzy."

"Everything is crazy-frenzy around here," says Violet with a painful glance towards the cabin and a catch in her voice, "Especially Christine. 'Crazy-frenzy' must be catching."

"The 'period of ecstasy', to be precise, is the overpowering necessity for Nature in the Northern climes to reproduce before Dame Flora doffs her summer frock and clothes herself in winter fur," quotes Lars memory-perfect from 'Old Mr Svensson's Garden Companion', a treasured gift from Lars's mum whose thumbs are also viridian.

"You don't say," grunts Violet who watches for another moment, peering intensely at Lars's deft manoeuvres amongst his impeccably cared-for strawberry plants. She blows her nose, says "Weeding then?"

"Ja."

"Oh."

She watches another moment, blows her nose again.

"Weeding, then?"

"Ja, veeding. As said."

"Oh."

Poor Vi's heart just isn't in it, not just now whilst her own Chrissie shares that fucking, funny-fluid with a florid stranger. Even if today is not by any means a fertile window, due to Violet's pseudo-scientific tampering with Christine's already cooked reproduction schedule. But one simply cannot be sure, can one?! Chrissie's fertile windows are entirely anomalous in the first place and terribly difficult to fudge with any certainty. Violet would have thrown the thermometer out a fertile window long ago but Chrissie still insists upon it. Besides, all those Humane Reproduction brochures they've studied have only served, in large part, to confuse them. So together they have depended much more on their Instinctual Knowledge classes which have proved to be far more reassuring. Until now, when Chrissie has wilfully turned everything upside down and possibly ruined her, Violet-the-rat's life. At least for the foreseeable future.

Violet frowns but attempts to be pleasant. She has been

altogether too irritable and so utterly unlike her true appealing self. "What are you weeding?" she asks, attempting to grin but falling miserably short as her upper lip sticks to a tooth (her mouth is dry these days too!). Her quivering lower lip now sags in a totally wrong direction and she must turn to dash away another incipient tear.

"Strawberries." says Lars patiently, "I am weeding strawberries."

"Strawberries? Those are strawberries? But they're so red!"

"Ja."

"Oh. I'd forgotten what real strawberries look like. Chrissie eats only frozen ones. Says they're more hygienic. One forgets, doesn't one?"

"Ja, apparently."

"Real strawberries are only a hazy memory," sighs Violet, "now I eat frozen, mushy ones just like Chrissie. Have for five years. They're beige."

Violet blows her nose again, dabs at her watering eyes, casts a jaundiced gaze over the whole landscape, says "I am allergic to fresh wood," and sneezes.

"Ja? Then 173,787 square miles of woodland is no picnic."

Violet bends close, scudding her shirtsleeve against her runny, reddening nose, "What are those funny little viney things trailing off from each plant? Weeds?"

She snatches up a strawberry runner.

"Those is runners. Each plant has got them. They vine out and take root and become new little plants. That is how they replicate."

In miserable wonderment, her voice cracking, Violet rasps, "On their very own?!"

"The bees give them a hand now and then."

"Oh."

Violet squats beside Lars, yanks at another runner, peers intently at it, whispers "Like a little tiny umbilical cord. A new, little tiny baby at its end. A new, little tiny life. And they do it all by themselves?"

"Ja."

"I wish..." A sob catches in Violet's throat, "I wish Christine was a strawberry."

"Poor Violet," says Lars who thinks: Poor, poor Violet. How fortunate are we men that we are never on heat.

16

Christine is elated over her recent loquacious machinations and springs knees-up under her pile of blankets. "Dennis!" she cries causing him to jump, "Do you like Violet?"

As Dennis considers this exceedingly delicate question, Violet, a tiny, distant figure framed in the window behind him, sobs, flails her arms, charges down the road kicking at pebbles.

"Well, do you like Violet?" repeats Christine. Dennis is about to say "That's an exceedingly delicate question," reconsiders, says: "I...err...hardly know her."

"To know her," murmurs Christine, "is to adore her."

"I sincerely hope so," replies Dennis before he can stop himself, covers it quickly with: "I've been missing so much, haven't I? But I hardly know you, Christine."

"Make that 'Chris', honeybuns. Well, for a start, I'm the impulsive type. Of course I've got it all worked out to the very last, niggling detail before I make my first impulsive move. However, Vi does the scheduling and carries Nana's petite demi-tasse, the turkey-baster, my thermometer, my Fertile Windows Notebook, and our Humane Reproduction study brochures wherever we go. This material is kept achingly au courant. My slightest twinge is noted by Vi, timed, located and accurately recorded. I'd be flying blind without Violet. I.... OUCH! Dennis! I am being invaded! It's begun! We are about to make a baby!"

Violet, some distance down the road and still sobbing, pauses breathless, drops herself on a mossy rock and wipes her flooding eyes. She looks up and sees naked -- but for his MP3 player and money belt -- earphoned Brad, almost upon her. She screams but Brad notices nothing, hears nothing and passes by wearing almost nothing, a thin ribbon of fungi ciggie-smoke wisping past his beauteous bald buttocks.

"Poor Dexter," sighs Christine, "We quizzed him for hours. Kept him up all night talking about you, Dennis, "We didn't give him a moment's peace." A tinkling laugh as she lies back, punching her pillow.
    "So he said."
    "Did he?"
    "Not in so few words."
    "We know everything about you. From your first measles jabs to your ancestral uncle at the Battle of Hastings with but one testicle."
    "Sadly, my uncle at Hastings was on the losing side."
    "What do you expect with only one sodding testicle? But fret not, love. He is dead and no longer a serious threat to your robust Viking lineage."
    "I had no idea Dexter was so well informed."
    Christine suddenly sits up, kicks her heels together, cries "Oh Denny, you are battering my fortress walls. The thrill of a lifetime! Thrills don't get any more thrilling than this! Isn't it thrilling?!
    "I'm thrilled," replies Dennis, "But can you actually feel that, Christine? I thought the whole event was somewhat more subtle and undetectable until rather later."
    "For the callous individual, perhaps -- but I and Violet are frightfully aware, almost hideously sensitive."
    "Really? I hadn't noticed."
    "Incidentally, what's Lars like in bed? Who conquers whom? We vary, I and Vi. But I'm told it's an entirely different kettle of fish with men. He who starts on the bottom stays on the bottom! Who's the bottom man, Denny? Eh? Nudge, nudge? Know what I mean?"
    Christine laughs merrily. Dennis is dismayed, thinks, I wish to God she wouldn't call me 'Denny' but says "Would you like a cup of coffee or something?"

"God no, Denny! Coffee is a stimulant! Might beef-up my ovum's walls and force your teeny weenie warriors to pound their pointy heads to a pulp attempting to breach them."

Christine lunges from her bed. Dennis jumps back in terror.

"I won't bite you, honeybuns!"

Christine licks her little finger, sticks it in the air, cries "Joke"!

"I'd better leave you now," says Dennis who wonders why he hasn't said this much sooner, like yesterday. No. He knows. One simply cannot inseminate a fellow human being, of either sex, then disappear. At least not if one is a gentleman which, upon reflection, one must necessarily be to do so. Odd, that. "The others will be back soon and I can make them all a nice cup of..."

Christine grabs Dennis's hand before he can dodge away and pulls him closer. "You're awfully jumpy, love."

Dennis, twitching markedly, says "Not at all!"

"You are," insists Christine, "you're twitching."

"No, I'm not. That's a tic. I have long suffered from a tic."

"No, Denny, dear, it is not a tic. It is a twitch." Christine stabs a finger into Dennis's now bright, blushing cheek and, tracing with her finger, says, "This twitch starts directly under your right eye and moves down to the right corner of your mouth and subsequently repeats itself in no particular pattern."

She holds his head with one hand and pokes another finger into Dennis's other cheek, just below his left eye. "Now it is travelling from your left eye to the left corner of your mouth." she says, again tracing its progress in his sweating, ever more pinkening flesh.

"Christine, please," moans twitching Dennis. But Christine is inexorable.

"A tic, on the other hand, is thoroughly defined as an habitual, patterned, spasmodic contraction of the muscles, particularly of the face", she says, not yet releasing his head. "This phenomenon, have I and Violet recently researched in our Domestic Psychology evening-class. A twitch, on the other hand, is erratic. Your random facial event, Dennis, is not a tic. It is a twitch." Christine at last removes her finger from Dennis's ever more twitching, sweating face, and with a twinkle in her eye gives him a genial but firmly conclusive and only slightly painful pat on each now lividly scarlet cheek. "Dear Denny, it is pointless to argue. I know a twitch when I see one. Violet often twitches during sustained conversation. Particularly when we quibble. But you and I are assuredly not quibbling."

"I assure you, Christine, that you and I are assuredly quibbling. But whether we are or not, I repeat, what I am suffering is a tic, has always been a tic and will forever remain a tic. World without end, amen!"

"Ha! The Church rears its ubiquitous though truly reverent head. Do not change the subject, honeybuns. Christine is now about to whistle to you. Violet loves it when I whistle. It calms her down. It'll calm you down too, Denny. You've twitched your last."

She owes it to him. He has been a brick! Done all this for her and Violet and their little tiny Isabella -- even if he is a man. Which, of course, he couldn't have if he weren't. Odd, that, and even a bit disappointing that a woman can't too! But Mother Nature, as Christine knows, seeks unceasingly to improve herself. And one day she'll simply cast off those unwieldy skirts and all hell will break loose -- Liberty! as they say, Equality! Sorority! Christine grins at the thought as she licks each lip till it glistens, fixes a penetrating eye on the now spasmodically twitching Dennis, grips his hand and begins to whistle the old standard, 'Come to me my melancholy baby'. Which her father had often sung to her mother who wouldn't. At least not often and only when it suited her. Which as far as Christine knew, suited him. One must trust ones own instinct even if the whole world disagrees. One must always be ones own person. This, Christine tried unstintingly to be. She had succeeded admirably.

17

"Hello there!" calls Lars from the strawberry patch to naked Brad who tosses him an innocently goony smile, "If you are

Brad, you are a day late!" calls Lars.

"Where's the nearest loo?" calls Brad, very cleverly lifting an earphone for the answer.

"Over there!" calls Lars, and points him towards a little red outhouse.

Christine, whose eyes remain unnervingly fixed upon Dennis, brings her superbly whistled rendering of "Melancholy Baby" to a technically difficult, multi-trilled conclusion. She almost -- no, does -- feel a certain affection for this poor, tense, twitch-ravaged man whose no doubt bewildered spunk now fights for precedence in her intimate battleground. Yes. A certain affection. Nothing to shout about and certainly unrelated to her love for Violet which remains inviolate. But she must not speak of this certain, albeit limited, affection to Violet. Lest Violet become "Violent". It takes great effort for Christine to resist licking her little finger and waving it about and shouting "Joke!" and further flummoxing poor Dennis.

For his part, Dennis is relieved and applauds gratefully at the conclusion of Christine's tedious, pursed-lipped warble. Which, actually, was cracking good whistling.

"Violet loves it when I whistle. She's forever saying to me: 'Chrissie, whistle Vi-Vi's cares away.' Do you whistle, Dennis?"

"Never."

"Why ever not?"

"I errr just never seem to find the time." He's twitching again.

"Never mind, honeybuns, Chrissie will teach you."

"Prepare for a shock, Christine. I am an exceptionally slow learner and I am not very bright."

"Don't worry your pretty head, honeybuns, I'm bright enough for the both of us."

Christine grabs up the sticky demitasse, tosses it to Dennis who catches it with some difficulty as he was never a good catcher and always spent school games on the bench. "Could you do the honours, love? Rubba-dub-dub?"

"Yes, of course!" he cries and leaps from the room, a free, for the time-being, man.

61

He slams the guestroom door leaving Christine to her fecund fate, sets the 'petite' demitasse on the rustic, beautifully-waxed-by-Lars bar, starts to answer the jangling telephone but stops, apprehensive, just stares at it. It continues to ring. It couldn't be Mum, not at this reasonable hour.

"Why can't they leave me alone?! It's only five hundred pounds not five hundred thousand! Biff and Bart, go back to your Sicilian Mob masters and leave me alone!"

The telephone continues to ring. He drops to the sofa, answers the phone, holding it well away from his ear, listens.

Dennis's Mum stirs soup, Dennis's favourite, but of course he's not here to eat it but at the moment, she suspects, there, at the other end of the line inside that telephone that's perched on her ruffled aproned shoulder (she's had a few -- it's well after four). "Dennis?"

Dennis, still quivering from Christine's warbling water-torture, not to mention that artificial yet all too real insemination, says nothing, tries to locate his thoughts.

"It's me, Dennis, your mother. Remember me?"

Dennis is still at a loss to speak because the minute he opens his mouth she'll know everything and everything has still to be resolved. He has never been able to conceal anything from dear Mum, feels himself the guilty child at every turn. He's not quite sure how he feels about what has just happened, not even sure, exactly, how Lars might feel about it now the diabolical deed is done. But Dennis must...

"I know you're there, Dennis. I can hear you breathing. I know something is wrong. Do you know how I know something is wrong? Because I am your mother and you are my son and that is precisely how I know something is wrong. Desperately, perhaps even irretrievably wrong."

How right you are, Mummy, thinks Dennis and takes several deep breaths, girding, a trifle too late as it were, his loins. Finally, as nonchalantly as he can manage, "Oh, hello, Mum! Sorry, love, I was just pulling a fluff ball off my jumper."

"Jumper, Dennis? It is high summer and I assume we are still in the same hemisphere?"

Mum stirs her soup, tastes it with a big wooden spoon. "I'm warming up your favourite soup, darling, chicken tomato." Then, ominously: "What is it, darling, what is troubling you?"

"Hard to talk, Mummy, guests."

"Guests? I knew it! What sort of guests?"

"Err...women."

"Women?!"

"Err...yes. female guests."

"Are these female guests lesbians?! Are these females lesbians, my son?!"

"Err...allegedly, Mummy. Up here on a visit."

"Up there on a visit?! Why, I implore you, dear, why have these alleged lesbians ventured so far North?

"Very nice too...they...err...are. I think."

"How many lesbians?"

"Only two."

"Two? One would be sufficient."

"You can say that again."

"What do they want?"

Dennis ponders how to -- and he must because Mum will find out anyhow -- phrase this.

"Well?" says Mum giving her warming chicken tomato soup an affirmative stir, "Well, what do they want?

"A baby!" blurts Dennis, at the verge of tears.

Mum by reflex executes a broad, wobbly stir, upsetting the fortunately still lukewarm chicken tomato. Her telephone topples off her shoulder and she drops into a chair and fans herself with the wooden spoon, too dazed to notice the viscous droplets of delicious soup that spatter and roll slowly down her cheeks and drip to the floor to join the small lake of chunky chicken tomato spreading across the kitchen. Her expression leaps jerkily from surprise to puzzlement to severe puzzlement to earth-shaking puzzlement to fledgling hope, ordinary hope, extraordinary hope and finally, to glowing, face the heavens, eyes-closed, divine hope. She is speechless with joy.

"Mummy? Mummy, are you there?!"

Dennis hangs up the telephone. Mummy is getting so

forgetful. She often forgets to say goodbye! The point is though, about her incessant telephoning, it's just the human contact she needs. She is lonely, poor Mummy. "You're the head of the house now" -- as she has repeatedly told him since his "deceased" father's precipitous departure. Mummy is a doll -- of sorts -- and Dad was a fool to run off with that twenty-five year old! That twenty-five year old...boy.

"It's alive! cries Dexter, dashing through the door, "Brad is alive! My Brad is arrived and alive! He's stark naked in the outside loo and he's safe! God! I need a drink!"

Dexter rushes to the bar, grabs the first object to hand, slops it full of whiskey, brings it to his lips, it is sticky, he instantly realizes it must be Nana's notorious 'petite' demitasse as it seems a bit viscous, like Dennis's Mum's chunky chicken tomato soup which Dexter adores. But isn't Dennis his best friend and aren't Dennis and Lars paired for life like Canadian Snow Geese? So what's a little spunk between friends? Besides, he likes the taste. And it wouldn't be the first time. Nor will it be -- come the vaccine -- the last. So Dexter shrugs and quaffs and belches a happy little burp. Fortified, he must now see to Brad! Where is that new pair of designer lederhosen? Ah! All wrapped and ready along with the new pair of designer briefs! He rushes away to find his precious gifts.

"Are you quite finished?!" sneezes Violet, poking her head suddenly at Dennis through an open window, her narrowed, allergy-ridden eyes trained on that shut, mysterious guestroom, her heart breaking, "Are you quite, quite finished?!" Then, for emphasis, though she regrets it before the word has left her frowning lips, "Wanker!"

"Yes," sighs Dennis, "Yes, Violet, I believe I am. Finished. I am quite wanked over."

"Dennis?" says Mum from the telephone receiver ajar in its cradle, "Denny-den-Dennis?"

But Dennis is fanning his over-excited friend, Dexter, who has collapsed on the sofa beside his open fake alligator suitcase, delightedly close to tears of abject joy.

18

In the balmy, late afternoon glow, this lazy beginning of another interminable twilight, sit Violet, Christine, Dexter, Brad, Dennis and Lars on the lakeside deck of a rustic outdoor restaurant just having eaten, everyone of them, especially Dennis, too much.

Lars gazes over a wooden balcony at the shimmering, sailboat-cluttered lake beyond. He ponders precisely how many sailboats crammed end-to-end it would take to reach the other side of this crystal-blue, pine-edged body of water. He patiently shifts them in his mind's eye from here to there to here and remembers when he and his mother used to sail with his long-gone, deserter father. He remembers his mother's joy when his errant Daddy bolted never to return. His Mum and his Dad were ships that passed in the night but the cargo, himself, was left with Mum. Now Mum is a successful interior designer who's done hotels and public buildings all over Scandinavia. She had been very helpful when he and Dennis bought their cabin in the woods, had actually, well, paid for it in full and set Dennis up in his DVD studio and built a sizeable hothouse for them to raise tomatoes off-season and a state of the art chicken farm to supplement their income. But now, well, things weren't going so bloomin' well -- as that long ago lady guest of his and Mum's might have said. He loves that quaint English expression, "bloomin'". Although his mother's friend was actually Irish.

Another sailboat pushes off from the little pier and Lars, in his mind's eye, sets it precisely where it belongs in his mental measuring queue. How satisfying to have a place for everything and everything in its place. How very satisfying that his place is with Dennis and Dennis's with him. How very, very satisfying it is to belong and be belonged to. Even if the bloomin' tomatoes ain't bloomin' and their irascible rooster is an occasional handful.

Dennis is thinking almost identical thoughts with the

notable exception of piling those sailboats end-to-end; and with the harrowing addition of whatever can be happening down there in Christine's ever-roiling womb? He wishes she could just get on with it and stop bleating about it. He has done his part and that was an end to it. Or a beginning? His heart beats a little faster and sweat again beads on his forehead almost as though he still held that infernal 'petite' demitasse in his fatigued and shaking right hand. He wonders if this 'little tiny Isabella Victoria Gloria' will cause tension with Lars. He thinks not but...

"What is he thinking of?!" asks Violet thrusting her index finger in earphoned, foot-thumping Brad's direction.

"Nothing," says Dexter fondly, "Nothing at all. He's listening to his 'space music'."

"I thought he looked spaced out. But not on music. What's he smoking?"

"Tree fungi," replies Dexter, "berries, variegated mushrooms, elk-poop? He's a health freak."

"He's a freak," says Violet contemptuously, sorry, of course, the moment she's said it. Why she must ceaselessly explain to herself that she's not this way at all. Am I, Chrissie? she almost asks but checks herself as she sees Christine gazing at Dennis's pink cheeks and thinks instead: He's been at them again! They'll fall off in a minute. That would teach him! And her! No, Violet Heather Rose! squeals her much abused conscience, don't be this way! It's unbecoming! He's only a man and doesn't know any better. You were married once. You know! Men are strangers to subtlety. My God! Only a man would pinch his cheeks to appear attractive to a woman! And that hair of his! If it isn't bleached I'll shave my legs! Violet! You're fraught, love, slow down. He can't harm you. What's done is done and being nasty can only alienate you from your Chrissie! All right, says Violet to herself, I'll behave, for now, but if that multi-coloured middle-aged...

"Does Brad know he was a day late?" asks Lars as he pours fresh coffee for everyone from the glistening pot that cute waiter has just left on the table for them.

"I don't think so," replies Dexter.

"How do we tell him?" asks Dennis.

"Oh we don't," says Dexter, "I never tell him anything. It only confuses him."

"What on earth is space music'?" asks Christine.

"Music that skinny little gits play," snaps Violet, "The skinny little git."

Lars brightly: "Violet, exactly how many sailboats end to end would it take to reach onto the other side of the lake?"

"Too many!" snaps Violet, unrepentant and a martyr to her alleged Christine-induced, uncontrollable moods.

Coffee finished, they all walk to a low stone wall on the water's edge, sit, take off their shoes and dangle their feet in the warmish shallow water. Christine gazes, to Violet's seething displeasure, at Dennis. Christine wonders if a restraint corset could correct his sloppy posture, makes a mental note: is posture a genetic trait? Consult Humane Reproduction brochure. Violet watches Christine watching Dennis who watches Lars who is now convinced his earlier sailboat calculations were faulty -- the lake is somewhat larger than he'd reckoned -- a trick of the clear, early evening air. He must Google soon about Atmospheric Distortion at this latitude.

Dexter peers unashamedly at shirtless Brad who is bumping to his earphoned beat, wondering why the submerged portions of his toes appear larger than the rest. But Brad soon abandons wondering as it makes his pretty head hurt.

Dennis's Mum, telephone in that useful device on her shoulder, dials as she hastily flings clothes at a small suitcase. The telephone rings again and again and of course is not answered. No one is home at that cabin in the copse.

As the ceaseless Nordic twilight stubbornly continues, the little group surrounds a tall, thinnish Viking Rune stone, bright pink in the light of the tardily setting sun. Brad has wound himself around this noble stone and, still reflexively keeping time, has dozed off, an unlit mysterious ciggie dangling from his luscious lips. Violet observes him with some distaste and is stunned as Christine, some distance away, laughs at something Dennis has just said. Is there no limit to Violet Heather Rose's suffering?

Dexter pats the sleeping Brad's head while Violet, fed-up and doesn't care who knows it, attempts to extricate Brad from the Rune stone. Dexter slaps her hands and a serious tussle nearly ensues but Dexter avoids it by crossing his arms over his chest and bowing low to the simmering Violet.

"Here, legend tells us," translates Dennis the peace-maker from a tourist sign, "here, legend tells us, the Viking housewife..."

"I beg your pardon," says Christine, "Viking Housewife?!"

Dennis nods pleasantly, "That is what it says, love, 'Here the Viking housewife, grief-stricken and crazed at the slaughter-death of her Viking husband and drenched in said husband's blood and gore, in a titanic fit of rage, with his sword in her bloody hand slew his fourteen murderers."

"A wery brave voman," says Lars.

"Temper, temper!" gasps Dexter who has just joined them.

"God! Can't you ever be serious?" snaps Violet who rushes up flushed and puffing from attempting in vain to rescue the Rune stone. "You prattle on like some bimbo from a 1940's B-movie!"

"Skirting the issues?" replies Dexter, "Madam, I'll have you know that Hollywood did not reach its artistic zenith by the fruits of its labour! Nay, madam, but by the labour of its fruits!"

Violet can stand it no longer and rushes back to Brad, grabs him by his tank-top, "Stop that! Stop squeezing that stone! It's old and weak! You'll break it! Have you no respect for archae-ology?" God! thinks Violet, Christine has got me so upset I'm pulling twits from rocks!

"Would that I were that Rune stone," sighs Dexter. Violet throws up her hands up, marches away shouting "I curse the world at this 'ridiculous latitude'!"

Violet's been so out of sorts lately, thinks Christine, she's even quoting Dexter. I don't know what's got into her. Certainly not what's got into me! she almost says. But doesn't. Ever so fortunately. At least in front of Vi.

Violet retreats to a bench, glowers into the everlasting sunset, brushes a hand against her teary eyes. She's bursting with tormenting doubt as she's not, just now, dead certain that her judicious juggling of Chrissie's fertile windows has been a complete success.

"We are standing upon," says Lars, ever eager to explain the recondite, fickle mysteries of Nature, and primarily, one of his favourite subjects, Geology, "a enormous pile of ancient compacted, granite gravel, grinded and scattered, as it were, in haste, geologically speaking, by a rapidly, relatively speaking, retreating glacier, remnant of the Great Ice Age. This mountainous assemblage of impacted gravel is known as a 'moraine'.

"Thank you, Lars," says Dennis, "that was desperately informative. Lars knows about these things as his second master's degree -- or is it his second Ph.D? -- was in..."

"Big deal." says Violet. "We've hundreds of moraines in Britain. Thousands of 'em! I've sat on a quite a few. Every mother's daughter of them is at least twice as big as this one. You don't need a Ph.D to know that!"

"Impossible!" interjects Lars, "Swedish moraines is this planet's veritable Ice Age leaders. This is a bloomin' fact!"

"Nonsense!" says Violet, "We Brits have funfair roller-coasters that would dwarf this piddly moron!"

"Moraine, darling," corrects Christine.

"That is veritably impossible, Violet," replies Lars, "This bloomin' moraine could easily contain, several dozen horizontal Empire State Buildings, the Battersea Park Funfair, Disney World, the Millennium Dome and a whole village to boot if it were hollow!"

Violet jumps up from her bench, and pulling her whole imposing frame to attention, struts up to Lars, thrusts her grinning face directly into his, "But it's not hollow, is it?!"

"Dexter?"

"Yes Brad?"

"Ain't it bee-yoo-tee-ful up here?"

"We are standing atop a moraine, dear boy."

"Dexter, what's a mor-aine?"

"Something to do with several dozen horizontal, Empire State Buildings, the Battersea Park Funfair, the Millenium Dome, and a whole village to boot."

"Ohhh, wowwwww!"

"And it's hollow."

Violet can contain herself no longer, "It is not hollow!"

"It feels hollow," says Dexter. Stamp your dainty foot, Vi. No. On second thoughts, don't."

Dennis's mum, telephone in hand and dressed to the nines, her suitcase beside her, taps her fingers impatiently as she waits for an answer. "Where can they be?! God! There are two of them plus two lesbians! And lord only knows how many more visitors! Can't anybody be there?!" A taxi beeps in the street. She slams down the telephone. "Must hurry! I'll miss my plane!"

19

The little group descends the last stone steps from an ancient churchyard through an iron gate, their usual moods and the nearly permanent sunset securely intact: Christine, closely studying Dennis, his pink cheeks, curly golden hair, perfect teeth and not completely unpleasant body geometry immediately transfers this pleasing ensemble to little tiny you-know-who and nearly giggles at the pleasant prospect; Violet, closely studying Christine and bored to death by her blabbing about Dennis's desirable coloring; Dexter, a definitive romantic-erotic, closely studying -- rather than the notable Nordic-Romanesque architecture -- Brad, who seems to study his exposed navel but with dishy Brad, you never know. Actually, Brad's borrowed tank top is simply too short for him as he bumps along to his earphoned, now gangsta-rap, beat; Lars, watching with profound Nordic detachment as all are finally assembled in the mini-bus, settles into the driver's seat and smiles sardonically.

Knowing precisely what that word means, though he often feigns ignorance to tease Dennis, starts up and they're off.

The speeding taxi carrying Mum races down the street. "Stop!" cries Mum. The taxi screeches to a halt. "I'll be right back!" She jumps out and hurries into a shop, "Little Babykins Infant Wear".

"Stop!" cries Violet. The mini-bus screeches to a halt beside their jacked-up, rental car. "We lost our wheel nuts here."

"You lost our wheel nuts here," replies Dexter.

"I think it is about time we got this vehicle rolling again. It is our responsibility. Let's find 'em!"

"We couldn't find them before, Violet, dear," says Christine, "Let's just leave the car here and rent another one."

"Where?" says Lars, "the nearest car-renting town is many miles. Many, many miles."

Violet leaps out. "On your knees, everybody! It should be easy with all of us looking."

Everyone reluctantly climbs out of the mini-bus. But Brad, looking dazed behind his earphones, wanders alone into the forest. Dexter is instantly beside him, grabs his arm, pulls him back, pushes him gently to his knees to search for wheel nuts with the others -- to be a team player. Brad, beginning to bump to his earphones, giggles. "A game?!" he giggles, "A new game?!"

"Yes, dear boy," replies Dexter, "a new game."

Brad giggles again and on his hands and knees crawls beneath a giant fern. Dexter follows, barks: "Woof! Woof!"

"Dexter!" snaps Violet, "You'll stoop to anything!"

"I stoop to conquer!" replies Dexter from beneath the fern. Brad giggles again. Dexter giggles.

"Stop!" giggles Brad, "That tickles!"

"Does it, dear boy? Oh does it? Here, let old Dexter help."

"Stop!" giggles Brad, precisely as before, "That tickles!"

"Sissies," mumbles Violet.

"Be nice, Violet," says Christine from her knees, "To each his own. It takes all types."

"You can say that again," growls Violet immediately before raging guilt rushes in to quench her irritability.

"I'd take both the blue and the pink, if I was you, dear," says the saleswomen as Mum contemplates the two piles of baby clothes on the counter before her, "It might be fraternal twins."
"Oh? D'you really think so?!" gasps Mum bubbling with delight.
"You never can tell," whispers the saleswoman conspiratorially, "Especially these days."
Mum anxiously glances at her watch, "May I use your telephone? I'll pay."

The mini-bus, driven by Lars and containing Dennis, Dexter and Brad, is followed by the rental car driven by the triumphant Violet with Christine close beside her who says emphatically: "You needn't have been so pompous, Violet. Even if you did find the wheel nuts. Men don't like women who win, you know."
"The point is, our sodding vehicle is again functional in case we need to make a quick getaway when I do something rash," says Violet and adds, "which is very likely".
"But as you may remember, love. Our vehicle is rented in Dexter's name."
"I could shave my armpits and pose as Dexter."
"It would never work, Vi. You'd have to shave your legs too."
"That I would never do! But I could wear heels!"
"Darling," laughs Christine, "there aren't a pair of heels within a hundred miles!"
"Unless Dennis hides them in his closet!" Violet ponders for a moment, and suddenly blurts "Since when have you cared about what men like?!"
"I care about a lot of things, Violet. Including you. Remember, love, as parents you and I will have exceptionally comprehensive responsibilities and Rome wasn't built in a day -- not even in three. Violet, we must learn to be versatile."
"Versatile?" asks Violet suspiciously, "What does that sodding mean?"

"The longest journey," replies Christine, begins with a single footstep!"

"How would you know?!"

"Fluffy, darling, we must learn to compromise to achieve our dreams."

"Why? We've never compromised before," retorts Violet, instantly aware that repellent compromise and duplicity have been at the very core of her being for the past two days. But nobody, not even her reproductively rampant lover seems to give a damn!

"We have, thus far," says Christine, dealt effectively with men. A first for us I believe you will agree. We have, Vi, through our traditional feminine wiles, extracted almost a quarter of an ounce of spunk from an extraordinarily reluctant donor. A goal achieved is a goal...well...a goal achieved."

"Your goal, not mine! cries Violet, "You have veered radically and I must say, selfishly, from our original concept. Had we not met Dexter with his sodding photo in Norway, you would, as I speak, be lying spread-eagled, your darling Venus's mound heavenward, on a sterile slab in Earls Court being deftly syringed up your twat by the rubber-gloved fingers of a skilled and highly personable Icelandic sperm technician named Gunilla Harridansdottir!"

"Yes, Vi! But who knows with what result? Anonymous spunk?! Absolutely not! It's my womb, Fluffy. Though together we shall share its fruit, the decision is ultimately mine."

"You and your womb! I'm sick to death of your sodding womb! It used to be our sodding womb! Now it's only your sodding womb! Christine, you've changed."

"Of course I've changed you silly, devoted girl. I am probably preggers as we speak."

"Enceinte?"

"Oui, oui! I shall know any moment now. A clarion call will echo through my pertinent paraphernalia."

I love her desperately, thinks Violet, but she's totally mad whilst on heat. Even at the best of times her hormones are significantly askew.

Suddenly Christine, arms outstretched, catapults across the car seat towards her dearest Violet to bestow a healing hug when she blinks, stops, and eyes wide, emits a tiny scream "Oh, Fluffy! The proverbial trumpet has sounded! Dennis has succeeded. I am ablaze with new life! Isabella is an unassailable fact!"

Violet slams on the brakes, leaps out of the car and leans pathetically on its bonnet, her mind a mass of searing doubt. How can this pregnancy be possible?! Given my cooking the books Chrissie should by all of the laws of her peculiarly unique physiological nature have been at that crucial moment in time, utterly not fertile! Not even of any kind! That's what all our brochures said! -- and doubly so, given Christine's nearly insoluble systemic inconstancies! But, has Instinctual Knowledge just spoken?! Oh, God! thinks Vi, I pray not!

20

Mum carrying the bag of pink baby clothes on one arm and the bag of blue on the other, springs from the taxi at Heathrow. "I'm going to be a grandmother!" she cries to the driver. "A grandmother!"

She rushes away. "Your suitcase, madam!" calls the driver after her. Mum twirls and returns, her mind a pink and blue carousel of perfect happiness.

"A grandmother!" she repeats to the driver as he places her suitcase on a luggage cart, "A grandmother!"

She throws her ticket on the check-in counter. "I'm going to be a grandmother!" she exclaims to all the personnel at Check-In, "A grandmother!"

At passport control she cries "I'm going to be a grandmother!"

At security control she cries "I'm going to be a grandmother!" as her cabin luggage passes through X-Ray. Her exultant cry is instantly regarded as a suspicious distraction and she is questioned and her knitting needles briefly appropriated.

As the cabin attendant welcomes her aboard she cries "I'm going to be a grandmother!" and cannot help wonder why everyone isn't quite as excited as she is. Life has been tough since she and Dennis's father decided to part ways...but that's all behind her now. A grandchild will fix everything. Why else did people have children, except for their doting grandmothers? Why else should they, damn them! She draws her tiny silver flask from her bag, uncorks it and nipping the last nip, settles herself comfortably into her seat, anxious to be under way, anxious also, for the imminent arrival of the drinks trolley.

Violet and Christine arrive at the cabin and screech to a stop behind the mini-bus from which are scrambling Dexter, Brad, Dennis and Lars, though Lars never actually 'scrambles' but disembarks with great dignity, his thoughts dwelling on various, long accepted exactitudes and how to improve upon them.

Dennis gazes affectionately after him as Lars returns sedately through his perfectly cared-for garden to the cabin to prepare their usual sumptuous dinner. He does everything to perfection and then some, thinks Dennis, If only I could produce a perfect Safe Sex DVD. If only our tomatoes would bloom. If only that horrid rooster would leave me alone. If only these women would leave me alone. If only I could find and complete to perfection my epic novel. Am I going to be a father? Will Lars still love me when I'm sixty-four? This is a shallow approximation of the muddle in Dennis's mind -- whirling as much as his exultant, swiftly approaching, Mum's -- but for very different reasons. Unless, of course, floating anxiety is inherited and Mum is just now as chronically flummoxed as he is. Now, here is something new and horrid to chew on. And he does so, bite after gulping bite. Dennis considers himself a bit of a failure with everything but Lars. Ah, here is comfort at last! Dwell on Lars. Yes. Forget all...

These thoughts are, as increasingly everything is, interrupted by Christine. "I have just conceived! I am burning with new life! Little tiny Isabella Victoria Gloria has begun to arrive!"

she announces to all.

"Gloria in excelsis oestrus!" intones Dexter, who adds "But darling, you were only inseminated this afternoon, she must indeed be little and tiny."

"Christine was inseminated at four-forty p.m. precisely," says Violet, "Chrissie carved it on the bottom of her guestroom bedstead with my hunting knife." Of course, thinks Violet, this is a flat-out impossibility, given...

"I feel...wondrous!" cries Christine.

"Are you sure it's not just spontaneous combustion?" asks Dexter.

"If it was," snaps Violet, "I would know about it! What do you know about spontaneous combustion?!"

"I may not be spontaneous, darling, but I am definitely combustible."

"You look burned-out to me."

"Oh Violet! There you go again. Be nice. We'll be leaving tomorrow now the deed is done! Show some fortitude!" soothes Christine, rubbing her tummy with both hands and summoning up memories of newly pregnant, incognito heroines in startling turn-of-the-century novels recently explored in evening-class. The very book, in fact, that she is now reading to Violet.

Violet, irritatingly a-jumble, assists Christine, now dazed with joy, towards the cabin. What if Chrissie really is preggers?! How shall I deal with this pink-cheeked, golden-haired, reason-ably intelligent -- though I have yet to see irrefutable signs of that -- interloper who will indubitably intrude more and more, as a much-feared Father Figure? Will Dennis become more important to Chrissie than I am? wonders Violet with a series of fully visible shudders.

"Ohhhhhhhh......Wowwwwwwwww!" moans Brad, bumping behind those earphones as he squats and peers goofily at a scolding squirrel gathering acorns from the grass.

"Get real, dickhead!" snaps Violet at Brad as she and Christine pass on to the cabin. Then softly, slipping her arm around Christine she says, eyes narrowing with deceit: "You'd better lie down, Chrissie. Little tiny Isabella's had a busy day."

"Yes, Vi-Vi, I wouldn't want to shake anything loose," murmurs Christine into Violet's comforting shoulder, "Not now. We well know of my perilous perch syndrome and..."

"Yes, Chrissie, darling, we well know," says Violet, her head a battlefield, strewn with the terrible debris of Earls Court. I shall soon go mad! Thinks Violet, if I am not already mad!

"Violet, love, I think you ought to know, darling, that now I am definitively preggers I could be inclined to edginess. Actually, I feel a tinge of edginess coming on right this minute."

"Yes, of course, Chrissie! That's what our brochures say, isn't it?!" replies Violet, wondering how pregnancy could possibly be the case.

"Keep your bloody voice down, Violet!" roars Christine who instantly recants, says "Sorry, Vi-Vi. Mother Nature's ways are indeed a mystery, aren't they, love?"

"Indeed they are," sighs Violet.

Dennis pauses in the fading light, watches the women disappear into the cabin, sees Dexter remove chemically content, squatting Brad from the spell of the scolding squirrel and guide him lovingly into the cabin.

I am a happy man, thinks Dennis, in spite of my failures, as he sees Lars in the kitchen window, working his miracles. Just as he has with my life, thinks Dennis. Oh, unworthy me. Blessed be us poor in spirit, for Lars is a worker of miracles.

21

Dinner is over, the dishes are washed, the table, tidied -- all by Lars who will have it no other way. His kitchen is a veritable shrine and he is its saint -- in all likelihood.

Outside, in the clear air under brilliant stars that seem to crackle, Brad simultaneously lights up two tree-fungi ciggies, takes one from his lips and offers it to Dexter who blissfully accepts it. They drop themselves on a Lars-carpentered split log bench and inhale great puffs until non-smoker Dexter gags. Brad blinks sleepily at him, claps him on the back and Dexter quietens down, sucks gently at his exotic fungi ciggie. Brad takes off his earphones, pats them with ineffable tenderness over Dexter's ears, thinks "Good old..." and would have added "Dexter", if his attention had not been diverted by a friendly ladybird making itself at home on his deliciously bare knee.

Though the music dismays him, Dexter is ecstatic under Brad's earphones for he has never had such meltingly intimate attention from Brad and suffers it gladly. Feigning interest, he even thumps feebly and out-of-time to this mind-numbing beat, begins somehow to grasp Brad's dilemma about just where he, fabulous Brad, is at any given point in time, and space -- grasps even the universal ambiguity of existence! But of course he knows, in his love-addled head, that it's just the fungi ciggie. Or is it?

Brad, now diverted from the friendly ladybird watches Dexter for a moment almost with interest, then dozes off and his handsome head flops onto Dexter's shoulder. Dexter's eyes move from Brad's thick, shining hair towards those crackling stars and he realizes that there are guardian angels up there somewhere that brought his Brad safely back to him through this endless jungle of pine. Dexter sighs and murmurs "Thank you, one and all."

A hint of a breeze, suspiciously like that occasional, familiar voice in Brad's head says distinctly, "You're very, very welcome!"

"Magic," concludes Dexter, who feels a warm glow moving up his legs, settling somewhere between his thighs and navel, an area that has been off-limits for a seeming millennium, "Sheer magic." Well, perhaps not.

Dennis brushes his perfect, Christine-vetted teeth, notes in the basin mirror Lars's tilted head, eager, as usual in his cook book. Tonight's feast had been bliss and perfectly conceived and created. A feather in the chef's hat of his accomplished Swede.

Dennis rinses his mouth, drops on the bed beside Lars who does not look up from his cookbook. Dennis says "Jag älskar dig, I love you."

"Is good," says Lars into tomorrow's recipes. Dennis smiles. Lars, behind his book smiles too. He always hears every word Dennis says. But to appear too attentive would spoil Dennis even more. If that were possible.

In the guestroom below, Violet runs her fingers through Christine's hair as Christine clutches Nana's petite demitasse, contemplates its recent contents with some reverence then spits on it for good luck and dries it on her sleeve. A distant cuckoo calls from somewhere in the still, starlit night. "What was that?" asks Christine, "It sounded like a Swiss clock."

Violet, rather sadly: "A cuckoo, Chrissie. It's a funny bird that lays its eggs in other bird's nests."

"It must be mad."

The cuckoo calls again and again and the two women regard each other, eyes shimmering with their combined futures. Love like theirs, they assure one another, in fits and starts, does not grow on trees, and certainly not the common pine. Love like theirs is magic.

"Sheer magic," says Christine and sets down Nana's demitasse and embraces Violet and says "Love is the truest thing I know."

They laugh, pushing Dennis to the farthest reaches of their minds, and Violet and Christine, relaxed for the first time in days, fall backward on the bed, frolicking in mutual affection and with little tiny Isabella tucked comfortably, Christine is firmly convinced, in her willing womb.

Outside, on their split-log bench, Dexter and Brad are still as statues, sculpted under a moon that rises rapidly, gloriously annihilating the brightness of the crackling stars. The muffled beat from Brad's earphones, still on Dexter's martyred ears, is relieved only by the call of that distant cuckoo -- again and again.

The little cabin seems a toy, dwarfed by the massive moon and endless forest that sweeps from horizon to horizon. The cuckoo calls once more, then once again. And is silent.

22

"Fight attendant!"

"Yes, dear?"

"I would so appreciate another little drinkie."

"Of course, dear."

"Johnny Walker Black, love. Make it a double. There's a lovey-love."

The flight attendant nods cheerfully and leaves Mum to her knitting. In her lap lie two completed baby-booties: one blue, one pink. She begins to knit their mates but drops the yarn which rolls several seats back in the sparsely occupied plane. Kneeling to fetch it she sees a woman of about her age gazing morosely at a photo of a beautiful baby. Mum bends close. "What an adorable child! What a perfectly adorable child!"

"Umm," says the woman.

"Your grandchild?"

"Umm."

The woman hands the photo to her. Mum admires it, says "I'm going to be a grandmother too!"

"Good for you, dear," says the woman, forlorn expression intact, "but be careful. It's not all it's cracked up to be."

"Boy or girl?"

"Girl."

"Perfectly adorable! Where is she now?"

"Just behind you, love."

Mum rises from her knees, stands, and with a welcoming smile and loving thoughts too numerous to count, turns and meets the much made-up eyes of a towering adolescent with purple hair; several rings through her nose, ears, lips and bare navel; tattoos on both her bare arms; black plastic short shorts; black sequinned, net stockings and a deadly, spiked dog collar tight around her neck. Mum's smile disintegrates but immediately reinstalls as the girl shoves roughly by and drops herself into the seat beside her grandmother where she grabs up a glittering mobile phone and begins to play an exceedingly noisy game on it.

Mum is still smiling as she stares in mute fascination at the girl who suddenly looks up, glares at her. "What's wif you, then, you steamin' old dyke?!"

Mum nods a quick nod to the girl's grandmother and is rescued by the flight attendant who hands her a whiskey. Mum quaffs it, hands the glass back to the surprised attendant, requests another and returns to her seat, dazed. She fastens her seat belt, takes up her knitting, crouches there, knitting by reflex, her fingers unconnected to the tangle of conflicting emotions passing behind her troubled brow. It's a funny old world, thinks Mum, and getting funnier every minute. But my grandchild will be different! She smiles to herself, accepts another whiskey from the attendant, sips, sets it down, smiles again to reassure herself, attempts to forget this rude teenie-giant, has a sudden insidious doubt, with effort dismisses it, smiles courageously again. Knits. Knits. Knits! And knits some more.

"Gosh!" sings Christine, after an eventful day of sightseeing and a simply superb dinner, as she pats her tummy and pushes herself away from the dining table, "Preggers at last! I feel divine!"

"Delusions of grandeur, dearest Miss," quips Dexter.

"Can I have a glass of water, Vi-vi," lisps Christine like a small child, "I'm firsty."

Violet is always an instant dupe for Christine's child-act and pours her a large glass of ice-water. Christine takes it in both hands and, still the child, gazing innocently from the top of her eyes at everyone round the table, drains the glass. Mummy trained her well. Their attention she has!

But...

"That's your seventh glass of water today, Chrissie," dotes Violet, "If our sainted Kate Hepburn were yet amongst us she would be proud of you."

"You give your baby too much vater," says Lars

matter-of-factly. Who is Katja Hepburn?"

"Who is this man?!" cries Violet, "What does he know about it?!"

"Lars," intones Dexter, "as well as co-producing socially-conscious pornography for the unenlightened of the same sex and plump, red, firm -- not mushy, certainly not beige -- strawberries for our table and oddly bloomless tomatoes in a medium-sized hothouse at the wrong latitude, is a stand-by nutrition consultant for the Swedish government. His latest article, 'Too Much Water: How we drink ourselves to death' appeared only last week as a series of brochures..."

"Brochures?!" cries Christine, only too familiar with the power of the mini-press.

"Brochures?!" cries Violet, "A whole series?"

"Yes," says Dexter, "a whole series published under the auspices of the Royal Swedish Health Department and picked up on the Net by at least fifty thousand blogs and websites not to mention every major newspaper in Sweden!"

Christine is horrified, shoots up from the table toppling the accused, accursed water glass. "Lars!" she gasps, "Is this true?!"

"In all likelihood," says Lars with his usual, studied diffidence but nevertheless leaping with a cloth to ameliorate the spreading water stain.

"Swedes never lie," adds Dexter at his serious best.

"Then, seven glasses of water a day are err...dangerous when one is, when one is...enceinte?"

"Or even pregnant," says Dexter.

"Anything is bloomin' possible," replies Lars, "Veritably."

"Leave her alone! She's suffering for two!" cries Violet, hoping wretchedly not.

"Ach du lieber! Poor little tiny Isabella!" shrieks Christine, freely lapsing into evening-class German.

"Mon Dieu!" cries Violet, not to be linguistically outdone but hiding her pleasure in a frown whilst covertly hoping that this present Isabella, if she actually does exist, would be reasonable, just be reasonable and float away in at least one or two of those seven glasses of water.

"Oh, my God!" cries Christine.

"Calm down, Christine," says Dexter, "Isabella may have water on the brain but she'll be a damned good swimmer."

"Oh my God!" cries Christine yet again, and with a violent clatter of dishes and cutlery she crumples in her chair and bursts into huge, wet, flying tears. Violet thrusts her arms around Christine, throws a sulphuric scowl at everyone, cries "Now look what you've gone and done! Don't you know she's edgy?!"

"Lars, move away a bit, love," says Dennis, "out of Violet's range."

Violet rises to her full, frightening height, confronts the men and says again, louder, if possible, "Now look what you've gone and done!"

Christine's sobbing head, at Violet's abrupt rise, drops with another crash of cutlery and china onto the table, her hair lashing the butter dish which Lars deftly removes. Head on the table though safely out of the butter she continues to sob. 'Misery loves an audience' comes to mind, as her dear designing Mum has always advised her, and 'Misery is power.' Christine's tears have now morphed to sobs of a deep, gulping nature punctuated by small shrieks in which "Isabella" or "Victoria" or "Gloria" and even "little tiny" can be distinctly heard. She pulls away from Violet and shrieking wildly, disappears into their guestroom.

"Can't you imbeciles see she's edgy?!" wails Violet, "Her incessant need to procreate makes her edgy!"

"Her incessant need to procreate makes me edgy too," ventures Dennis, going where no man, at least recently, has dared to venture.

"The world thinks and I think too," says Dexter, "that both of our lady friends are edgy."

Violet well knows through her Domestic Psychology course that ultimately her terrible anger can be laid directly on Dennis's damnable 'colouring' which has been busily ungluing a perfectly functioning, self-sufficient, exclusive relationship and insidiously diluting the devotion they had shown one another for five wonderfully exciting years. A devotion based on she and she that had now begun to founder, at least ostensibly, on she and he.

Violet moves towards...who will it be first? -- she'll save Dennis for last! Ah!...towards jiving Brad, thumps him on his head, fails to get his attention. On to Dexter: "You perfumed, strutting little phrase-maker," she spits, "Why couldn't you keep your sick little rogue's gallery of photos to yourself?!"

Dexter flattens himself in his chair, has no idea what Violet is screaming about. On to Lars: "You think you know everything about water, do you?!" cries Violet, "You think you're some kind of...of...of H-2-O specialist, do you?! Well you're not! Kate Hepburn drank seven glasses of water a day, rest her steely soul, and had more knowledge of H-2-O in her shiny old latex douche bag than you've got in your whole...body!"

"Who is Katja Hepburn?" asks Lars.

Violet ignores him, goes on to the major culprit, Dennis, who is about to rise and flee the room but is shoved roughly back into his chair. "And you!" hisses Violet, "You and your petite demi-tasse of sticky little tadpoles! Have you no shame?!"

"It wasn't my idea at all, Violet, it wasn't even my petite demitasse! It was Christine's great grandmother's! It was Nana's! Christine told me herself!"

"Belt up! you, you...cuckoo!"

"Really, Violet, if you've finished with your melodrama we can..."

But Dexter is drowned out by a bellow the likes of which he hadn't experienced since he slipped in bullshit in Pamplona and was lightly gored by a raging bull -- all quite by accident several years before when, unduly heightened by an aspiring bullfighter's tight pantaloons, he'd fallen right through the open window of his armoured tour bus.

The bellow in question, emanates from Christine in the guestroom: "Don't you understand, you idiots?! Women are fragiiiiiiiiiiiiiiiiiiiile!"

The men, save Brad who does not hear it, huddle together, pelted by Violet's additional, ascending decibels. "You bullies!"

she cries, "You sissy-bullies!" her last restraints in tatters, as she slams into the guestroom to console her disconsolate lover.

"Some wine, Dexter? To disperse your edginess?" asks Lars as he offers, on a lovely silver tray compliments of his mum, an engraved crystal, impossibly long-stemmed goblet of wine. Dexter accepts, sips, his face a blank.

"Is good?" asks Lars who hovers beside him, "Is good?"

"Err..." says connoisseur Dexter, "is...challenging."

"Ah! Is good then!" says Lars who loves a challenge.

"Ummnn," says Dexter, "challenging, darling. Err (sip) most challenging."

"Ah," says Lars, returning to his perfect kitchen, "Is good."

23

"I'm going to be a grandmother!" cries Mum tipsily thrusting her bags of assorted blue and pink infant apparel at the Swedish passport control officer. The woman eyes her glassily, puts a finger to her lips, whispers, "Please, Mrs, Sweden is sedate country. Shhhhhhh."

"Sedate!?" replies Mum, "Sssshhhh!?"

"Sssshhhh," says the woman, "We have multitude of grand-mamas in Sweden which do not loudly shout."

Mum, not quite sussing what's up, tucks her assorted baby clothes and knitting basket under one arm, takes up her small suitcase on the other and tiptoes into sedate Sweden.

Lars, having refilled the coffee cups, rises from the dining table. "I fetch the Svedish butter cream meringue torte."

"Can I help?" asks Dexter.

"No," says Lars through the kitchen door, "No."

"He's more comfortable alone in the kitchen," says Dennis, "He's very efficient."

"What bliss, dear boy. It's vice versa with Brad and me no matter what room we're in."

Dexter leans lovingly across the table, taps Brad who, glazen-eyed, thumps his beat on the dining table as he puffs absently at his latest fungi ciggie. "Hello? Brad?! Are you really in there somewhere, Laddie?"

Brad peeps over his shoulder and his face alight with a perfect coquette's smile, takes a deep drag on his ciggie.

"I never say anything to him unless it is very important," says Dexter, "And even then I don't."

"He's rather charming. In his distant way," replies Dennis.

"Oh? D'you think so? Our relationship, Dennis, what there is of it, is a complete mystery to me. Because I'm usually attracted to older men -- which, recently, in my twilight years of sad necessity, usually includes me and my own disconcertingly large reflection in the ceiling mirror above my empty -- save but me -- bed."

"You poor kid," commiserates Dennis.

But Dexter is pleased when others also appreciate Brad's peculiar genius for appearing to do, to think, absolutely nothing. This is what had originally attracted him to Brad -- notwithstanding his drop-dead good looks and Praxiteles physique. It was this all-consuming vagueness of his, this otherness, this more than otherness, this, well, nothingness, this...

"But how do you communicate?" asks Dennis, breaking Dexter's homoerotic contemplation with an admiring nod at Brad's shapely T-shirted back.

Dexter grins, taps Brad again, says: "A smile is worth a thousand words."

Brad lurches round, smiles a perfect, identical reprise over his shoulder. "See what I mean," clucks Dexter more loving than a fussing flock of mother hens.

"Disarming," replies Dennis, genuinely moved, "singularly disarming. How old is the boy?"

"Nineteen, I believe. But he could be fifty. Cretins never age," sighs Dexter, "Just call me Kelvin. I've stumbled upon absolute zero."

"Poor Dexter, having to operate in a vacuum."

"It's better than nothing," murmurs Dexter, leering longingly at Brad, "But sometimes I almost wish I were a lesbian so I might then be attracted to females. At my age, life would be so much simpler."

"Good God, how!?" asks Dennis with a nervous glance towards the guestroom within whose walls now lurks direst discontent.

Lars enters with a stunner of a torte which Dennis and Dexter eye approvingly, warming Lars to the depths of his over-organized soul. Even Brad surfaces, sees Lar's luscious confection and wags his head from side to side, brings splayed fingers to his perfect forehead, brushes his magnificent hair from his dazzled eyes, moans "Ohhh wowwwwwww..."

Mum sways into an airport telephone kiosk -- sorry she'd had that last whisky on the plane. But the cabin attendant was so sweet to pour them herself that Mum lost count.

Mum now attempts, scattering baby booties like rose petals, to operate the telephone with a handful of British coins that with a wrenching clatter, rocket right back at her from the coin return. God! Why hadn't she ever learned to use a mobile telephone?!

"Uhh," says Dennis to the sullen, silent Violet who has just now stomped back from the guestroom and dropped herself with a disconcerting thud on the sofa opposite him, "Would you care, Violet, for some of Lars's super aromatic espresso and delectable Swedish butter cream meringue torte? We're just sampling it."

What can he say to this impossible woman? Or to her equally impossible mate? They have wrecked havoc upon his sacred household. Have shaken him to the very roots of his authentically golden hair. Have questioned his every motive and have wrung from him his...his very essence!

"Christine is involved with you, in her way," snarls Violet, "I know the signs!"

"Ah, yes, the signs," announces Dexter. "Like the sign of the double cross. Women say they'll enlighten you, show you the

True Cross. But all they ever do is make certain you suffer upon it."

"And men say they want to be your mate," replies Violet somewhat louder, "Correction! Your checkmate!"

Violet remembers sadly the footloose early days of hers and Chrissie's relationship: the water polo, beginner's Judo, the marathon runs and, oh! those bar-room brawls! Back to back, she and Chrissie were invincible! Where had it all gone? Up Christine's fallopian tubes! Violet now ignores Dexter and, eyes fixed on Dennis and vibrating with some nerve-jangling emotion that Dennis has never before encountered, hisses "Christine is involved with you, in her way."

Dennis's espresso quivers in his hand. This was completely unexpected! But he manages, "Errr...whatever can this mean?"

Lars appears, serves more tantalizing torte, places a dish in Violet's hand. She silently accepts it, takes a large, sloshy bite and again fastens her eyes on Dennis and chews menacingly, "I'll tell you what it means," she replies, "I'll tell you precisely what it means."

"Oh, do tell us!" cries Dexter and claps his hands, "Precisely what it means!"

Violet silences him with a glower from deepest Hell.

"It means," continues Violet, "It means that Christine may wish to read books with you, Dennis. And discuss them."

"Oh God no!" cries Dexter, "Surely not discuss them?!"

Lars approaches, hovers near, studies Violet's reaction to his delectable torte. "Is good?" he asks.

Violet ignores him, takes another sloshy bite, chews, her eyes still glued on Dennis. "What did you do to Christine?"

Another bite of delectable torte, a noisy swill of super aromatic espresso.

Lars says "Is good?"

"Naff off, Lars! Dennis, what are we going to do about this?"

"Enjoy, Vi-Vi!" says Dexter waving a hunk of torte on his fork. Real danger lurks in her withering look. Dexter stops chewing, lays down his fork, sticks his nose in a magazine.

"I want it straight, Dennis, what did you do to Christine?"

"Exclusive of my jizzum?" peeps Dennis, taking a large bite of his lover's delectable torte.

"Exclusive of your so-called jizzum."

"Nothing, then. I did absolutely nothing."

"Nada," adds Dexter.

"What?" asks Violet.

"In Spanish, one language you have apparently not yet conquered in evening-class. 'Nada' means 'nothing.'"

"Is good?" asks Lars, serving Dennis another piece of torte.

"Is good," replies Dennis.

"Is not good," snaps Violet, "You've done some 'man' thing to Christine! What was it, sirrah?! 'Fess up, Sir! Chocolates or flowers?!"

"Sir? You're labouring under the impression, ma'am, that I have been knighted. I assure you, this is not the case." The woman is mad, thinks Dennis, mad, sad, and exceedingly dangerous to know. But he adds, good Samaritan that he is: precisely as he himself would be if some interloper had attempted to inseminate Lars. Yes, he must try to understand it in this way. Possibly win her affection this way. He can't bear disapproval, even hers...oh God! He's pandering again! Turning himself inside out for a peck and a pat! It's debilitating! But worse, obsessive!

"Is good?" asks Lars of Brad, who takes a bite of torte, replies Oh wow!"

"Is good!" says Lars and disappears into the kitchen with a satisfied smirk and a stack of dirty dishes. He is so helpful to others, most particularly Dennis. I am, thinks Lars, helpful but at the same time my own man.

Lars's logic will have it no other way: In these stressful times, I love Dennis even more. Dennis loves me. I help Dennis. I help Dennis's friends if it helps Dennis. This helping helps me by helping Dennis. Because Dennis is my raison d'etre, thinks Lars, borrowing a bit of that French that seems lately to be so bandied about -- he'd take evening language classes too if they weren't so bloomin' far away. There was another world, he knew, far beyond weights and measures and this prodigious plenitude of pines. Though he cannot see it. Yes, he thinks, It must be there.

I need glasses too.

Lars sets the dirty dishes on the kitchen sink. Them two ladies ain't too bad, thinks Lars, I bloomin' like them. They got spunk! He chuckles, spunk, in more ways than one! He chuckles again, amused that he can entertain himself so spontaneously -- almost whistling as he works. Ja, spunk is a good thing to have. He takes a half goblet of wine from a nearby shelf, quaffs it, pours another, sips -- it is his fifth. But back to the matter at hand and raison d'etres aside, I am my very own man but I am also incomplete without the love of Dennis. Why shouldn't I be? Anybody who don't think so can go to bloomin' hell!

Lars suddenly has an overwhelming desire to embrace Dennis, to have ear-splitting sex with him! Oestrus Sunday is abroad in the land thinks Lars, a cultured phrase that might be worthy even of Dennis. Lars is pleased with himself yet again. He loves to contemplate love. It calms away his incessant and even annoying preoccupation with minutiae. He chuckles and, minutiae abandoned, lays the dishes into the sudsy water. Excellent dishwater, Excellent. I will have clean, shining dishes. I know just how much liquid soap to use, which brand, and the ideal warmth for the water. "These is important facts," he says aloud, volubly returning to minutiae which, of course, he had never left, "important facts for every homemaker, or homo-maker!" He laughs, raises his little finger in the air, cries "Joke!" and takes another swig of wine and humming merrily begins to wash the dishes with an excellent, stiff-bristled, brush. Red. His favourite colour. He is fond of yellow too, of course. And blue. All three primary colours, in fact. In all likelihood, he...

24

A uniformed man directs Mum to a waiting bus. She rushes for it, skids over a handful of flying baby booties, stoops to retrieve them and the bus leaves without her. She frowns, hiccups, gathers and repacks the baby booties into her knitting basket and returns to the terminal foyer and finds that the foreign exchange window has closed. Dejected, she checks the bus schedule, sits and begins to knit, angry with herself that she hasn't got a mobile phone or an international credit card or anything to facilitate her progress, spiritual and/or practical, through this new foreign reality.

The older woman from the plane and her horrid grand-daughter pass by. Mum studiously avoids the girl's damning eyes. The woman, distinctly cooler, without turning, waves over her shoulder to Mum and disappears out the terminal's revolving glass door with her slouching, half-naked, adolescent giant. I'm going to be a grandmother, thinks Mum, but that woman and her grandchild are now convinced I'm a lesbian. Not that there's anything wrong with that! But Mum's own grandchild will be the enlightened guide to her future. "It is soon to be their brave new world!" says Mum aloud, and hiccups. "And it will have such fine young people in it!"

"Dennis is an innocent, Violet," soothes Dexter, "Truly, darling. One of our last. Treat him good."

"Not chocolates. Not flowers," mumbles Violet, "Then it *is* his colouring. His sodding colouring."

Hardly knowing what to think now -- her evening-classes and their multiple brochures having signally failed her -- Violet slumps back in her chair, sadly munches torte. They all munch for a while as a contented Lars returns with more super aromatic espresso and announces that the dishes are soaking nicely in their perfectly heated, sudsy environment.

The guestroom door now ominously creaks open and Christine enters as though sleepwalking. She waits for the others' full attention then slumps pathetically at the centre of the room where she pats her tummy and begins softly to sob. Violet is at her side in an instant, and leads Christine to the sofa, gently sits her down and drops beside her and embraces her tenderly. But how dare I! This duplicitous Judas known as Vi! Thinks Violet knowing that Christine's fertile windows were now a hopeless jumble amidst her, Violet's, duplicitous modifications.

"It didn't work," moans Christine confirming what Violet had all along prayerfully insisted to herself, "It was a failure."

"But how do you know, baby?" asks Violet, painfully concealing her treacherous but necessary role in this tragic reproductive failure as her hopeful heart jumps several beats.

"I just know, Vi. I felt that little tiny, vainly fertilized egg quiver, lose her perilous perch and tumble..." Christine wipes her flooding eyes, "...tumble..." she traces with a shaking finger from her stomach to the fly of her jeans, "tumble down to..." she pats her crotch..."oblivion. It was only the egg that tumbled," moans Christine with the mystical certainty born of avid absorption in many a pertinent Instinctual Knowledge brochure, "The egg, the whole egg and nothing but the egg. Though my thoroughly engorged uterine lining remains intact and desperately craves company, I am not, I fear, in the family-way."

"Don't cry, darling," comforts Violet, " I'm sure you've got another egg for next time."

"Yes, Christine," says Dexter, "but you must be exceedingly careful to hold onto it. To lose one egg may be regarded as a misfortune, to lose another sounds like carelessness."

"I simply do not believe it is possible for her to know such things!" whispers Dennis to Dexter, "where does she get them?"

"Hush, dear boy," says Dexter, "I do not approve of anything that tampers with natural ignorance."

"Shut up, Dexter, says Violet, her heart leaping but not quite ready to surrender to this happy news, "We know what we know. It's Instinctual Knowledge! And we've got the brochures to prove it! Never mind, Chrissie, baby. Just wait till next month in Earls Court. I'm sure you've got another egg up your sleeve. Maybe even two."

"Perhaps I have, Vi," mews Christine, dabbing an eye, "But perhaps I haven't. Perhaps I have decanted never to decant again? It can happen. I read about such a case only recently. 'Woman loses last egg.' I quote from my painfully indelible photographic memory: 'I shall never be a Mum, screamed Ms Mary Fishlock, as before several startled witnesses, she flung herself into South Croydon Sewage Cleansing Pond number Seven-B and was stirred to death before their horrified eyes'."

Christine yanks a hanky from her pocket, wipes her eyes, blows her nose, announces, "I can hardly conceive of a crueller fate. Imagine. Barren, tormented, battered by gigantic mixing blades -- ones last drowning breath, a putrid cocktail of human excrement!"

"The mind boggles," says Dexter.

"Svedish butter cream meringue torte?" asks Lars, thrusting a dish at Christine who nods a pathetic little nod and snatches it, tucking in with surprising enthusiasm given her recent announcement.

"But still eating for two, I see?" says Dexter.

"Super aromatic espresso?" asks Lars.

"Why not? What have I got to lose now?" sighs Christine.

"Another egg?" ventures Dexter, "Your mind?"

Violet says, "There, there, darling," and clutches Christine's shoulders, rocks her gently back and forth. "Vi! Desist!" cries Christine, "You'll make me seasick!"

"It's all that water," says Dexter with a naughty leer.

Christine ignores him, tries desperately to forget her dubiously departed egg, concentrates on a certain good nutrition brochure sprung to mind in the turmoil of the moment. Good nutrition is a must, thinks Christine and takes another excessively large bite of torte, which she easily manages.

"Is good?" asks Lars.

Christine munches noisily for a moment, begins to sniffle then sob.

"Is not good?" asks Lars.

"Don't cry, Chrissie," says Violet, gripping Christine's arm as a barrage of butter cream flies from Christine's fork, "You can try again, baby..." she throws a nasty frown at Dennis, "...with a human."

Even as she's said this Violet realises that she would have vehemently resented anyone who attempted to inseminate Christine. Poor Dennis, she thinks, I am unfair. But I can't help it. True love can make a person cru-el.

"But I don't want to try again with a human, Vi! I want to try again with him!"

"It's his colouring, isn't it?" sighs Violet.

"Yes! Yes! Yes! Yes! Yes!" screams Christine.

"Admit it," replies Violet who appears not to have heard.

Christine, her eyes frantic and awry, suddenly pivots to Dennis, cries "Denny! Denny, honeybuns!.."

"No!" says Dennis, "You can keep your 'petite' demitasse and that gigantic eye-dropper to yourself, Christine. I will no longer be a party to this midsummer madness. That is my final and very last word on the subject!"

Christine, her eyes askew, glares at Dennis and goes berserk. She flails her arms, shrieks "Isabella! This is for you!" as she leaps into the air and lands behind Dennis. With a Judo chop to the back of his knees, he topples. She throws herself on him, pins him to the floor and screams "Dennis, I will not allow you to thwart little tiny Isabella Victoria Gloria! I'll have your jizzum if it's the last orgasm you ever have!"

Christine, straddling poor, dazed Dennis, unzips his trousers, yanks them to his knees. "Violet! Don't stand there like a ninny!" she screams, "fetch the fucking demitasse! Dennis, you're amongst friends, doff those designer Y-fronts and wank!"

"No! No!" Cries Dennis, slowly coming to his senses as he struggles to escape Christine's vise-like grasp on each of his not insignificantly muscled arms, "No! No!" Rape! No! No!"

"Dennis," smiles Dexter, hovering, what seems to Dennis, miles above him, "Dear boy, don't you realise that 'no' always means 'yes'?"

25

"Isn't it wonderful, Chrissie?!" puffs Violet as she and Christine in their identical vermilion sweat-suits jog down the dusty forest road, "now that we're going to a properly licensed sperm bank for our merchandise? We'll leave tomorrow, won't we, Chrissie? I'll ring Earls Court and make a semen reservation. Oh, it's so exciting! Back to plan one! We will be excellent parents, won't we, Chrissie, with certified spunk?"

"Of course we will, Violet," replies Christine reluctantly. She's got something of greater import on her mind.

"Isabella won't miss having a father, will she, Chrissie?"

"Stuff fathers. You'll be her father. You'll make an excellent father."

But Christine's attention is still divided, bemused.

"I'll make an excellent father," repeats Violet, worried that Chrissie seems even more than usual not herself.

A few puffing silent strides.

"You'll certainly make a better father than my father," manages Christine. "My father was a brute."

"A brute?!" cries Violet, grabbing Christine and pulling her to a grinding stop in the dusty road.

"He forced me..." Christine breaks off and turns away, the humiliating recollection of that shameful day emerging more real than ever, from the deepest vault of memory to which she had assigned it so long ago.

Violet is alarmed, grabs Christine's shoulder, shakes her. "Forced you to what, baby?!"

Christine sniffles but continues with extreme difficulty, "He forced me to..." She breaks off again.

"What, Chrissie, darling, what?!"

"He forced me to wear a little white pinafore with awful, puffy sleeves and pink, fluttery ribbons and obscenely shiny little black shoes with tiny straps and white, pleated satin bows and..."

"And?! That filthy beast! What else, Chrissie? Do tell! What else?!"

"And he painted my tiny fingernails pink and..."

"And?!" cries Violet, temper rising.

"And...he forced me to..." Christine chokes on a massive sob.

"Yes, darling, yes? You can tell your own, loving Vi-Vi."

"Oh, Violet! He forced me to bake fake cherry tarts in a tiny fake toy oven in a little toy kitchen!" cries Christine and throws herself into Violet's welcoming, comforting arms.

"Oh my GOD! Why haven't you told me this before, baby?!"

"I felt...violated," sobs Christine. I felt... I felt as if it was, somehow, all my fault."

"Oh, darling," coos Violet, "it must have been torture to keep this dreadful secret to yourself all these years."

"We would never force our little tiny Isabella into a fake toy kitchen, to bake fake cherry tarts in a fake toy oven, would we, Violet?"

"Certainly not!" cries Violet, her ire ascending to new and terrifying levels.

"Our little Isabella," sniffs Christine, "will be taught to play golf on her very own miniature golf course!"

"Whether the little brat likes it or not!" snaps Violet, unable momentarily, to quench her stratospheric rage.

"Calm down, darling, I do love your righteous anger in defence of moi but we have other things to think of just now," murmurs Christine, fully recovered and nuzzling against her raison -- Isabella aside, of course -- d'etre.

"You'll make a better mother than my mother," says Violet, under control now and planning rapidly ahead.

"Yes, I will. Of that, I am quite certain!" replies Christine.

"What did you mean by that, Chrissie?" asks Violet plaintively, as Violet does love her Mum.

"Nothing, Vi, darling. Your mother is wizard, in her way. Especially now she's won the lottery. Money often loosens ones heart strings. Let us pray this will be the case with your loving mum."

"I've seen the signs. She'll come round. You'll see. She might even begin to speak to you."

I do hope so, Vi. I'm so special. So very special. But..."

"Of course you are, Chrissie, exceedingly special. And with properly accredited spunk you'll prove it! Little tiny Isabella will become a faultless fact of life, won't she?"

"All will come right in Earls Court."

"When we find the right cum?"

They both laugh, Christine, a bit hysterically.

Says Violet, "Earls Court will come through for us."

Making the best of it Christine manages a tiny crooked grin, "In Earls Court they hardly know whether they're coming or going anyway."

"I daresay," says Violet, exulting in Chrissie's tiny, crooked grin, "At the sperm bank, I daresay, mostly coming!"

"Yes, home. We must go home!" cries Christine, and they begin again to jog.

"For a homecoming!" adds Violet.

"Violet! Violet!" cries Christine, her eyes blazing as she stops short in a rut on the road.

"Yes, Chrissie?!"

"Would you buy a pig in a poke?!"

Christine now jogs in place, eyes wide, her fists clenched as Violet puzzles. "Well?" says Christine, "Well?"

"I'm not familiar with that term, Chrissie, 'a pig in a poke'."

"It is an archaic Scottish-American idiomatic phrase. 'Poke' being 'bag', 'pig' being 'pig'.

"I don't follow you, Chrissie."

"A pig in a poke for God's sake! It means a pig hidden in a bag, for God's sake!"

"Chrissie, darling, I am not sure what this has to do with our little tiny Isabella Victoria Gloria."

"Think! Violet, think! The 'poke' or bag equals a container. The 'pig' equals spermatozoans. Billions of them. Anonymous strangers. Hidden in the bag."

"What pig, Chrissie?" replies Violet, reddening, saddening, "What bag? Are you speaking of the swine flu, darling?"

"The sodding 'poke' which means, 'bag' in archaic idiomatic Scottish-American English, damn it!"

"Language! And you don't have to shout!"

"What I am trying to say, Vi, perhaps a bit more allegorically than you are able, at this moment, to absorb -- for reasons known only to yourself because I simply cannot explain your recent aberrant behaviour -- is that going to a sperm bank, accredited, or not, cracking Icelandic sperm technician or not, does not insure that our little tiny Isabella will have golden blond hair and pink cheeks like Dennis's."

"He pinches them pink!"

"Violet! Will you let me continue! You know I've always longed for a little golden girl! What I am trying to tell you is that our Viking Dennis, paunch and all, is a known quantity! And Dennis is not precisely stupid. I mean he didn't fall for it when I jumped him and tried to dupe him into ejaculating. From a sperm bank one might end up after a perfectly grotesque gestation, end up with -- well -- they could fumble the label on a sodding test-tube at a sperm bank and voila! Horns, a forked tail and dreadful pointy teeth! They could slip us some macabre mickey at a sperm bank! Besides...besides..."

"Besides what, Chrissie?" says Vi, dabbing away an oncoming tear and dreading what's to come.

"Violet, I may as well come out and say it. I am certain I have another egg ready and waiting. Right now! I am certain of it!"

"Two superbly ripe eggs in one day, baby? You'll surely over-stress your sodding ovaries and God only knows what'll happen then!"

"It's my anomalies, Vi, my sodding anomalies working overtime. I'm special, you said it yourself. I have never been so unequivocally convinced about anything in my entire life."

Christine begins again to jog, "I can feel this little tiny egg gyrating, pulsating, poised to pop out, plummet and perch in my still conveniently engorged uterine lining."

"But Chrissie..."

"If we can just grab Dennis by his designer Y-fronts and force him to ejaculate an encore into Nana's petite demitasse..."

"But Chrissie, you just tried that and it didn't work!"

"I thought we might scare it out of him. You were no help at all, Vi."

"Chrissie, darling, I thought we had decided to go back to plan one. Our fully licensed sperm bank in Earls Court where that nice Icelandic..."

"Stuff Earls Court! Stuff Gunilla Harridansdottir or whatever the hell her name is! Stuff Iceland -- their sodding volocano will blow us all apart one day! Violet, I have just explained all that! Hello?! Besides, that was before I was certain I had another

98

eager egg up my chute rarin' to go."

A few more silent, solemn strides then: "Christine?, did you actually feel anything for Dennis yesterday?"

"When he presented his jizzum in Nana's petite demitasse and I inseminated myself with the turkey-baster?"

"Yes... then," says Violet, but not without difficulty.

"Let's face it. I was moved. He gave of...of himself."

"Rubbish, Christine! They enjoy ejaculating!"

Snoring gently, Mum snoozes, various half-knitted bits of pink and blue yarn scattered from her ancient, knitting basket over her lap and the adjoining seat in her speeding bus. The night sky, deepest indigo at one horizon, lightens into the gaseous glow of a shallowly hidden sun at the other. Purple monoliths of granite, sentinels topped with carpets of pine, lurk at either side of the highway as Mum hurtles, inexorably, though somewhat tardily and totally unexpected, towards that cunningly coiffed cabin in the copse.

"Oh, Vi, I have the strangest feeling," sighs Christine, "that Dennis will never fill my petite demitasse again."

"He never filled it in the first place, stingy little git.

A few more silent, sullen strides during which Violet's face twists into a terrifying sneer and she hisses: "There has always been, for men, a distinct aspect of mutilation in the sex act. Do you know what 'vagina' is called in Greek?"

"Of course not!"

"Dexter, told me yesterday. Vagina, in Greek, is 'mystee-kee-plee-ee' which means... Mysterious wound!"

"Oh my God! What's Greek for penis?" cries Christine.

"Probably 'glorious weapon'."

"That would be just like them, wouldn't it? Even the homo-phile Greeks were against us!"

"That is why we must find an anonymous donor, baby," says Violet, "we simply do not need some known bellicose male prancing about wagging his militant member and frightening our little tiny Isabella!"

Ancient Sven on his dilapidated bicycle hurtles up behind them at some speed, "Hello, boys!" he shouts and shoots neatly between them, swaying as he disappears around a piney bend. Violet regains her balance, shakes her fists, screams "Damn you, Sven!" then they both catch sight of ciggie-lipped Brad, naked but for his MP3 player, chasing after a leaping toad. "Damn all of you!" screams Violet, "You couldn't find your own ballocks, Brad, if they were pinned between your legs!"

"They *are* pinned between his legs, Violet."

Brad sees the women, waves happily.

"He is rather cute, Violet. You do get upset, love. I'm the one who should be edgy."

"But you're not preggers, Chrissie, not just now."

"So I'm not. But I was until quite recently, love, until I spontaneously chucked that other egg. It's residual edginess, I'm certain. and we must deal intelligently with it. I'll expect from you a comprehensive, refiguring of my fertile windows beginning today! It was not for naught that we so thoroughly immersed ourselves in Humane Reproduction! "

"Chrissie?"

"Yes, Violet?"

"I'm gutted! Whistle to me."

"No."

"Chrissieeeeeeee..."

"Oh, all right. What shall I whistle?"

"Bluebirds Over."

Christine wipes her mouth, puffs out her lips in a practise-pucker, begins to whistle. Violet slips her arm through Christine's and they jog along. But Christine suddenly stops whistling, pulls Violet's arm away. "I'd rather jog alone, Violet. I've got a lot to think about. Besides, whistling throws me off-balance and jogging entwined makes me seasick."

Christine jogs faster, leaves Violet puzzling in the dust. I love Chrissie but crikey, she's become impossible. Impossible! And Violet knows precisely why. Men. Cherchez el hombre! she thinks, as had her lover, supplying an alternate gender to this venerated though highly prejudicial proverb. Dennis is the cause of it all! thinks Violet. His pink cheeks. His golden hair. His sodding semen! And Christine is after it again -- after that shabby spunk! That degenerated jizzum! That spurious specimen!

26

"Have you seen Brad?" hollers Dexter from the centre of Lars's perfectly trimmed lawn as Christine, followed by Violet, jogs into view.

"He's naked again!" cries Christine.

"You must do something about that, Dexter!" cries Violet from the road.

"I've tried," replies Dexter, leaning longingly into his lawn chair, "tried and tried. And, happily, failed."

Violet, mumbling "that masochist!" darts into the house, returns with two towels and she and Christine strip off their sweatshirts revealing identical red striped tank-tops and furry armpits.

"I thought girls shaved their armpits," says Dexter in some awe.

"'Girls might," replies Violet, "Informed Women do not. Do you shave yours?"

"Yes," says Dexter.

"I thought so. Sissies do," says Violet, leering at Dexter, "invariably."

"Leave him alone, Vi," says Christine from the grass where she has thrown herself and begun a series of perfectly coordinated push-ups. "This is how I stay fit!" she calls to Dexter, "I never eat breakfast before I've worked up a good sweat."

"Take it easy, Christine!" says Dennis exiting the cabin with a large stack of Lars's Swedish waffles and a vat of whipped cream which he sets on the outdoor dining table, "You'll shake something loose."

"I'm all right, just now," replies Christine, "Specific exercises can strengthen a dodgy egg's perch whilst others can diminish it. I know my fallopian tubes like the palm of my hand."

"And how is that managed?" ventures Dennis.

"Instinct! replies Christine, "Instinctual Knowledge and Humane Reproduction!" She now uses only one arm for her next strenuous push-up.

"Oh," says Dennis, "Of course. How completely silly of me."

"Dennis'll be a pushover," whispers Christine to Vi, "I'll have his spunk by nightfall."

Violet casts a worried look into that forbidding forest, wonders where this not-fun-ride of conflicting feelings and tattered master plans is leading them. Wonders what must now be her next dirty-rat-action.

"I never take my vital functions for granted, Dexter," grunts Christine.

"At our gym," says Violet, they call her Little Ms Big calves!"

"At my gym," says Dexter, "they always call me Old Big Dong. I never mind the 'old' as long as the 'Big' always precedes the 'Dong'."

Christine stops her push-ups, sits up, accepts an espresso from Lars, takes a swallow, hands the cup back to Violet, sighs, says, "You do not shock me with your juvenile preoccupation with the size of your procreative organ, Dexter. You began this childish banter in Trondheim before that harrowingly-hung bronze statue of The Great Horse of the North. It was boring then. It is boring now. A lot of sound and fury signifying what surely must be almost nothing."

"Say it, Christine," exults Dexter, "Say it: 'dick'!"

"A most puerile obsession," continues Christine, "common to the male gender."

"Who just happen to have," replies Dexter, "dongs."

"Naff off, Dexter," snaps Violet, "or I'll thump you,"

"Say it, Christine, say it! Dick! Dong!"

"Leave her alone, you cad!" cries Violet.

Dexter dances round Christine who ignores him. Dennis and Lars, though amused by the silly chatter, have nonetheless begun to attack the stack of Swedish waffles and whipped cream and thick, gooseberry jam Lars has so effortlessly conjured.

"You silly men and your...members," mutters Christine whose push-ups have begun again in earnest.

Dexter will not be deterred. "Dicks!" he shouts, "Cut or uncut! Straight or scalloped! Pricks! Dicks! Dongs! Accoutrements! Doo-dads! Them darling danglies! God bless 'em all! The long and the short and the tall! Hot cock and plenty of it! World without end, amen! Christine!"

Dexter stops short, suddenly realises, his eyes like saucers. "My God, Christine! You've never even seen a penis have you?!"

Christine pauses, cheek to Lars's faultlessly clipped grass, contemplates for a moment. She sits up, catches her breath and wipes her brow with a towel Violet has swooped into her hand. "As a matter of fact," she says, "I have seen one. But have you ever seen a magnificent vagina, cunningly equipped with a spectacularly serviceable clitoris?!"

"Err...not exactly," replies Dexter.

"Then belt up!" snaps Christine and continues "I also, when very young and somewhat undiscriminating dreamwise, had a nightmare about many tiny willies. There were swarms of them, each with four tiny legs, clambering upon my bed whilst I slept and violating me. Squirming and writhing and pushing into me. And, suddenly I can't move and I can't scream. My bed starts to rock then pitches, whirls and rises into the sky with this great swarm of unspeakables clinging to it, their millions of tiny spindly legs flailing the fetid air. Then it becomes dark and I can't see and I can't breathe but I know the myriad little buggers are there because I can hear them go 'squish-squish-squish' until they begin to squeal like tiny piglets searching for some great hidden sow. Their squeals and tiny snorts become shriller and shriller and then I wake up. Oh, yes, I've seen... willies."

Christine calmly, lovingly, pats Violet's hand.

"Once very long ago -- long before I met you, Violet -- I encountered a willie in person. Chalk it up to my extreme youth coupled with my sharp, inquisitive mind. He was twelve and I was eleven. We were sitting in a darkened cinema and his willie-thing crept out in the dim light of the film -- I forget what film, it may have been a re-issue of 'The Wizard of Oz'. No. I believe it was a re-issue of 'Meet Me In St Louis' as I remember tiny Margaret O'Brien's tantrum as she rushed out into the snow and with a stick beat down her little family of snow people. Yes. That was it. Anyhow, this willie-thing that crept out from my young companion's deliberately unzipped fly appeared to be a wrinkly, fleshy, unpleasantly pulsating cylinder topped with a mushroom in which was set one obnoxious cyclopean eye. It was accompanied by several straggly, incidental hairs and had a mottled, uneven complexion and a gruesome purplish colour at its mushroom tip. Plus a most curious odour. It quivered disagreeably and suddenly reared up and peered at me like there was no tomorrow."

"Oh darling!" cries Violet, "More awful secrets!"

"Christine, says Dennis, You have just snatched all romance from this life as we know it."

"Well," says Christine, ignoring Dennis, "I looked right into this sinister willie-thing's cyclopean eye and do you know what I said?"

A gasping silence from all.

"Do you know what I said?!"

"We haven't the foggiest," says Dennis, nonchalantly downing a remarkably large forkful of waffle and whipped cream, "but do tell! Your tale is riveting."

"I said," says Christine, "I said SO WHAT!"

Christine sighs, lets herself down on her arms again, begins a second series of perfect push-ups, "You men do go on about your willies."

"Why you pre-pubescent provocateur!" says Dexter.

"Dexter, it is high time you got serious about something, stopped being so frivolous. You must attempt to discover an edifying pursuit. You must cast frivolity aside, transform yourself in some noble way. Anyone who can speak a bit of French can't be all bad. Have you never thought of..." Christine casts about, attempts to glean something pertinent from her uplifting and recent evening-class lectures where a lot of knowledge can be a dangerous thing, and settles on a recent religious tract she briefly scanned after it was slipped under her classroom door: "Ah! The Church, Dexter. The Church is a snug perch for sissies. Have you never thought of the Church?"

"Really, darling," replies Dexter, "when I need religion I just bugger a priest."

"Blasphemer!" cries Violet.

"Or," continues Dexter, "he buggers me."

"Braggart!" says Dennis.

"Or sometimes I bugger two priests. En brochette!"

"I don't believe a word of it," says Dennis.

"Dexter, how appalling! You call that self-improvement?"

"You'd be surprised, Christine, what sermons men of the cloth -- preferably biting the cloth -- will shriek when suitably inspired."

"Having been reared in a convent," roars Violet, outraged, "I must protest!"

"I would too, Vi-Vi, but perhaps not half so strenuously."

"Dexter," whispers Lars, "Was that a fact about the priests?"

"Of course not, dear boy, what do you think I am, a pervert?"

"Be that as it may," says Christine, "I see that Lars, our chef-in-residence, has prepared for us a splendid Hunt Breakfast! Violet! Fetch our sodding hunting vests!"

27

Mum, watching the Nordic landscape fly by, pops a chocolate in her mouth and chases it down with a swig from her initialled silver flask -- compliments of that long fled husband. A child in the aisle peeps over the edge of the empty bus-seat beside her and to Mum's dismay grabs a handful of chocolates -- one or two could have been looked upon as perfectly childlike. But this was GREED spelt large! Worst than the excesses of the French Revolution! Mum snatches the box from the seat. The gobbling child, sticks out its revolting, chocolate slathered tongue and scrambles away. Mum sighs and, sadder but wiser, settles in again -- to watch the endlessly coniferous landscape fly by.

Meanwhile, Lars and Dennis and Dexter watch in awe as Christine and Violet, having donned their tartan hunting vests, put away vast amounts of whipped-cream smothered Swedish waffles, two soft-boiled eggs and one fried, apiece, endless strips of bacon, and at least three cups of coffee each, not to mention a towering stack of crunchy toast drowning in prodigious amounts of marmalade and melting butter.

"One must establish healthy eating habits whilst one is young," says Christine, through a swampy mouthful of butter and toast, immediately after draining her fourth cup of coffee.

"You are closing the pigsty gate, Christine, long after the sow has bolted," sniffs Dexter. Christine grabs another slice of toast, trowels on more butter, "Dexter, if you must continually interrupt, please keep to the subject at hand. Level with me, Dennis. What do you do for exercise?"

Pause. Then, "I read."

"Read? Read to keep fit?" titters Christine.

"A healthy mind in a healthy body," continues Dennis, "the Greeks had a word for it..."

"Sloth," says Dexter.

"But how do you keep your weight down, Denny?"

"He obviously doesn't," snaps Violet, "And his name is 'Dennis'!

"Behave, Vi!" says Christine.

"I errr..." attempts Dennis, "I errr..."

"Remember, Dennis, less is more," prompts Christine.

"More or less," adds Dexter.

Christine gouges at the butter mound, trowels on more butter, chomps.

"I'm glad we got plen-ty butter," says Lars, "With lady guests we got to have plen-ty butter."

"Apparently," adds Dennis.

"What's all this about butter? He's always going on about butter," snaps Violet.

"Butter is his fetish," volunteers Dexter.

"Nonsense! A fetish is a shoe. I've taken Domestic Psychology," replies Violet. "Remind me later and I'll give you a free brochure."

"Perhaps, Violet, Domestic Psychology has taken you?"

"Don't change the subject, Dexter. Exercise, Dennis? Exercise?" burbles Christine through a mouthful of waffle, cream and gooseberry jam. "You must have done something to build that spectacular bottom!"

"I would greatly appreciate it, Christine, if you would leave my secondary sexual characteristics alone."

"Honeybuns, you have not answered my question. What else do you do to thwart those bundles of cholesterol that, as we speak, may be clogging every other vein and artery in your sagging body?"

"Well. I do those things...you know...what you were doing... uhhh...where you lift yourself up on your errr arms and uhhh..."

"Push-ups! Like moi! Like I was doing just now!"

"Like she was doing just now!" splutters Violet through coffee-logged waffle.

"Errr, not precisely," says Dennis.

"Seconded!" says Dexter with a giggle.

"Then show me, Denny" cries Christine, thinking: healthy body equals healthy spunk.

"His name is Dennis!" snaps Violet.

"Show her, Denny!" cries Dexter.

"No," replies Dennis.

"Show her, Denny," says Lars who winks at Christine, adds "Is good!"

The intimidated Dennis, thinking this is really too much but still wishing to be a good sport and adored by all -- a problem he chronically acknowledges he must and will one day simply have to come to grips with in a very big way -- acquiesces. He wipes his whipped-creamed lips on a fine, initialled serviette intricately embroidered by Lars, rises from the breakfast table, squats and lets himself creakily down on his stomach on Lars's newly clipped -- only this morning! -- lawn.

"Well?" asks Christine.

"Well?" scoffs Violet who guiltily enjoys Dennis on the chopping block.

Puffing, Dennis on two shaky though not entirely undeveloped arms, pulls himself irresolutely up from his prone position. Peering imperiously at piteous Dennis, both women munch more much-buttered toast closely watched by Lars who again mutters "With guests we got to have plen-ty butter."

Christine downs a great hunk of butter-slathered toast with a swill of coffee, "Crikey!" she cries, "You call that a push-up?!"

"Well that is what I do," replies Dennis, his ample stomach flattened on Lars's perfect lawn, "and I don't feel like doing it on a full stomach."

"A very full stomach," adds Dexter.

"Shut up, Dexter," snaps Dennis, "You perpetrator!"

"How many?" asks Christine.

"How many what?" replies Dennis, still prone and puffing.

"How many of these alleged (gulp of coffee) 'push-ups' do you manage?"

Dennis colours, hesitates.

"That's the lot," says Dexter.

"Shut up, Dexter," snaps Violet, spewing waffle.

"How many?" mumbles Christine, mouth full of marmalade, butter and toast.

"Four," says Lars.

"Four," says Dexter.

Christine chokes on a great gob of waffle, "Four?!"

"A veek," says Lars.

"A veek?! Four push-ups a veek?!" cries Christine.

"When he remembers," replies Lars.

"Oh my God!" exclaims Christine and slams a great slab of ham into her mouth. "What else do you do for exercise?!"

Dennis feels himself sinking into the lawn, wishes he would sink faster, farther, wishes these women would leave him and his fatal cholesterol alone. Why must he perform unto abject humiliation? Is he descended from a dynasty of doormats?! Were his ancestors court jesters, courtesans, dogsbodies, flunkies? He must ask Mum next time he sees her. It wouldn't do to ask her on the telephone -- she is sure to be offended, especially if she's tipsy which she is these days, more often than not. She needs some happy distraction. And it's his fault! His alone! The dear, lonely grand-childless woman has no alternative! I'm wrecking Mummy's life! Oh why can't he, Dennis the so-called Viking, be an ordinary man and not a mouse?! Or at least a father!? "I... errr...walk," murmurs Dennis, mouse-like, "I... errr... walk for exercise."

"You mean like 'hike'?" replies Christine hopefully, thrusting out the empty butter dish for Lars to fill.

"Yes," mutters Dennis, pulling himself to his knees, "Hike. I hike."

"Ja!" says Lars, "Från sovrummet till köket och sen till toaletten och tillbaka till sovrummet."

"What?!" say Christine and Violet who simultaneously drop their forks.

"He 'hikes'. 'From the bedroom to the kitchen to the toilet and back to the bedroom'. 'Hikes'."

"Lars. dearie-dear, you appear to adhere to a reasonably strict diet and exercise program. You're adequately trim."

"Most gay men are, Christine," says Dexter, "With notable exceptions, of course, and present company excluded. If we can't get into our own pants it's relatively certain that no one else will."

"I'm going to the loo. Got any magazines, anybody?" says Brad.

"In loo," says Lars.

"In lieu of what?" asks Dexter, bored with his comment before the phrase had left his lips.

Brad swings round a corner of the cabin, lovingly eyed by Dexter who sighs and pushes himself away from the garden table, drops with a book into a canvas chair.

"How old are you, Dennis? Exactly?" asks Christine.

Dennis is caught off-guard but rallies instantly, as he had so many, many times before with the age-old defense, "How old do you think?" -- planning of course to add or subtract a few years at either side depending on Christine's estimate. But he is humiliatingly foiled by his lover, logical Lars.

"Dennis is forty. Four-O."

"FORTY?!" gasps Christine, "FORTY?!"

She stares at Dennis, murmurs "Crikey. He looks much younger."

Christine takes a deep breath as she always does to calm herself. Her head reels. Is she doing the right thing -- the right thing for little tiny Isabella?

"It's his sodding colouring!" pipes Dexter from behind his book.

"As well as the fact," adds Lars informatively, "that he is fat. All wrinkles have disappeared."

"He's as smooth as an over-cooked sausage," adds Dexter.

"This is all your fault, Dexter!" cries Dennis who never raises his voice except to express excess acute anxiety and deep personal inadequacy.

"This is a matter of life and death," says Christine, in sonorous tones not employed since jettisoning her 'very last' egg. "Is it true, Dennis, that you are forty years of age?"

"Ja," says Lars.

"Ja." says Dexter.

"I imagine so," manages Dennis, "if it's any of your business."

"Crikey."

Christine slumps in her chair, sinks into a grim quandary, her forehead furrows, her fingers run through her healthily tousled hair, her unpainted, immaculate toenails tremble in the tight-clipped grass of the cool lawn. "Crikey!" she mumbles, "Crikey! He's old enough to be Isabella's grandfather! FORTY! That bugger!"

"But life begins at..."

"Belt up, Dexter!" snaps Violet (happily). As a new, thoroughly Dennis-free world seems now to beckon.

Christine frowns, continues to teeter through her colossal confusion. The quality of spunk, she reasons, unlike that of mercy, declines with age and rarely droppeth from heaven as the gentle rain. But her personal experience of aging spunk

-- indeed spunk of any age -- is nil and not at all likely to expand. So she thumps her temples, summoning up verbatim -- her memory is phenomenal if not photographic -- that absolutely seminal brochure, 'Sperm, What On Earth Is It?', read in Humane Reproduction last term: For example: MOTILITY! How mobile, after forty, is each tiny wriggling warrior? How able to survive the 'slings and arrows' of outrageous womb-dom? And STAMINA! How equipped are these microscopic swimmers to batter at the perimeters of Isabella's robust ovum, poking their pointy heads again and again and yet again into said protein ovaloid, this very stuff of life? And POTENCY! Is at least one of Dennis's aging little buggers likely to fertilize an intransigent egg at a single bound?! DENSITY! How many billion spermatozoans to a cubic inch?! -- Crikey! This could be Lars speaking! -- And, ah yes! QUANTITY! How much, per each repulsive emission of the horrid, gooey stuff? A teaspoonful? A thimbleful? A petite demitasse?! Clearly, Dennis will have to do better with his specimen! But really! How sound anyway is the semen of a forty-year-old, rather plump, lethargic person with a wobbly bottom haphazardly assembled from the intemperate consumption of junk carbohydrates? (Lars must monitor his torte-baking habits!) Will wee Isabella Victoria Gloria hold me alone responsible for her impromptu conception from shabby, second-rate male material?! For getting the wrong end of her genealogical lollipop?! But! OH! NANA! His colouring! Dennis's glorious Viking colouring! I am turgid, thinks Christine, with possibilities both radiant and ruinous. I am, as it were, impaled on the horns of a dilemma! With the distinct possibility of being hoist on my own petard!

Christine, fraught with interior agony, snatches up a large bit of toast, lathers it with what appears to be nearly a quarter of a pound of butter as Lars, more fascinated by now than worried, watches.

"With guests we got to have plen-ty butter," says Dexter, peeping from behind his book.

Christine takes a large bite of toast, mumbles "Dennis. You'll need a sperm count."

Dennis stares in disbelief. Is there no end to her impertinence?! Is there no end to his humiliation?! It's an imperfect world and he, Dennis, thinks Dennis in all his shimmering imperfection, should feel perfectly imperfect within it! But oh no! In an imperfect world there is no justice. To what absurd lengths has he already allowed himself to be...manipulated? Or rather, self-manipulated?

"And possibly, Dennis," continues Christine, "you'll require a crash program of hormonal injections. "We'll pay for everything, of course. Violet's mum won the lottery."

Christine engineers, with a certain difficulty, what she imagines to be a particularly lovely smile and employs with innocent ease, her lilting evening-class "N'est-ce-pas?"

28

Mum's bus approaches a ferry landing at the shore of what appears to be an inland sea. She cups her hand over an eye, attempts to see to the other side. Not succeeding, she uncaps her recently replenished silver flask, takes a swig, snatches her box of chocolates from the grubby fingers of that ruthless child who has continued to stalk her, and takes up her knitting basket. The bus rolls slowly, creakily up the ramp to the ferry, entirely in tune with poor Mum's flagging disposition.

Brad, having relieved himself, saunters back to the little group in the garden, pushes up his earphones and, with the meditative look of a pleasant but simple person who has entertained a single, searing thought for several hours, announces: "We all love each other. Ain't that what counts anyways? Ain't it?"

Taken very much by surprise, all nod.

"That's what counts, ain't it, Dexter? Anyways?"

Dexter nods, speechless with gratitude, hands clasped in a silent prayer, "Umm, you're so right, dear boy. Anyways."

"Ain't it, Dennis?"

"Why, errr, yes, of course errr Brad, more or less."

"Ain't it, Lars?"

"Why not. Is good?"

Brad moves uncomfortably close to Violet. "Love is what counts, ain't it, Violet? Anyways?"

"I suppose so, you little fool. Now back off," snaps Violet without a hint of guilt. She's inured now, been through a three day school of hard knocks from which even her Domestic Psychology cannot now rescue her. She may believe in love but she no longer believes in happiness.

Brad, wiping a teary eye on a torn magazine he carries, moves on to Christine. "Ain't it, anyways, Christine? Ain't love what counts?"

"Isn't it, anyways," says Christine, "Isn't it love that counts anyways."

"Uh-huh," says Brad, slipping his earphones back in place, "It sure as heck is."

All watch solemnly as Brad toddles to the edge of the forest, disrobes for the umpteenth time, revealing a fresh ivy-adorned jock-strap (Dexter's) skimpily covering those luscious loins, lights a fungi ciggie, piles his -- actually Dexter's too-tight fitting clothes -- on a handy stump and wanders into a shadowy glade.

Everyone is watching Brad but Christine. She peers contentedly at Dennis and daydreams of viscous petite demitasses bursting with spunk as they dance a secret, pine-wooded tarantella. Violet watches Christine and despairs. She knows precisely what Chrissie is thinking. But the scheming Violet soon rises again, victorious -- Isabella Victorious -- an Isabella who, if Violet succeeds, will be spawned, a nascent Venus, from a glimmering frozen cylinder. Where? My goodness! In an Earls Court sperm bank, of course! Where there is a very great deal of coming and going!

Mum, comfortably sprawled in a deck chair and several nips on, knits lazily, half enjoying the passing lake, apparently "the largest in Scandinavia". Several passengers wander about the ferry giving Mum curious looks. But Mum is intent on the pink and blue array of infant's wear that will soon find its way from her nimble fingers into Dennis's anxious, imperfect world. Actually, 'imperfect world' was one of Dennis's favourite utterances and she, as his mother, should know. She drops her knitting in her lap, takes another nip from her silver flask, receives another curious look from a fellow passenger, smiles at him, pipes yet another: "I'm going to be a grandmother!"

He nods gallantly enough, although he understands not a word of English and turns away, and that child, that chocolate-thieving child, that brat, creeps up, gags itself, and vomits on the deck directly beside Mum.

"You did that on purpose!" cries Mum.

"So?" says the child in an unmistakable American accent, "Sue me!"

29

"Crikey! What's the big deal? As Gertrude Stein would say: A sperm count is a sperm count is a sperm count!" stage-whispers Christine into the back of Dennis's neck.

"Christine," says Dexter, "Crew-cut Gertie never encountered a sperm in her life. They dared not come -- if you'll pardon the pun -- near her."

"Poops to you, Dexter," says Violet, "Gertrude Stein was a saint!"

"Correction, Violet, Four Saints in Three Acts," smiles Dexter. "We knew that!"

Christine sits beside Dexter in the second back seat of Dennis and Lars's mini-bus -- also purchased for them by Lar's loving mum who, incidentally, provides the fuel. Dennis is beside Violet in the first back seat and is deeply angry, mostly at himself for allowing this preposterous situation to arise. What a calamitous mistake he'd made yesterday when he careened, trousers whipping round his thighs, down the stairs with countless millions of spermatozoa in a demitasse destined for this insatiable virago seated directly behind him. And the woman beside him is even worse! Though, fortuitously, had not yet made demands upon his sagging genome. But anything can happen. In Dennis's case, thinks Dennis, it usually does. He would think twice now, before allowing unknown lesbians into the peaceful though unpredictable core of his and Lars's comfy world. A world where ostensibly innocuous, hump-able safe-sex porno actors could be mob-molls, where irate roosters harbour grudges and where hothouse tomatoes never bloom. An unpredictable world that -- at least before this deafening duo arrived on the scene -- was predictably unpredictable.

"A sperm count is a sperm count is a sperm count," repeats Christine.

"Get out the magnifying glass," cries Dexter. Violet reaches back, thumps him soundly.

"Ouch" peeps Dexter.

"We got a magnifying glass," mutters Lars who is driving. "It came with compact edition of Oxford English Dictionary."

Oddly, Brad who is sitting beside Lars and is uncharacteristically sans earphones has been listening to actual human conversation. "Ohhhh wowwww! Them two behemoth tomes with all them itsy-bitsy words inside?!" he moans.

"The same," replies Dexter, convinced that Brad and books, any books but comic books, would make strange bedfellows. One day, perhaps, they would find themselves in some strange bed and Dexter would prove his point. Strange bedfellows indeed! Why oh why won't beauteous Brad give him a tiny tumble?! But if Brad did? What then? Indeed, what then!

"What a turn-on!" says Brad in his grand-parentally acquired mid-nineteen seventies mode, "all them itsy-bitsy words! And that crazy magnifying glass! Oh, wowwww!"

"Look, anyone," says Christine, "Is there a doctor nearby? A clinic? A first-aid station? A MASH Unit? Something civilized?! We are poised amidst the Northern reaches of the European sodding Union, are we not? Is nothing nearby?"

"Nothing is nearby, Christine," replies Dennis over his shoulder, "That is the reason Lars and I have chosen to live in the middle of a forest, miles from temptation. In this blissfully mobile-phone-free paradise. That is why we are medically 'safe'. That is why you chose me for your Frankenstein caper. Remember?"

"We shall leave at three o'clock tomorrow morning," says Christine, "There must be some city, any city, within five hours that would..."

"Don't be hasty, Chrissie!" cries Violet.

"Life is flying by! Vi! I am twenty-something! We must make hay whilst the sun shines!"

"Your beau-tee-ful, Christine," says Brad, whose head, twisted round at the oddest angle, has been studying her through sleepy, glistening lids, "Ain't that what counts? Anyways?"

"You bet," says Dexter, who thinks: 'and counts and counts and counts.' If I'd only been beautiful I'd have conquered Brad long ago! Peut-etre. And then? He simply cannot stretch this scenario any further, abandons it with a sigh.

"Thank you, honeybuns," replies Christine to Brad, "That was a very nice thing to say," then in the same breath: "Now, Denny..."

"My name is Dennis!"

"His name is Dennis," snaps Violet.

"I am going nowhere," says Dennis, "especially in haste, except to our destination -- to experience an exceptionally scenic view from the top of the next hill."

"But honeybuns, if you need hormones," pleads Christine, "it can only be ascertained by a sperm count!"

"You can count them yourself, Christine," says Dexter, "You're real fast! Ain't she, Brad?"

"Oh yeahhhhh," says Brad, "Oh yeahhhh. That's what counts!"

Violet reaches back, gives Dexter a desultory thump, regrets it. Her conscience has begun to act up again. Dexter winces, exclaims "A microscope! A microscope! Christine's kingdom for a microscope!"

"Dexter!" snaps Violet, a handy maxim dashing to the fore, "Must you continually overcompensate?!"

"We got a microscope," says Lars nonchalantly shifting down a gear for an approaching hill.

"Then give it to Dexter," snaps Violet, "so he can find his willie."

"I don't want a microscope!" cries Christine to the newly vacuumed ceiling of the mini-bus.

"Dexter cannot help it if he is small in his nether region," says Lars, who has accidentally seen and appreciates Dexter's dubious dilemma, as he shifts to yet a lower gear on this ever steepening though scenic hill.

"My white knight," sighs Dexter, "But make that almost never region. And, dear boy, "as to the 'small', It ain't necessarily so."

"Even tiny people can be cruel, Lars," says Christine, "Remember that, dear."

"I vill!" says Lars and pulls off the road and stops with a bone-shaking jerk, "Ve is here."

30

As the others climb out of the mini-bus, Dexter, and Christine with a firm grip on Dexter's arm, have remained in the second back seat, deeply engrossed.

"Darling," says Dexter, what difference does it make? It takes only one tiny sperm. Either it wags its wispy tail and proceeds merrily up your breath-taking uterine canal or it don't."

"Doesn't," corrects Christine, "And we're talking healthy spunk, Dexter. Indefatigable spermatozoans."

"Don't you mean 'spermatozoa', Christine?" asks Dexter, "Or perhaps 'Amazoans'?"

"Whatever," says Christine, frowning. "There a direct correlation between how fast the little buggers wag those tiny wispy tails and the general health of the child-to-be."

"I doubt Dennis's little tiny buggers would be layabouts."

Christine's eyes stray to Dennis's plodding rear as he and the others -- Violet peering suspiciously back -- climb towards the crest the hill-with-a-view. "Oh, he looks vigorous enough but let's face it. Dennis is fat with a capital 'F'. Or at the very least, plump with a capital 'P'. Dexter, you're his friend, why won't Dennis cooperate?"

Dexter sighs. When Christine is like this, so needy -- need he understands -- he likes her. Almost a lot. He secretly feels too, that she likes him, in an oddly oblique way that even she doesn't understand. "You are hitting Dennis where he lives, darling. Where every man lives, just below his belt."

Christine's eyes blink and widen. "Whatever do you mean?!"

"You are attacking Dennis's age, his physical fitness, his spunk. "

"My God you men are touchy! At least you sissies!"

Try as she may, Dexter is still fond, in his way, of Christine. "Darling," he implores, "Penises, for men, are very personal things."

Christine grabs Dexter's hand, places it squarely on one of her breasts. He snatches back his hand, she grabs it again, slams it on her other breast. "So are these," she cries, 'personal things!' What about these then?!"

She presses his fingers, pumps them around the breast in question, repeats, "What about these?!"

"What about them?"

"I certainly don't mind discussing these, do I?!"

"Apparently not."

Christine, jamming his struggling hand against her breast, stares intently at Dexter, suddenly grabs his other hand and crams it between her legs. "What about this, then?!"

Dexter is sweating and as uncomfortable as he can ever remember being -- unless it was the time when he was five and he and his six year old cousin, Mona, were playing doctor and he put bright red nail polish up her kee-kee and she put nail-polish remover up his toddler's pee-pee. It burned!

"What about what?" cries Dexter, struggling to free both his

118

hands from Christine's iron grip.

Violet, curious of Christine and Dexter, had stealthily returned and now crept up to the rocking mini-bus and peeped into the window as Christine, in a fury, gave Dexter's imprisoned hand on her be-jeaned crotch a healthy thrust. "Here!" she cries, "What about here?!"

Violet wails, slams the mini-bus with a fist, twirls and dashes back up the hill.

"Here!" cries Christine, ignoring Violet's piteous plaint and continues to mishandle Dexter's reluctant hand.

"But there's nothing there." peeps Dexter.

"Be serious! I am simply demonstrating that we should be more open, more sensible about our humane biological paraphernalia. I am simply saying that our private parts aren't sacred. That there is more to life than tits and twats!"

"You have inadvertently touched upon my very fondest hope," moans Dexter.

"You simply can't be serious!" snaps Christine who now allows Dexter to remove his hands from her seething breast and most mysterious, to Dexter, crotch.

"Now," says Christine, "Let's be frank."

"Let's," says Dexter without a trace of a smile.

"If I touched you there, Dexter, you'd have shat your designer Y-fronts."

"Bullseye!" cries a much relieved Dexter, his two trembling though well-manicured paws now safely installed in his pockets.

Violet, with numerous pouting glances down the hill at the rocking mini-bus wherein Christine and Dexter quasi-battle, drops herself abruptly on a mossy rock and mopes attempting to consider, among so many other things, the limitless panorama of hills and pine forest below her.

"Ain't life bee-uu-tee-ful?" says Brad who sits down beside her.

"No," she answers, "Absolutely not!"

Brad sticks his grinning face in hers, repeats, this time lifting his earphones for the answer, "Ain't life bee-uu-ti-ful?"

"Fuck off," says Violet, wiping her streaming eyes on an already sodden hanky.

But Brad is not to be discouraged. He rests a hand tenderly on her shoulder. She scowls but allows it as he begins, gently, to massage.

"A little to the left," she sniffs and sneezes allergically.

Brad moves his hand gently to the left, kneads her shoulder and together they quietly contemplate this endless panoply of pines. Violet is comforted by Brad's gentle fingers but says nothing. Wishes she could because he is being considerate which is a lot more consideration than she's had from you-know-who in the last few...

"Ohhh wowwww," says Brad, "What a turn on! Touching a feee-male intimate."

Violet is instantly glad she'd made no contented comment to him, glad she'd shown no gratitude. He's being stupid again! What is it with men?! Suddenly she's sorry she was silent. Should've said something sweet to him. Like 'that's nice,' or even 'thank you.' What if he dies in the next moment. What if she dies in the next moment? What is it with women?! It's only because I'm worried, she thinks. Why does she permit Christine to keep her in this perpetually over-alert, anxious state? She comforts herself, thinks: Chrissie can't help it. She is in Oestrus. By definition: 'A recurring period of sexual receptivity in female mammals. From the Greek: Gadfly frenzy'. They'd read that together, hadn't they, taken from their massive library of bound brochures? And Chrissie is a 'mammal', isn't she?! And she is certainly behaving like a 'Gadfly!' So I, the clear-headed, the sane partner, must be patient, thinks thwarted Vi. Patient for little tiny Isabella's sake. But I do suffer so, adds Violet in her head and looks over at Brad, whose tender massage has at least calmed the tensions in her taut shoulders. She says softly "Thank you, honey."

But, bumping again to his secret rhythms, he doesn't hear her.

120

Somewhat later, in the fading light of another endless twilight, the little group returns to their mini-bus. Dennis studiously avoids eye-contact with Christine; Violet studiously avoids eye-contact with Christine; Dexter, each hand adamantly submerged in each trouser pocket lest it be snatched and thrust somewhere unknown, studiously avoids eye-contact with both Christine, unnervingly near on the seat beside him, and Violet -- he's been thumped too often lately -- in the seat in front.

Brad avoids, but not deliberately, eye contact with everyone as he puffs a fungi ciggie and thumps away to the comfortingly meaningless beat of his earphones.

Lars starts up the mini-bus and they roll down the hill away from that unforgettable scenic view that has so impressed them all -- in such very different ways. Lars had seen it many times before, anyway. But with lady guests you got to have plen-ty scenic views.

31

"Violet won't speak to me," moans Christine, "I've really balls-upped on this one, haven't I?"

Christine rolls her eyes as Dexter looks up from his two current pursuits, a book of smashing Gore Vidal essays, and intermittent gazing at Brad lying on his stomach, his shapely, designer-clad buttocks thrust ceiling-ward and clenching and unclenching in sync as he scans his exciting comic book. Dexter, clenching and unclenching in perfect unison with his beloved, whispers: "God only knows, Christine," though he's already forgotten her question.

"Violet's got her blanket over her head."

"The poor dear's probably caught a cold," says Dexter surfacing momentarily from Brad-watching, "Either that or she loathes you."

Christine ignores this patent impossibility. "Dennis didn't say much at dinner either, did he?"

"Nope."

"I believe he actually thinks I'm pressuring him. I should have worked a bit harder to convince him otherwise."

"Yes, darling, I'm afraid your artifice is only skin-deep."

"I've really balls-upped on this one, haven't I?"

"In a manner of speaking."

"Should I apologise to him, Dexter?"

"If you wish to be inseminated it might be a grand idea."

"Where is Dennis?"

"Up the stairs," says Lars wiping the last of the dinner crumbs from the dining table and returning to the kitchen.

Christine ponders for the briefest moment then: "He needs me!" she cries and darts from the room as Lars enters in his gardening gloves wielding a huge weeding prong. "God!" cries Dexter, "You're not into artificial insemination as well?!"

"I veed the strawberries. Hell Storm is late. Om-mee-nous. The pressure drops and it still don't come."

"Odd," says Dexter, "That's my problem too."

Brad, thumping to his earphones, cocks his head, dreamily looks up at Dexter and washes him with a soul-destroying though thoroughly blank grin. "Dexter," he says.

"Yes?! Yes?! Yes?!"

"Dexter. Ain't life bee-yoo-tee-ful? Anyways?"

"No," sighs Dexter, "No, it ain't!"

"Yeah, I know," exults Brad, "Ain't it just!"

"Denny?" whispers Christine, upstairs and tapping softly on his and Lars's bedroom door, "Denny, it's only me."

"Only?" mutters Dennis, crouched on his bed, his book suddenly clutched, white-knuckled, in his hand. Solitude -- where had it gone? Why don't these woman depart and leave him and his privates alone?

Christine nudges the bedroom door open, enters sheepishly, eyes downcast, the contrite child. "May I come in? I've been a very naughty girl."

"Forget it," sighs Dennis, trying desperately himself to do so,

122

"It's all right."

"It's not all right," mews Christine who enters and plumps herself rather too near Dennis on the bed, "It is not at all all right."

"It is," says Dennis, "It is all right. Wonderfully all right, unbelievably all right. Galactically all right. Now if you'll just leave me to my Oscar Wilde I will..."

"Look darling," says Christine who sniffles, looks slyly up, daubs her faux tears with a hanky.

"Please don't do that, Christine, It won't make any difference. A woman's tears have absolutely no effect on me. I am a proud, practising homosexualist, as dear Mr Gore Vidal might himself have put it in one of his astonishingly excellent essays."

Christine, for good measure, sniffles for another moment, gazes pathetically at Dennis with her great, sad, child-eyes shtick, just manages, in her new child's voice, "When I was a wee golden girl, Dennis, I was so... I was...I was..."

"Wotan!" wails Dennis, eyes to the ceiling, "Wotan, Mighty God of the North, wherever you are, whatever *she* was, spare me!"

Distant, ominous thunder from that tardy Hell Storm seems to come in portentous response to Dennis's pitiable plea. Christine, after a few more sniffles and at least one fully audible sob, says "As a wee, golden girl -- I'm still deliciously blonde, aren't I? -- But as a wee girl I was so unbelievably lonely. I longed for another wee golden girl just like me. Another wee golden girl to be my playmate, my life-mate, to clamber up trees with me. To play football and basketball and hockey, To rock-climb and lay bricks and do various crude carpentry. So I grew up..."

"As one is wont to."

"...and I still hadn't found my wee, pink-cheeked, flaxen-haired darling. My l'amour toujours. My wee golden girl play-mate. In other words..."

"Yes," sighs Dennis, "*Other* words, please."

""...in other words, here I am, suddenly grown -- my lonely childhood past. And I shall never have my wee girl unless I can actually *have* my wee girl. If you can possibly, given your somewhat cruder gender, fervently grasp my meaning."

Her meaning, thinks, Dennis, is most assuredly the only part of her that I shall ever fervently, or otherwise, grasp.

"So I must become a mother. Dennis, the mother of my own wee, gilded vixen. I must replicate. And soon. Is that so difficult?"

"If you're planning to do it with me it is," says Dennis."

"Darling Denny, we'll drive into the city tomorrow, see the sights, have a tasty meal at an excellent Chinese restaurant, you'll have a sperm count and we'll say no more about it."

"Imagine. Weeding strawberries at eleven at night," says Dexter, still surveying Brad's serenely sculpted posterior.

"They von't vait. Hell Storm," says Lars, disappearing out the front door with his garden gloves and weeding fork.

"I love you!" calls Dexter to Brad's behind. Brad, thumping to his earphones, cocks his head, looks up dreamily at Dexter, washes him with that soul-destroying blank smile.

"Goddamn you! Goddamn you! I love you!" cries Dexter.

Brad lazily removes his earphones, continues to smile. "What'd you say, Dexter?"

"Nothing."

"Dexter?"

"Yes, my darling?"

"Dexter. Ain't life bee-uu-tee-ful?"

"Yes" and after a long, masochistic pause, "Positively scrumptious."

Crumbs are falling and they're filling -- if there are enough of them, thinks Dexter. That's so. That is certainly so. If there are enough of them. At the moment I'm famished!

"What'd you say, Dexter?" asks Brad, pulling an earphone aside.

"Life is beautiful," says Dexter.

"Yeah!" says Brad, snapping the earphone back over a perfect ear, "Ain't it just!

32

Upstairs, continued: "Please don't do that!" begs Dennis, "It won't make any difference. I've told you, tears have no effect on me."

Christine, sniffling, looks slyly up, wipes her eyes, looks slyly down, sniffles, dabs with a hanky, creates a flawless, impromptu sob deep in her throat.

"Please don't do that, Christine! It's just irritating. I'm sorry. I'm a complete bastard."

"No, you're not." sniffles Christine, "No, you are not."

Dennis, the intimidated gentleman, longing to be loved by the entire human race is destined, by his own admission, to be forever disillusioned. But, irretrievably tangled in the more merciful mores of another age, swings a comforting arm around Christine whose sniffles now morph into gulping sobs -- compliments of her Mum who is an excellent teacher -- must ring Mum, thank her, thinks Christine, eyes squinched, alligator tears flying.

"Where's Christine?!" bawls Violet, casting her head-covering blanket aside and bursting into the living-room. Brad and Dexter, lost in mutual bliss and sharing Brad's earphones thump their entwined fingers on the sofa arm, ignore her.

"Can either of you sissies tell me where my Chrissie is?" snaps Violet, sorry she's said it. She really must treat men better, particularly homosexuals -- they're miles more sensitive than the other brands. Yes, she really must treat men better, after all she was once married to one. No, she reconsiders. Not a good reason!

Dexter who has slid his shared earphone sideways, says mischievously "She is with Dennis in Dennis and Lars's bedroom upstairs."

Violet dashes up the stairs, sails into the bedroom, sees Dennis and Christine sitting together on the bed, shrieks, sails

125

out again, shoots down the stairs, spins past Dexter and Brad and slams back into the guestroom.

Christine pulls herself gently from Dennis's comforting arm, ceases sniffling, dabs her eyes one last time for good measure, girds her loins, prepares now to perform a hastily arranged ruse, a deception she feels not the least guilty for. "I'm an honest woman, honeybuns," says Christine, inaccurately in this case, "So I'll level with you."

"Christinnnnne!" wails Violet, plainly audible from the guestroom below, "Christinnnne, baby! Are you still up there?!"

Violet cocks her ear towards the ceiling, waits for an answer. None comes.

"Christinnnnne!" whines Violet.

"She feels deeply," whispers Christine to Dennis, "Ignore her."

"Christinnnnnnnnnnne!"

"Just ignore her," whispers Christine.

"I'm trying," sighs Dennis.

Lars swings open the bedroom door, takes off his gardening gloves, says casually "I veeded the strawberries. Veeds grow crazy frenzy in summer."

"I'm an honest woman, Lars," says Christine, inaccurately again, "so I'll level with you."

Lars shoots a look at Dennis who only shrugs.

"Christinnnnnnne!" cries Violet from below.

"Belt up, darling!" calls Christine into the vibrating floorboards. "Lars, I may be involved, in a very special way, with Dennis."

"Ja?"

"Ja. I'm terribly sorry, honeybuns, but desperate measures are called for. I'm only human. These things just happen."

"Ja?"

"Ja."

"Christinnnne!" wails Violet from below.

"Belt up, dear! Don't be upset, Lars."

"Chrissieeeeeeee!"

"It would be folly to interfere with Dennis and me, Lars -- poor Vi, she loves me so! -- and it would only encourage me. Be warned. I perform best in adversity."

"Christinnnnnne! Baby, I love you!"

"Will you listen to that devoted girl?!"

"Have we any choice?" says Dennis.

Christine gives Dennis a good natured prod and a chuckle then back to business: "Now, Lars, I said may be involved, I may be involved with Dennis. In a very special way. It's not a commitment."

"Vould you like to see strawberries?"

"I've seen strawberries. They're mushy and beige."

"Strawberries is not mushy and beige. Strawberries is firm and red and shiny," says Lars, as affronted as he ever becomes about strawberries. Or possibly butter.

"But how can you see the sodding strawberries? It is almost dark," insists Christine.

Dennis, from a far corner of the bed: "He's got a flashlight."

"Christinnnnnne!" wails Violet in a particularly heart-rending timbre.

"Your strawberries are frozen. My strawberries are fresh," says Lars.

"To hell with the sodding strawberries! Did you hear what I said, Lars? Involved with Dennis?"

"Ja."

"Good. then it's settled. You've got to be straight about these things or you just frighten people away. Now. I and Violet and Dennis are going into a city, any city, tomorrow, Lars. Dennis will need a sperm count and it may be necessary to pump him up with a few male hormones."

"Maybe you could give him some of yours?"

"What?"

"I beg your pardon, Christine," says Dennis with some emphasis, "but I am going nowhere!"

"But Denny, you promised!"

"My name is Dennis and I am going nowhere."

"But you implied you would, with an amiable look. A

positively pliant look!"

"That was either pure terror or a tic. And I did not."

"You led me on!"

"I did not."

"Well you didn't resist."

"I did so! Passively."

"You did not! I know passive resistance when I see it! People lie about in ill-fitting clothes, in groups! On tarmac!"

"Watch my lips! I am lying in this bed and I am going nowhere! Not even for ready money. Not even if you club me."

"Oh, Dennis, rise from your fully recumbent position and help me!"

"No."

"That's why you're so sodding plump! You just lie about! You never do anything! You need to be clubbed into action! Clubbed! Clubbed! Clubbed!"

From below: "Christinnnnnnne! I neeeed you!"

"Oh Dennis! Why do you thwart me?!"

"You need thwarting! You're too damned aggressive!"

"Ha! That old shibboleth! As soon as a woman has needs she's aggressive! A man with needs is a victim but a woman with needs is a bitch!"

From below: "Christinnnnnnnne!"

"Belt up, you howling bitch!" shrieks Christine to the floor, then back to Dennis: "A man who stands up for himself is a 'go-getter'! But a woman who stands up for herself is a monster! You men and your world! It's yours, isn't?! Even you sissies! It's yours! Yours! Yours!"

"Take my fucking semen!" cries Dennis.

"She has," interjects Lars.

"But do not ask me how old I am or..."

"You're Forty! Forty! Forty!"

"...Or if I exercise properly or if my cum wiggles!"

"I wouldn't take your fucking spunk now..."

"...If he gave it to you in a petite demitasse," says Lars.

Christine leaps from the bed, "Lars! You're a traitor!" Then, to the floor, "Vi-o-lettttttt?!"

"Chrissssssieeeeeee?!" comes the plaintive reply from below.

"For God's sake!" cries Dennis.

"I would have gone to the sodding ends of the earth for you, Dennis!"

Christine flings an arm at the window. "I have gone to the sodding ends of the earth for you!" Then, to the floor, "Violettttt?! Are you down there, darling?!" Then to Dennis, "All I ever wanted from you was a fucking baby!"

"A 'fucking-less' baby," corrects Lars, "I think I veed my shiny, red strawberries."

"Lars! Don't you dare leave me!" cries Dennis.

"Hell Storm is coming."

"Hell Storm is here, Lars, here in this very room!"

"They von't vait," replies Lars and exits.

"Vhat does he veed them vith?!" cries Christine, "His fucking flashlight?!"

The door flies open, in tumbles Violet. "Chrissie! What has he done to you?!"

Violet violently embraces Christine who scowls and pulls away. Violet lurches blindly towards Dennis who now cowers behind his book. Dexter rushes in, Brad's earphones tangled round his neck, confronts Violet. "Don't you dare touch our Dennis, you brute!"

"Take off those earphones, you look a perfect fool!" cries Violet.

"To think I once...once... desired this man!" spits Christine, with a poisonous glance at Dennis.

"Envied, Christine. Penis only," says Dexter.

"Ha!" cries Violet, "That old shibboleth! But Chrissie, what do you mean, baby? You once desired Dennis?" murmurs the now bereft Violet.

"A figure of speech. A bloody ruse! He's not quite as dumb as I thought! Come, Violet, let us pack!"

Brad in his designer briefs bumbles in, a berry ciggie on his lip, Violet thumps him on the head. "Put your trousers on and grow up!" she cries as she and Christine slam out the door. Brad, undaunted and grinning, sticks out a hand to Dexter who returns his MP3 and earphones. "Ain't my music bee-uu-tee-ful, Dexter?"

Brad pulls on his earphones leans against a wall, thumps an awkward rhythm on the wash-basin plumbing. Dexter watches with a confused mixture of paternal love and tempestuous desire, hopelessly unable to distinguish between them. Brad throws a goony grin at Dennis, then at Dexter. "Geez, you guys, ain't life..."

"I vant," moans Dennis, huddled behind his unread book and quivering atop his rumpled bed, "I vant to be alone."

The telephone rings and, terrified, Dennis answers, holding the phone well away from his ear. "What? What? Biff? Bart? Sicily? Sicily?! Fuck Sicily!"

Dennis slams down the telephone. "Oh my God! What have I done?! I've signed my own death warrant! I'll be shot at dawn!"

33

"But the car! The car! Our sodding rented car, Chrissie! It's rented to sodding Dexter and he's got the sodding keys and he wouldn't sodding give them to me!"

The woman, frantic and puffing, march without a nod past Dexter and Brad who are already vigorously moving from the living-room floor into the newly vacated guestroom.

Lugging their enormous backpacks the furious women burst out the front door into the thundering though still rainless night. They pause on the porch steps, fumbling with their backpacks and worriedly noting lightning flashes in not-so-distant ebony storm clouds. They huddle together shivering and listening fearfully to this Hell Storm's menacing rumble.

"We'll walk! Brad walked, didn't he?!" snaps Christine.

"That idiot!" snaps Violet.

"If that idiot can walk, so can we! We'll hike to the main road and thumb a ride. Two girlies on their own won't have any trouble thumbing a ride!"

"No trouble at all, Chrissie!" snaps Violet, "Not for us two demure little girlies."

"That's the way of the world, isn't it?!" shrieks Christine, "Men made the sodding bed, didn't they?! So us two girlies will just lie in it!"

"I've never in my life seen a man make a bed!" cries Violet.

"Well, we'll lie in it anyway! Complete with all our charms! We'll use what God gave us, Violet! And then some!"

"What did God give us, Chrissie, in particular?" moans Violet.

"God gave us poise, Vi! Yes, that's it! Poise and sensitivity and...My God! Pheromones! Why didn't I think of that before?!"

"What, Chrissie, what?!"

"Never mind, darling. It's much too late now. Let's get hopping. Let's get out of the woods and onto that sodding highway. We'll follow the yellow brick road to that sodding ride!"

Violet, grim and frightened, because she's got no taste for trawling about in an alien forest and on a stormy night to boot, but happy at the same time to be rid of that florid, fake Viking's spunk, says "We'll show our best sides."

"Our very best sides!" adds Christine.

"Sides don't get any better than that, do they, Chrissie?"

"You betcha, Fluffy, our best sides are the very best!"

Then with a touch of sadness, and suddenly, given the forbidding night ahead, not so sure, Violet adds "They'd better be the best. Those sides."

"Larrrrrrrrrrs! Larrrrrrrrrrs!" calls Dennis from the bedroom window.

"Coming, Denny!" answers Lars signalling now with his flashlight not from the strawberries but from that hothouse's hopeless, bloomless tomato patch.

"Sissies!" cry Christine and Violet in unison as they hurry, courageously girded for a stormy night, down the dusty road into mysterious forest. Lightning flashes, ever nearer thunder crashes. They exchange brave but apprehensive looks and disappear around a piny bend watched by Lars from the lawn,

Dexter, from the porch and Dennis, from his window.

"Vimmen! Come back! Hell Storm is approaching expeditiously in all likelihood!" calls Lars after Christine and Violet who in a blinding flash of lightning turn and peer grimly back, having absolutely no intention of returning. Ever, ever, ever!

And Dennis knows, from this lightning-illumined moment, that 'La Belle Dame Sans Merci', as he has ever suspected since the arrival of this now departing pair, is surely a lesbian. No! Two lesbians! And it is he who was 'en brochette'!

Mum's bus is stalled in rain-drowned gravel at the side of the road. The driver attempts without success to activate his mobile telephone. By a streaming window Mum nips from her little silver flask and knits and stares into the driving rain. Nips and knits. Knits and nips. The nasty, chocolate-smeared child sleeps across the aisle dreaming, no doubt, in perfect Americanese, thinks Mum.

In the half-light that passes for night in the far north, Christine and Violet lie side by side in their sleeping bags, munching emergency chocolate bars and watching a full moon appear then rapidly disappear in masses of swiftly moving, lightning-lit clouds. The women, more angry than exhausted have decided to call it a day and conserve their fractious energies for the harrowing journey ahead. After a long perplexed moment of deepest contemplation, her eyes now anxiously fixed on Christine, Violet speaks. "I've been thinking, Chrissie."

"Yes, love, I've always encouraged that -- what is it?" replies Christine, managing a sleepy smile.

"Isabella Victoria Gloria? Gloria rhymes with Victoria. I never thought of it till now but don't you think that it sounds a wee bit peculiar?"

"What sounds a wee bit peculiar?" says Christine, yawning and faintly alarmed though still groggy.

"Isabella Victoria Gloria. It sounds a wee bit peculiar."

"No, I'm afraid, Violet Iris Heather Rose, it does not sound a wee bit peculiar. Not in the least!" snaps Christine, now fully alarmed.

"Well, I'm afraid it does sound a wee bit peculiar. It's got a peculiar ring to it. It's...it's well, disquieting."

"It is not."

"It is. I never thought of it before but it disquiets me." says Violet, profoundly disquieted and not at all eased by the hard pebbly ground upon which their sleeping bags lie. Ground that is not alleviated by their twin, thinnish foam-rubber pads. "Seriously disquiets me" adds Violet for good measure.

"Then you are easily seriously disquieted," snaps Christine.

"I am not."

"Violet. It does not disquiet me."

"It should."

"But it doesn't," says Christine.

"It would if you were easily seriously disquieted," adds Violet sarcastically. "Like me."

"Well, I'm not, am I? Not about proper nouns anyway."

"We'll be forced to live with those proper nouns, Christine, for the rest of our sodding lives."

"We perfected those proper nouns, years ago, Violet, the day we met. They are lovely proper nouns: Isabella Victoria Gloria. These three proper nouns flow trippingly off the tongue and they have never disquieted you before. Have they? You are simply seriously disquieted because you are not a happy camper. We are at this harrowing moment, camping and you happen to loathe The Great Outdoors."

Violet wishes she could cry. She and Chrissie are in one of their loop the loops. A game she never wins -- never ever wins. "I do not loathe The Great Outdoors. I only happen to loathe this particular Great Outdoors. Nothing but boring old pine trees as far as the eye can see in every direction. Every sodding direction!"

"Fluffy, it's a sodding forest, for God's sake. It's very typical for this latitude, I promise you."

"Why do the sodding Swedes bother to kill themselves in such numbers when they could so easily be bored to death by their own sodding scenery?"

"Fluffy, you hated Hyde Park. Your bucolic dislikes have simply expanded exponentially."

"Negative, Christine, my dislikes are familiarly intact and peculiarly constant."

"Hence, you have always loathed extended periods of being outside. Wherever it may be. This has clouded your usual good sense. Isabella Victoria Gloria is a perfect name -- inspiring, uplifting, transfiguring."

"Then why, pray, did Dexter make fun of it?!"

"Because Dexter is devastatingly insecure."

"Pray, Christine, I defy you to name me one man who isn't devastatingly insecure."

"Violet, what is all this 'pray' nonsense? You've been reading too many Victorian novels."

"One man, Christine, pray name one man who isn't devastatingly insecure."

"Dennis. Dennis isn't."

"Yes he is! Devastatingly! He is devastatingly plump too! Plump with a capital 'P'. And you, Chrissie, are devastatingly obtuse! Obtuse with a capital 'O'!"

"I have never been called devastatingly obtuse with a capital 'O' in my entire life! Violet, you are seriously, but hopefully not terminally disquieted, dear girl. We shall immediately seek assistance from the nearest authority upon our return to civilisation!"

Thunder rumbles, closer and more pervasive and a strong wind rushes savagely through the superfluous pines. Suddenly a sharp rustle seems to explode beside the women causing them to shoot up, alert and frightened from their sleeping bags.

"What was that!" cries Christine.

"The wind?" replies Violet, determined not to surrender to her primal fear of the wild.

"I sincerely hope so," whispers Christine.

"But what if it isn't the wind, Chrissie? What if it isn't? What if it's a bear?" whispers Violet, swiftly approaching the limit of her false courage.

"Then it won't be the wind, will it? It will be a bear," whispers

Christine.

"I hope it's not a snake," whispers Violet.

"How could it be a snake?!"

"Shhhhh! If it were it would be."

"Don't be absurd," whispers Christine, "St. Ingrid drove all the snakes out of Sweden eons ago."

"Belgium, Chrissie, St. Ingrid drove all the snakes out of Belgium."

"Wrong again, darling, St. Dennis drove all the snakes out of Belgium. They even named a cathedral after him somewhere."

"Then who drove all the snakes out of the whole sodding European Union?" whispers Violet.

"Nobody, whispers Christine, "We've still got 'em!"

Lars snuggles up to Dennis. They lie in bed, staring at the ceiling. "Them vimmen are real disorganized. They've got a million facts. I like facts. But their facts is all scrambled like eggs, in their heads. Though Christine did get a demitasse of jizzum out of you."

"It takes no organizing to get jizzum out of me."

"It does these days."

"A temporary anomaly," says Dennis. "I am being hunted down by organized crime and simultaneously being driven insane by my adoring Mum. Not to mention our recently departed, partially demented though dynamic duo."

"Ve must hope for the bloomin' best, mustn't ve?"

"Name just one woman who isn't disorganized," yawns Dennis, attempting to change the subject.

"My mother," yawns Lars, "My mother ain't."

"You got me there," yawns Dennis, "Your Mum is a peach."

"Christine drinks too much vater," says Lars, "how can she have a baby? She vill vash it away. Vash it away vith all her vater-soluble witamins. Her body cannot make its own vater-soluble witamins."

"Hers could. If she closed her eyes and clenched her fists and screamed. I wonder where the poor dears are right now?"

34

The women, tucked up again into their sleeping bags, are cosy, calmer and more disposed to gentle chat -- for the moment.

"Dennis does have a certain je ne sais quoi," says Christine.

"Je ne sais quoi? What does that mean, Chrissie? Precisely? I wasn't really listening when Ms La Fleur explained it in class. What precisely does je ne sais quoi mean?"

"Nothing, darling. Nothing in particular. Violet, you must re-examine your idiomatic phrases. I'm sure Ms La Fleur would be delighted to assist you. We must be able to communicate fluently with the nuns at Isabella's projected Parisian convent. Perhaps Dexter can coach you. His French is tres bon, n'est-ce-pas?"

"I shall speak perfect French, in due course, without the aid of la hommo!"

"Oui! Moi aussi!" says Christine.

"Bon!" replies Violet.

"Well done, darling!"

Then, in a much more serious vein, Violet, who simply must get this niggling thought out of her head, says, "You said you once desired Dennis, Chrissie. You said those exact words in their bedroom tonight. I was there. Did you, Chrissie, did you desire him?"

"Of course not, you big silliness! It was just a ruse to get him into town and count his spermatozoans. Men are so gullible. One must promise them the world but give them absolutely nothing!"

"Goodo, I knew you had a logical reason. But I could have told you it wouldn't work. Men are infants. They've got to be spoon-fed. Especially when it boils down to spunk."

"Oh go to sleep, Vi, we've got a very busy day tomorrow. We must reconnoitre. Perhaps we can locate some new floridly pigmented and equally isolated donor."

"When my ex-husband Jamie had his sperms counted and got his hormonal injections he had thousands of babies with that cow, Brenda," moans Violet. "That cow could have been me! We'd have had our little tiny Isabella as we speak!"

"Darling girl, Jamie had bad skin. Would you have wanted little tiny Isabella to resemble a puce crocodile? Darling. You've got your black belt now. You run our Judo school and I'll have all the infants we need."

"I could have had all the sodding infants we needed. And then some!"

"We only want one, love. Little tiny Isabella Victoria Gloria."

"I know what the brat's name is, Christine!"

"Why, Violet!"

"If that bastard Jamie had got his sodding hormones whilst he was married to me, you and I wouldn't be lying here in the sodding muck in this pine-tree hell depending upon the spurious spunk of a fat albino eunuch who makes mediocre porny movies!"

Violet is, of course, sorry to have employed such bitter language about poor Dennis who is simply a victim here, much as is she herself -- a victim of Christine's 'gadfly frenzy', her 'Oestrus Sunday'. Her reproductive extravaganza! Her three ring fertile-cycled circus! Why couldn't Christine have been a self-reproducing strawberry? It would have been so much simpler! Now, it seems, yet again, rather than that comfy sperm bank in Earls Court with comfy, Icelandic Gunilla, this insane hunt for Nordic colouring is about to commence anew! Is there no end to 'oestrus'?! Who invented it in the first sodding place! My God! It's unnatural!

"Dennis produces responsible porny movies, Violet. I think that's commendable even if he is a lazy lout as well as a selfish, sodding bastard. But the poor man is going bust -- Lars's mother is the only thing that keeps them afloat. Besides, we are not depending upon his spunk any longer, are we, darling?"

"Christine? Why couldn't we have gone to an ordinary sperm bank? An accredited sperm bank?"

"I believe you've got a girlish crush on that Gunilla sperm

technician."

"Of course I haven't. I have got a crush on you! I love you, Chrissie. But why can't we be like nice, ordinary, every day people and get our sperm from a bank?"

"Darling! You're a genius! You've just given me a super idea! If we could trick Dennis into a sperm bank we could drug him, wank him with a wooden spoon and have his effluent frozen before he knew what hit him. We'd then spirit the spunk safely away into our freezer in London to inseminate later in the comfort of our own home!"

"Not a good Idea, Chrissie. We could be arrested for kidnapping and spunk-theft!"

"Yes, love, of course you're right," says Christine. "In any case, Dennis won't come near us, if you'll pardon the pun. For a sissy Dennis is unnaturally adamant."

The women lie there on their backs in cosy sleeping bags, churning with their separate anxieties and staring into the darkening sky. The swirling, windswept clouds shatter and flash more regularly now with great, jagged snakes of lightning and the frightening crackle of extremely close thunder. Violet takes Christine's hand, pats it lovingly, says "Chrissieeeeeee, whistle to me."

"Absolutely not. You're most uncooperative."

"Chrissie. Vi-Vi can't sleep. Whistle Vi-Vi's cares away."

"Oh, all right," says Christine -- she's so irritated, why so much flack from her chosen life's-mate?! "Violet, why can't you just settle down and do what I want for a change?"

"But Chrissie, I always do what you want!" replies Violet. Though certain rat-like necessities come contradictorily to mind -- with possibly more in store, all for their mutual good, of course. "I always do what you want, baby," she repeats, feebly attempting to keep her hateful duplicity at bay. "Your smallest wish has always been my heart's desire. I always do what you want."

"Then you should do it more often, Fluffy. It would relax me."

"Oh, I shall, darling! I'll do my very best!"

"My tubes are in a terrible twist, Fluffy, I am well and truly stressed out."

"Then whistle to me. It always relaxes you, too. Whistle 'Melancholy Baby', Chrissie. Vi-Vi's a melancholy baby tonight."

"Oh, all right." Christine sighs, licks her lips, puckers and grasps Violet's hand and squeezes. Then takes a long, deep breath. The women lie back. Violet sighs, shuts her eyes and, half-dozing, sings to Christine's enormously accomplished trills:

"Come to me my melancholy baby,
cuddle up and don't be blue..."

A terrifyingly near thunder clap causes the women to jump upright and frantically cling together. "It'll rain soon," says Christine whose words are no sooner out of her mouth when the heavens open in a sky-splitting deluge.

Swept by great wind-driven torrents of warmish summer rain, they scramble out of their sleeping bags and attempt, miserably, to pack.

35

"Dennis. You must sleep now," says Lars, leaning across in bed and kissing Dennis's nose, "I think tomorrow you have a busy day. The vimmin. They vill be back."

"I won't do it, love. I simply will not ejaculate on demand. Not ever again. Never! She's rude. They're both rude. I feel so used."

"I thought you wanted a little baby somewhere."

"It wouldn't be mine anyway."

"It would. It would have your genes, Dennis, you would become eternal."

"I never thought of that."

"It might be nice to be eternal."

"I suppose. Why?"

"Your baby," says Lars, "I could be Step-Daddy." And he might become a genius like me."

"He'd be a girl. Christine would see to that. She'd hijack my spermatozoa and twist their teeny-weeny tails till they begged to be females."

"Dennis, even girls can be geniuses."

"Christine has such mad ideas about biology. About everything. She's read a hundred thousand brochures and still I wonder whether the woman can even boil water."

"She can certainly drink it! If she can boil it too, I think she will throw you into it."

"A hot-watery death would be preferable," says Dennis, "to being forced to watch Biff and Bart again in my soul-destroying safe-sex DVD. A work by my own hand, pardon the pun, a visual testimony to my abject failure to accomplish -- at the moment -- my greatest aim in life. To strike a blow, pardon the additional pun, for safe sex!"

"I think you want to be eternal," says Lars.

"I wish you'd stop saying that. It sounds so permanent. I really must think about it, love. There. I've thought about it. NO!"

"But Dennis, you'd make a wonderful father."

"I suppose I would. In a way. I'm deeply intelligent, though jumpy. But eternity comes dear, doesn't it?"

"Ja, I think so. But is good."

"I wouldn't touch one dirty nappy not even for eternity. Nor wipe one snotty little nose."

"I would change a nappy," says Lars, "I would wipe a snotty nose. And I think you would too."

Dennis switches off the bedlamp. "Pie in the sky, love."

"Dennis?"

"Yes, love?"

"Who is Katja Hepburn?"

"What did we ever do to deserve this?!" shrieks Christine, as she and Violet, unimaginably miserable, silhouetted against the flashing, crashing sky, are battered by raging wind and slammed by pouring rain.

"Chrissie!" screams Violet through the pounding rain, "Just look over there!"

"Where?!" screams Christine, startled by Violet's outburst.

"In the world, sod it!" shrills Violet over the tempest, "In this sodding excuse for a world!"

The women, hobbled by backpacks and wringing wet, their way dimly lit by their feeble flashlights, grumble and bumble along between rising rivulets in the rutted road.

"Just look!" continues Violet above the howling wind, "Just look at all those procreating monsters who call themselves parents! Hurling unwanted offspring into this sodding world and forgetting 'em -- leaving them to the...elements! Deserting them uncultivated and unloved! Beating them! Starving them! Neglecting them! Exploiting them! Abusing those pitiful babes in unspeakable ways! And they say we aren't fit to raise a child! How dare they?! How dare they, Chrissie?! I say stuff them! Stuff them-stuff-them-stuff them!"

The women pause for breath, cower as a limb explodes on a nearby tree showering them with splinters and moss and the semi-dark becomes, for an instant, dazzling day.

"We mustn't be bitter, Vi!" cries Christine to her disconsolate, water-sodden lover, "Some of our best friends are heterosexualists and they occasionally, very occasionally, make perfectly adequate parents!"

The women attempt again to soldier-on but suddenly stop, wide-eyed. A short distance down the road, lit by continual flashes of lightning and hammered by torrential rain, a dark hulk, gargantuan and completely horrifying, shambles slowly towards them.

"What's that?!" screams Violet, "What is it?! King Kong?!"

"Oh my God!" screams Christine, "It's Godzilla!"

The women shriek and pitch themselves into a water filled ditch where they huddle together hiding beneath their backpacks, their eyes squinched shut as the enormous hulk proceeds closer and closer down the road towards them.

Had either woman opened her eyes at the moment this hulk lumbered by, they would have seen a giant elk -- wide-spanned antlers festooned with the tattered remains of Brad's backpack: shredded shirt, torn lederhosen, and what was once a pair of -- compliments again of Dexter -- transcendent designer briefs.

"Is it gone?" asks Christine, eyes still squinched shut.

"The hulk has passed," reassures Violet, "We are delivered. It walks funny. See it down the road?"

"No!" replies Christine, "Don't make me look! It'll make me feel strange! I don't wish to feel any stranger than I already feel!"

Violet hugs her, wipes the hair from Christine's eyes, says: "Your gadfly frenzy has certainly led us a merry chase."

"Sorry about that Vi-Vi."

"I understand, darling," replies Violet with stupefying devotion, "Totally."

Their eyes set longingly on the tiny distant blinking porch light of that cosy cabin some distance down this last stretch of road, the soaked and exhausted women trudge forward and fail to notice in the howling wind, Sven, on his bicycle as he bears down upon them from behind, a small, tethered Jersey cow trotting swiftly after.

"Hello, boys!" he hollers and splashes by.

"Damn you, Sven!" screams Violet after him. She should have been welcoming! Another human being in this watery hell should have been welcomed, succoured! But why oh why is that gnarled old Troll always sneaking up on one?!

"I fetch Ingeborg! Ja?!" he hollers over his shoulder, "She run avay! She is två year old, I am eight-ty-five! Farewell!"

He is gone as suddenly as he came. The rain pours ever harder, engulfs them, and the women begin to weep, knowing that comfort is only fifty sodding, sodden yards away over an immaculately clipped though now submerged lawn. They can even see Dexter's head in the yellow light of the bathroom window!

"There's old Dexter!" cries Christine through rain-diluted tears, amazed she'd ever be so happy to see him.

"Yes!" snuffles Violet, deeply penitent for past wrongs and determined never to thump him again, "Old Dexter! We've been much too hard on old Dexter, haven't we, Chrissie?"

Her face, streaming with rain and tears of empathy and desperation, mostly desperation, Christine nods pathetically.

36

Inside in the warmth of the cabin, insulated from the deafening storm by foot-thick logs, Dexter applies his face-finishing coup de grace, a fine imported oil, smooths it from ear to ear ever so gently on his throat. Lightning flashes, thunder crashes, Dexter smooths and smooths. He is certain he has never looked better -- he concentrates on his glorious new nose, mulling over its brief though delicious history: Two mutineers abreast could have walked the plank on my old snout. Then, a fleeting, though fortuitous affaire d'amour with a greying yet skilful plastic surgeon who must surely have seen in me experimental possibilities quite other than erotic. Yes! It was worth it. Even if I paid an arm and a leg for it, not to mention the occasional, freely bestowed intimate favour. This is the best I have ever looked. And life before Brad was a litany of loss and...

Dexter must immediately halt these insidious reservations that swarm when he's addled, as he often is. He must stanch these doubts pecking at his self-esteem like a flock of spiteful chicks mauling a newly hatched runt. Dexter has much in common with Dennis -- perhaps that is why they are life-long pals.

Yes! His new nose positively radiates bonhomie above his smashing yellow silk pyjamas and purple satin dressing gown. He postures, primping before the bathroom mirror as rain pounds savagely though nearly silently against the newly installed triple-glass window just by his head. After a moment, blissfully unaware of the ever mounting maelstrom outside, and rapturously comfortable with his new face, he reaches into his fake alligator vanity kit, finds a silvery tube of expensive face cream emblazoned with the gold insignia, 'Number 2', puts it back, roots, finds another tube emblazoned 'Number 3', puts it back, at last finds 'Number 1' and begins expertly to apply it beneath his eyes and on his neck. And ever so carefully at each glowing side as well as the bridge of his exceedingly pricey nasal masterwork.

Finishing with 'Number 1', he finds 'Number 2', applies it painstakingly to his forehead and the front and back portions of both ears, finishes. Then with his own initialled towel, fans gently to dry the cream. 'Number 3' he scrubs vigorously over his cheeks, chin, forehead and jowls. With a wet also initialled clothe he carefully pats his face clean, finds a small, elaborately decorated jar with the ornate label, 'Night Creme Extraordinaire', and soothes it over his now red, somewhat drooping, though not a lot, features, delights seeing them slowly firm and tighten.

The reverberating din of the storm outside fails to disturb Dexter's meticulous ablutions though an overhead light-bulb dims in accompaniment to the increasing turmoil of thunder, lightning, wind and rain through which -- at least a drenched twenty five yards away -- Christine and Violet struggle valiantly, step by step, oath by oath, back towards the cabin.

Brad, earphoned as always and immersed in his own private gangsta-rap, sprawls on his bed as seductively as ever in his designer briefs close beside the rain-lashed window in the guestroom. He peruses a comic book, occasionally pausing to puff a fungi and/or berry ciggie and laugh heartily, jolting his seminude, lithesome frame in a most provocative way; mercifully unseen by Dexter who would subsequently never get to sleep, and who continues his meticulous ablutions in the bathroom at the other end of the cabin.

"Dexter! Dear Dexter!" cries Christine.

"Dexter, old friend!" cries Violet as she and Christine, on their last wobbling legs, batter at the front door. But they are unheard and unseen in the dangerously close crackle of thunder.

Dexter smooths in more fine oil, taking deep delight in the sensuous feel of his fingers on his own throat, feels, in fact, a certain delicious warmth suffuse his long-untouched-by-another nether regions. Certainly beauteous Brad had never made the slightest move in this direction. But -- and this is an extraordinary admission certainly this late in the game (and game it is!) -- But if Brad had. Had...well...groped him -- how would Dexter, thinks Dexter, have responded? The question horrifies because the answer is more horrifying still and takes even him by surprise. These fantastical ruminations must be avoided at all costs. He had never, never seriously considered an erotic approach from Brad! If Brad, on his own, had chosen Dexter for a, however brief, liaison then there must obviously be something dreadfully wrong with Brad! Who could desire such wantonly spoiled goods?! Certainly not Dexter!

Dexter pauses, feels faint, grips the basin edge, recovers, applies more Night Crème Extraordinaire to his neck, takes several deep breaths to calm his thudding heart, his fluttering, oily fingers -- prays Brad will keep his fingers to himself. At least until Dexter works himself out of this new, painfully dichotomous catch-22.

While Dexter ruminates, Christine and Violet continue to hammer at the cabin's front door for what seems to them an eternity of dodging wind-shattered cats and dogs raindrops. They flatten themselves, shrieking, into the cabin's streaming logs. Deafening thunderclaps instantly follow blinding flashes of near fatal lightning as nearby bushes explode and burn with biblical ferocity.

Then they give up screaming at Dexter and, hugging the drenched log walls, creep round the cabin to toss muddy pebbles at Dennis and Lars's upstairs window. But the men sleep the deep sleep of babes -- mentally exhausted, put upon babes, impossible to wake even by the boisterous babble of two severely distressed, wringing-wet ladies of this howling night.

Thwarted again, the women move inch by inch -- backs uncomfortably flat against the riveted cabin logs to their erstwhile guestroom's window. Pushing great hanks of watery hair from their four eyes, they peer in. Here is Brad, sleeping soundly behind his earphones while his somnolent body as though from memory, writhes to that gangsta-rap beat.

Violet pastes her wet, streaming mouth against the flooding window and shouts "Brad! Brad! Let us in!"

"Brad! Brad!" cries Christine, "Remove your earphones, darling, and walk! Let us in! Oh, please let us in!"

To no avail. What shall they do?! Perhaps Dexter is still primping in the loo?! Yes! They'll inch their way back through the tempest along the streaming logs to the loo! Surely Dexter will hear them if they pound more heavily upon the bathroom window, perhaps even shatter it. Violet's mum will gladly foot the bill for a new one.

But Dexter, his fake alligator vanity kit under his arm, is just now leaving the bathroom and though Violet, who must leap to peer in this high bathroom window, sees him depart and shouts maniacally, he does not hear. "He's going that way!" screams Violet to Christine, "he'll pass the kitchen window in two seconds!" The women, shrieking under their heavy back-packs and as exhausted as ever in memory -- unless one includes that unsuccessful attempt on the Matterhorn -- scurry clumsily through the mud and downpour to the kitchen window, pound on it, but Dexter has already passed by. "Next window down!" cries Violet, "Pound hard!"

Desperate and drenched, Christine and Violet stumble through the deluge to the next window, batter frantically. But Dexter is gone, has disappeared into the guestroom where he must pause to catch his breath at the delectable sight of sleeping, semi-nude, rhythmically writhing Brad. So near yet so far away! -- on that twin-bed formerly occupied by Christine during her most seminally Oestrus Sunday. "Do I dare?" ponders Dexter, trembling here, "Do I dare to touch up this slumbering Narcissus, this snoozing Ganymede?!"

Dexter pauses, gazing down at Brad, turns away, thinks No! 'Twas beauty killed the beast. But how can such heavenly beauty be only skin-deep? Surely some glorious secret, some wondrous arcane wisdom must repose therein? Am I never to know? Are my waxen wings never to wilt contiguous this radiant son? Dexter bends near. Dare I steal a kiss? Then nearer yet. But what if I weren't rejected? How could I respect someone who desired little me? Such is the zenith of unpardonably poor taste! I must turn away!

Dexter, had meant, when he turned, to cast his eyes beseechingly towards the exploding heavens. But suddenly, here he is at the window face to face with Christine and Violet, their eyes wide with fear, their noses flattened against the streaming glass, each armed with a huge fallen tree-limb and about to break in. "Jesus H. Christ!" screams Dexter, tossing his alligator kit at the ceiling, "Jesus H. Christ!"

"Let us in, Dexter! Be a lamb and let us in!" screams Christine. now toppled on her back into the mud by the weight of her huge, sodden backpack, her arms and legs wriggling like an overturned tortoise.

"Let us in, Dexter! There's a good boy!" pleads Violet, sorry for every nasty word she'd ever uttered at this, this...warm... dry...comfy...male inside. They can say no more as the sky again explodes in a kaleidoscope of lightning and it seems the very cabin will shake apart in the ensuing mega-clap of thunder.

Violet struggles to help Christine to her feet and the women flatten themselves yet again onto the streaming log walls of the cabin as they inch their way through the downpour to pound for dear life at the front door. Dexter, meanwhile, bends ever so casually, retrieves his happily intact alligator kit, sets it on a chest of drawers and moves nonchalantly towards the quaking front door to the combined cries -- pitiful cries, most deservedly pitiful cries, thinks Dexter -- of these two preternaturally penitent women. He unlocks and swings wide the door, arches a deftly plucked eyebrow, cries "Apres le deluge, moi!"

37

"Wotan is angry tonight, n'est-ce-pas?" adds Dexter with a good natured leer -- two can play this Frenchie game. And he plays it well. Mon Dieu! As though he'd taught the subject! Had -- but lets not go into that, thinks Dexter.

The women ignore Dexter -- wondering whatever possessed them to see this strutting peacock in a gentler light -- and stomp resolutely towards the guestroom but Dexter, with a flutter of his purple satin dressing gown and a courtier's flick of his wrist, dances in front of them, bows low, announces "I'm afraid your bedroom reservations have been cancelled, girlies."

"We are *women!*" cries Violet, summoning surprising vigour amidst serious fatigue.

"Women," murmurs Christine, not quite up to Violet's bellicose example.

"Well," replies Dexter with a studied gape at their dripping, bedraggled state, "You could have fooled me! Whatever you are, darlings -- malheurusement! -- there is no room at the Inn. How about the manger, just a trot across the road? Ring a bell? Have you chaste darlings packed your swaddling clothes? There's something oddly appropriate about that manger, n'est-ce-pas?"

"Enough of your schoolboy French, Dexter!" thunders Violet, at the raw limit of her surprising vigour. She feels, at this point, no remorse at all. He's a dickhead!

"Of course, there's always the floor," replies Dexter, with a smirk as Lars and Dennis enter yawning down the staircase carrying two deflated inflatable, mattresses which each, the sleepy though perfect host, places to his lips and blows.

The women throw down their sodden backpacks and snatch the mattresses away. Carefully wiping the mouthpiece of both, they drop themselves to the floor and begin noisily to blow -- all the while glaring at Dennis, Dexter, Lars, and Brad who has just appeared, grinning at the guestroom door.

Violet rips the mattress mouthpiece from her lips, snaps: "Your air-mattresses aren't self-inflating!"

"Like some people we know," says Dexter, and Christine must grab Violet's arm to keep her from responding in a more physical way.

"Not, now, Vi-Vi!"

"Don't mind me, girlies," says Dexter, "I'm just an interesting bystander."

A flash of lightning fills the room, the lights dim out, dim up, and the women cling together by reflex until they realize the men are watching them.

"Geez, Dexter!" says Brad, lovingly scratching at the perfectly wondrous crotch of his second pair of many-flowered designer briefs, "Ain't thunderstorms the greatest?!"

"You bet!" replies attentive Dexter, "And so are thunderstorms!" as heartstrings zinging, he pulls Brad into the guestroom and slams the door.

"I trust you'll be all right with these?" yawns Dennis as the women resume inflating their mattresses, "Dexter and Brad used them last night. There were no complaints."

"We have no complaints, have we, Violet?"

"We are not complaining types!" replies Violet, "Even if we were, we wouldn't be."

"So if you'll just let us get on with it," says Christine, "we'll get on with it! We are exhausted!"

Vi stops blowing. "And wet!" (resumes blowing)

"Thoroughly miserable!" adds Christine.

"Cold," adds Violet (resumes blowing).

"And temporarily in your power!" says Christine, her head even now riddled with rudimentary, reproductive reconnoitres. Particularly one plan! She *will* get seed from this turnip!

"Well then," yawns Dennis, "We'll leave you to it."

"Well then. Just you do that," replies Christine, "Just you leave us to it."

"Just you do that," repeats Violet, totally, though covertly, dedicated to the failure of any new mysterious offshoot of Christine's sticky mission.

149

"We have every intention of doing just that," replies Dennis, "But would you like a fire?"

"No!" says Violet.

"Yes!" says Christine.

The women blow energetically on their air-mattresses, and pointedly ignore Dennis and Lars as the two proceed to build a lovely, warming fire. Lightning flashes, the lights dim, come up again, the women gaze longingly at the fire, regard one another apprehensively. Thunder crashes, they cling together and realise, yet again, that Dennis and Lars are watching. We must not expose our mutual frailties, thinks Christine. We must not expose our mutual frailties, thinks Violet almost but not quite simultaneously. As often happens with old married couples.

"Well goodnight then," says Dennis.

"Goodnight then," says Christine.

"Goodnight then," says Violet.

"Goodnight," says Lars.

"Goodnight," says Christine.

"Goodnight," says Violet.

Dennis and Lars have gone and Christine and Violet, damp and desperate, drag their air mattresses nearer the lovely roaring fire, crouch there, blowing, until Violet peeps sorrowfully up, stops blowing and whimpers "Christinnnnnne?"

Christine stops blowing. "Yes, Vi-Vi?"

"Christine, how dare they treat women like this?!"

Christine shoots her a sad look, blows hard for a moment, stops and mutters, "Men are hard," blows a bit more, stops, "Or soft." Blows more, stops, "they're either hard or they're soft." Resumes blowing, stops, "That's all that can be said about men." Resumes blowing.

"Chrissie?"

Christine stops blowing, "Yes, Vi-Vi?"

"Chrissie, Vi-Vi is humgry, blowing and storms makes your Vi-Vi humgry. I think I'll just nip into the kitchen and..."

"Violet," hisses Christine through clenched teeth. If you set so much as one unvarnished toenail into the kitchen of the enemy, I'll have your titties for tarmac!"

Violet is duly chastened and both women continue earnestly to blow on their air mattresses until Christine stops, looks miserably at Violet, says, "If we had dry clothes we could change into them. Oh, Vi-Vi! What have I done? What shall we do?!"

Christine throws herself into Violet's welcoming arms and they hug enthusiastically for several minutes then Christine rests her head on Violet's lap and Violet dries her hair with one of the many Lars-laundered, fine, fluffy towels Dennis has considerately left for them. There is something to be said for Dennis, thinks Violet, ever thankful for Domestic Psychology, as she briskly towels Christine's hair. Dennis did, in many cases, aim to please. He is rather sweet. But, she pauses, squinching her troubled brow, it did seem to be a 'pathological' -- did she get that word right? -- a 'pathological need to please'. Ah! So it must, unfortunately, be 'discounted'! Perhaps Dennis had tried to please because it fulfilled a desperate need in him?! His pleasing, then, was selfish pleasing, not really for other people -- only for his own delectation! What a sneak! But so, Violet sadly reflects, am I. In my way, I am a rat. A dirty rotten, duplicitous rat. And, if necessary, I shall remain so.

After a moment Christine seems to gain strength, perhaps it is her lover's loving fingers through her hair -- isn't love lovely? Yes, she thinks, that is certainly part of it. But perhaps the more empowering -- how she adores that word! -- the more empowering part is this new stratagem shaping itself behind eyes that now narrow with cunning. Christine's will returns with a vengeance and she cries, eyes no longer narrowed but wide and afire with new hope: "I'm feeling better already, Fluffy! Your soothing fingers, have revitalized me. But darling, I know what I am about to say will come as a shock to you. So prepare for it."

"Oh, God, Chrissie, what now?!"

"Are you prepared?"

"As prepared as I shall ever be," murmurs, Violet, her heart skipping several crucial beats and lodging in her throat.

"I intend tomorrow, my dearest darling Violet Heather Rose, to somehow," continues Christine, her eyes snapping towards the ceiling and the upstairs bedroom of Dennis and Lars, "to procreate with him!

38

"We were sleeping so soundly. The first time in two bloody days! How dare they?! Now I'm awake all I can think of is Biff and Bart, the Mob, our total bankruptcy, sudden death, and my poor, frustrated and unhappy Mum! Oh, God, Lars, I'm so desperately worried about our future!"

"Don't exaggerate," says Lars, placing an arm behind Dennis's head and pulling their bedclothes higher, "Go to sleep, Denny."

"That terrible day may come, love, when I'm able only to lie about and be spoiled by you and whine and worry and be jumpy and never bring any money into our household," whines worried Dennis.

"You're a creative person, Denny, and you can't be expected to be constantly productive. You overwhelmingly creative people work only when the mood strikes you. All creative people are like that. Creative people must be inspired first. Then the money rolls in."

"What if I'm never inspired again?"

"Don't worry, I've still got my Papa's Draft-Dodger's pension. I've saved every bit of it. But you will be inspired, Denny. Maybe one day your epic novel will turn up and you'll finish it and all our dreams will instantly come true."

"If only I *could* find it," moans Dennis. "Why hasn't Mum rung?! She should be dialling this very minute! Something's dreadfully wrong."

"No! No! Lady!" cries the bus-driver, kneeling on the road-shoulder beside his mired bus. Mum, in a raincoat and Sou'wester, lashed by wind, doused by rain, is about to lift the receiver on a roadside emergency telephone.

"Is dangerous, Lady!" cries the driver, "Telephone in storm!

Murder! Death!"

"Oh my!" calls Mum, hanging up the phone, and rushing quickly away, "Are you absolutely sure?!"

In divine answer, the telephone disintegrates in a blinding flash that warms Mum's face at thirty paces.

"Ja!" calls the driver from his knees, "I sure!"

"You know what I find ironic, really ironic?" says Dennis, pulling down the bedclothes as he's a bit warmish, "At least half the big time movie-star gods and goddesses have been homosexual!"

"Don't exaggerate," says Lars, pulling up the bedclothes as he's a bit coldish.

"No. Really. They were. Are. Even now, as we speak. I saw an interview on telly last week. A famous actor discussing a new film role in which he plays a homosexual -- you know, the usual cinema homosexual; depressed or diseased, or a drug addict, or up to his eyeballs in angst, in the closet contemplating suicide or holding twenty-five bawling four-year-old children hostage over a bed of glowing hot coals...you know the usual filmic homosexual."

"And?"

"Then came the scene, said this actor, in his interview, then came the scene that he must, actually, horror of horrors, roman-tically kiss another man!"

"Is good?"

"Is not good! He said how really difficult it was. What a wrenching act of will it required. Because it was, well, so far from his experience as a normal person. How he had forced himself, poor baby, to prepare for this horrific kiss by fantasis-ing for three months in advance, that the actor he was required to kiss on film was his latest voluptuous girlfriend, who, I assure you and the gossip columnists insist -- those filthy bastards -- is a lesbian anyhow. My, my, my! But this same, poor put-upon actor seems to have no aversion at all to playing serial killers, or psychotic wife disembowelers or genocidal dictators...!

"Calm down, Denny!"

"In any case, the bloke this actor was forced to kiss on film, I happen to know, is his real-life boyfriend. He got his male bimbo the part in the first place! Appearance and reality. The world is not as it seems."

"Are you just finding this out, my love?"

"It's an uphill battle all the way!"

"Unless you happen to live on top of a hollow moraine," sighs Lars and gives Dennis a peck on his cheek. They laugh and Dennis stretches his arms and says, "Nothing is as it should be." and Lars says, "Yes it is. You and me are. We are precisely as we should be. Now try to sleep."

"Thank God Biff and Bart are one hundred percent homo and perfectly gorgeous. Like us. Even in spite of the Sicily connection. Even though they can't act and are planning to erase me. There's comfort in that."

"That's comfort?"

"If you don't think that's comfort you'd better not go to college."

"Dennis, love, I been to college. Three of 'em. I got two bloomin' degrees and a Ph.D pending."

"Then, if you're the smart one, where will we ever get the five hundred pounds to pay Biff and Bart? They'll sue and we can't ask your mum again. She's already been far too generous and..."

"Borrow it from Dexter?"

"I've broached that. He can't spare it."

"He could sell his alligator suitcase."

"I've checked it. It's a fake. What shall we do, love?! Those two mafia molls will sue or something worse! Biff and Bart will put the squeeze on us, or a contract on our heads!"

"Your head," mutters Lars and yawns.

Dennis is spinning out of control. He often does in the wee hours, 'The wee-wee hours' for a man over forty as Lars often calls them.

Lars will be forty one day thinks Dennis, He'll know what it means to worry out of control, to toss and turn and have to pee every ten minutes and simply not be able to calm himself long enough to untangle the synapses (if that's what they're called) in ones whirling brain. Dennis considers the pair of dames sans merci below, bedded down beside that roaring fire, thinks, I have a most tenuous grasp on reality and even now my aging genome is collapsing in upon itself like a rotten peach! I am, as it were, clinging to the rattling edge of this world. Would that this semi-satanic pair one flimsy floor beneath were closer to that roaring fire, hands bound behind them, with a bit of straw stuffed, for good measure, under those simply awful tartan hunting vests! Of course I don't mean this, thinks poor ravaged Dennis, I don't mean this at all. But it is diverting. And fodder for my epic novel -- if only I could find it.

"Don't exaggerate, Dennis," yawns Lars -- as though he's been reading Dennis's thoughts which he often does -- and drops off.

Lars sleeps on through the storm's din. Dennis listens, when it's not thundering, to Lars's soft, even breathing. Asleep or awake he is my only comfort. Ah, comfort at last -- for a moment. Lars is his only comfort in this whirling world, this mendacious mortal coil. This vale of tears. But what if Lars grows exasperated, leaves him?! A new terrifying topic to teethe on! Yet another worry! It will last until dawn too, this new, gnawing anxiety. I'm half-mad! I must go into therapy! Or meditate, thinks Dennis. Or something... or something. Or find that bloody epic novel.

39

The women, side by side in their sleeping bags on their cosy, dry, at least partially inflated air mattresses, stare at the ceiling pondering their present predicament, attempting to leaven it with even a fillip from their sure-to-be fabulous future. "Our little tiny Isabella will never have to put up with what we have to put up with."

"We've had a lot to put up with, haven't we, Chrissie? But it'll be a different world when little tiny Isabella grows up, won't it?"

"You bet your black-belted ballocks, Vi!" mutters Christine, eyes seething with frightening determination.

"There won't be so much to put up with then, will there, Chrissie?"

"No. We've put up with the last things we'll ever have to put up with!" cries Christine.

"I've still got a lot to put up with," replies Violet.

"To whom it may concern," says Christine, "What have you got to put up with?"

"You, Chrissie. You and your scatterbrained Scandinavian insemination schemes."

"Nearly at an end, Fluffy. Put up with me just a bit more."

"Okay," says Violet with that guilty smile. Okay, Chrissie."

"Oh, Vi! We'll have the biggest Judo school in Earls Court! Tiny Isabella will speak French like a native and will cheer along with the nuns in her Parisian convent at all their sporting events! And, darling, she'll be rich!"

"She's already rich. Her grandmother won the lottery, didn't she? But Mum doesn't completely understand, Chrissie, does she, about you and me?"

"She will in time, Vi-Vi. She will in time."

"What if she doesn't?"

Christine takes Violet's hand, squeezes it, looks determinedly into Violet's questioning eyes. "If she doesn't. If she doesn't...Then stuff her!"

"But she won the lottery, love!" protests Violet.

"Then I take that back."

"You just never could hold a grudge, could you, baby?" grins Violet.

They squeeze hands several times, peer sideways into one another's loving eyes.

"You must tell me why you like Dennis so much," says Violet, "Besides his florid colouring."

"You're such a silly. I don't like him that much. But he's... well...sweet. And accommodating -- when he's not being horrid. Don't you think so?"

"Sure. If you like spineless, neurasthenic fat sissies."

A close crash of thunder catapults Christine into Violet's arms. "I'm a sissy, Vi, a Sissy with a capital 'S'!"

Violet hugs Christine tight, smooths her damp hair from her eyes, whispers lovingly "You're no sissy, Chrissie. You're just sensitive. You happen to be the most sensitive, caring and perceptive human being I have ever met."

"Really, Vi-Vi?"

Violet hugs her so tight Christine squeals with delight.

"Really," says Violet, "And that includes me!"

Christine is deeply gratified to have her personal theories about herself so definitively validated. "You darling girl," she murmurs sincerely into Violet's damp hair, "You darling, perceptive girl. You must always speak like that. Especially when others are present." Then louder: "This, surely, is the beginning of wisdom!"

"Darling *woman!*" corrects Violet, "I'm a darling, perceptive *woman.*"

"They both laugh a merry laugh then lie there peacefully contemplating their mutual happiness; Violet thinking hers would be complete if only she could spirit Christine away to Earls Court and get her properly knocked-up by Gunilla Harridansdottir, licensed sperm-technician; Christine hoping against too many shattered hopes that Dennis can be persuaded to relent and release a modicum of spunk into her cherished petite demitasse. This generous act would then amalgamate, after a suitable, admittedly excruciating duration (they've read those chilling brochures about natural childbirth!) into a golden blonde, pink-cheeked little tiny you-know-who whose initials are I.V.G.!

So Christine and Violet lie there, fingers entwined, tiptoeing through their separate wish-worlds, blinking at the lightning flashes, huddling together through the thunder, until their eyes, squinty and suspicious, swivel in unison towards the guestroom, in which lie Dexter and Brad. "I wonder," whispers Christine, "I wonder what those two buggers are doing in there, right now, on *our* beds?"

"Something revolting! You do realize that Dexter is a classic sado-masochistic martyr?" whispers Violet, gratefully drawing yet again on Domestic Psychology.

"Thank God for our evening-classes, Fluffy! We'd be so confused without them and their many incisive brochures! We'd be the blind leading the blind! Darling, do continue."

Violet's brows knit in deep concentration. "Dexter only hangs around Brad in order to be tortured. Brad will never give him a tumble."

"Do you think Brad even knows what a tumble is?" asks Christine, "I bet he can't even spell it."

"I can!" pipes Violet.

"If only he'd take those sodding earphones off his empty head! His tiny brain must be mush by now."

"Like frozen strawberries." replies Christine, "beige."

"Precisely," says Violet, determined to get frozen strawberries off their menu ASAP -- it churns her stomach even now, hundreds of miles from their detested, frozen strawberry-packed freezer in Earls Court.

"But sometimes I get the oddest feeling -- and you know how in Domestic Psych they encourage us to trust our instincts even if the fully-verified facts prove otherwise -- I get the oddest feeling that Brad is trying to think," says Christine, like...a thought is struggling to the surface in his swampy head."

"Anything is possible," says Violet, as she manoeuvres her sleeping bag closer to the hearth and lovely crackling fire. Christine does likewise, says with a certain awe, "Especially these days. Did you know that Tom-tits are even getting smarter?"

"Pooh, says Violet, Tom-tits have always been smart."

"Not as smart as they are today. They're really smart."

"Pooh," says Violet, "What can they do?"

"I saw it on telly," says Christine, "They know how to pull a little string with their wee beaks and get a whole handful of birdseed as a reward."

"Pooh! So could I," says Violet. "What's so smart about that? You can't live on birdseed."

"Tom-tits apparently can. You'll have to admit, Violet, that's pretty smart for a bird."

"Well, I think it's dumb and I say poops! Who wants bird-seed anyway?" snaps Violet.

"Tom-tits do," snaps Christine.

The women suddenly chuckle and begin to laugh and hug.

Christine sighs as they quieten down, and after a moment of gazing into the comforting fire, says, "Tom-tits aside, I like Dexter. He makes me laugh. We need to laugh, Violet, you and I, sometimes. We're far too serious. We need to laugh."

Violet's distress grows. "We do laugh, Chrissie."

"I mean," replies Christine, "Laugh with a capital 'L'. Ha-ha-ha!"

She laughs a lilting little sample laugh.

"We do laugh with a capital 'L'!"

Violet, too, laughs a sample laugh, "Ha-ha-ha! We laugh our sodding guts out. We're always laughing, Chrissie, you and I," says pouting Violet, "We are always sodding laughing!"

"Are, we, Fluffy? Are we?"

"Yes," says Violet, "Yes we are."

"Then we'd better stop, pronto, love. We can't let them see we're laughing. It only encourages them. They're too cheeky by half already, especially Dexter, though I do, somehow, like him."

Violet lies there for a muddled moment, deeply depressed, poking at the very foundations of evening-class Domestic Psychoanalysis for an answer to her present misery. We do laugh, Christine, you and I. We do laugh."

"Darling, we've just been through this. Let's move on. Dexter. Your candid opinion."

Violet, still in pain, considers, says "I like Dexter too, I suppose. He's boring with a capital 'B'. And he totally lacks of a sense of humour but I like him. I suppose. I do not like Dennis."

Really!? But Violet should like Dennis. Knows it. As a basically fair-minded and usually congenial person, she knows it. Especially as he so desperately wants to be liked -- even she can see this. What has he ever done to her except inseminate -- unsuccessfully thank the gods -- Christine? She should like Dennis. But alas, she thinks, I can't. I'm only human, she rationalizes -- that's it! She's rationalizing and that makes every-thing all right! I'm only human, she rationalizes and finds fleet-ing comfort, even joy in this profound self-knowledge.

"You're just jealous, Violet. With a capital 'J'," chides Christine.

"I'm not. I simply prefer men with mystery in their eyes. Like a woman's got. Have you ever seen mysterious eyes that were robin's egg blue? And stuck on either side of his nose which is so turned up that if he finally chose to walk upright and not slouch like a Neanderthal he'd drown in the rain!"

"We'll corset little Isabella in whale-bone from an early age just in case posture is genetic," says Christine then sighs happily. "But Dennis is so beautifully insecure, Vi, I adore that in a man. You have never really looked deep into his eyes as I have. You should have seen his eyes when he handed me Nana's petite demitasse -- sheer terror! It was adorable! No, Violet! You have never really looked into Dennis's eyes!"

"How can I?! They're slits! Every time I stare at him he looks away, sneaky-like. A fat sneak. Fat with a capital 'F'! Sneak with a capital 'S'!"

"Violet," murmurs Christine through her teeth, "Dennis is not that fat. Possibly Plump with a capital 'P' but certainly not Fat with a capital 'F'. And he is not," she whispers, "and darling girl, this will come as a shock to you, Dennis is not...completely gay."

"Not Gay with a capital 'G'?!" shrieks Violet, as flustered as she has been since their arrival, her confidence in The Very Nature of Things gravely diminished if not demolished.

"Darling," continues Christine in a reasonable tone as her latest strategy commences to clarify, "No man is completely homosexual!"

"Even if they're completely homosexual?!"

"Even if they are completely homosexual they are not completely homosexual."

"Oh, my God!" shrieks Violet.

"Men can't hide these things, Fluffy. Not from us. Not from our omniscient women's intuition. Dennis looks at me in an unmistakable way. It is an inherent weakness in all men, gay or not. They all succumb, in greater or lesser degree of course, they all succumb to... our pheromones."

"Pheromones?!" sputters Violet.

"I mentioned this earlier, darling, as you may recall. Now I intend to put it into practice. Pheromones, love, are those minute teeny tiny fantastically subtle chemicals that moths and you and I and all females worthy of that exalted moniker have extruded down through all the ages."

"Extruded?" asks Violet, curious though fearful.

"Extrude, Violet, 'To thrust out', extrude! Consult your dictionary, love. A male moth can sense a female moth's extruded pheromones at a distance of one hundred miles in any direction. No wind required!"

"Oh my *God*!"

"Our pheromones activate amenable responses in men, whatever their sexual orientation."

"Ugh!" says Violet with a grimace as broad as a Giant Cecropia's bold, powdery wings.

"Men smell us, you see," continues Christine, "Smell us in their mind's eye. Gay or not, deep in their tortured souls they cannot resist us. This helpless attraction varies from man to man, of course, but I have seen it in poor Dennis's robin's-egg-blue eyes."

"Well I haven't," replies Violet.

"These pheromones accumulate in our arm-pits, Vi, so I shall begin tomorrow, forty-five minutes before my fertile window slams open, to flap my arms vigorously, love, and waft my secret treasure, as it were. And thence, to subtly influence the speed, quality, and/or quantity of subsequent events. In other words, spunk! I wish I had put this divinely feminine coup d'etat into play sooner. But it never occurred to me that anyone could be so intransigent, so impervious to logical persuasion as Dennis. You must feel free to flap your arms too, darling, so we can saturate the air with our completely irresistible essence -- covertly, of course, so Dennis won't suss what is happening. Sooner or later, Violet, and I do believe sooner, Dennis the Viking will be lovely, runny putty again, in both our hands. The ideal man!

40

"I don't know why," yawns Dennis, to the half-dozing Lars beside him, "I don't know why, and this will sound crazy. But I kind of like Christine. I kind of like gruff old Violet too. Underneath that heaving breast beats a heart of gold."

"Or stainless steel? Like Katja's."

"Violet's bark is infinitely worse than her bite. I'm sure that if Christine were a bit more normal Violet might be the very picture of congeniality."

Dennis sighs and nuzzles Lars, "I don't know why I like them. Do you like them?"

"Ja," mutters Lars.

"Do you know why?" asks Dennis.

"Nej," mutters Lars and turns on his side, "Is a mystery."

"A complete mystery," says Dennis, who puzzles for a moment then dozes off. At last.

"We must play upon Dennis's completely unconscious attraction to my pheromones to get him into some populated town for a sperm count and hormonal jabs and back by nine-fifteen tomorrow night, which is my recalculated optimum period of oestrus. Is this not correct, Violet?" asks Christine, pulling herself upright in her sleeping bag and fastening her lovely, laser-like eyes on Violet.

Violet turns away, terrified and snatches her hand from Christine's, experiences a long, guilty moment, a moment Christine, not she should be experiencing! What has this animated, flush-faced, woman brought her to? Her beloved Christine, beside her on an unimaginably uncomfortable, semi-inflated air-mattress, issuing orders like a ...well...like a sodding man?!

"Is this not correct, Violet?" repeats Christine. "Nine-fifteen tomorrow night, give or take a few seconds is my next optimum, precisely scheduled fertile window of opportunity?!"

The day of reckoning had indeed arrived. "No!" cries Violet, asserting herself before it is too late! "No! No, it is not!"

"Fluffy?! Whatever do you mean?!"

"I mean 'no!'" cries Violet.

"Darling girl! First you said it was yesterday, Sunday. Then when I accidentally jettisoned that perilously perched egg you said tomorrow would be all right -- nine-fifteen tomorrow night! Crikey, Violet! I depend on you to know these things! You were the one who got an 'A' in Humane Reproduction. I only got a Pass. So when is it tomorrow?"

"It's not."

"Not, Fluffy, NOT?!"

"Your optimum oestrus was six hours ago. Nine-fifteen tonight. I mean last night. I, I...lied."

"Crikey! No wonder I felt so strange after dinner yesterday! I was ovulating, not aborting that egg! Do you mean to say that my little tiny egg has lain here all this time...abandoned?! Violet! You foolish girl! How could you! How could you?!"

"Oh Chrissie!" cries Violet, grabbing Christine's hand which Christine instantly snatches away, "Oh, Chrissie, you changed the rules in the middle of the game! And you seemed far too fond of Dennis!"

"Violet! Why do you thwart me?! As I explained at length, it was simply a delicate manoeuvre to get Dennis to pump specimen! To repeat -- one must promise them the world but give them nothing! Don't you see, you stupid, misguided, utterly devoted girl?! My God! What time is it?"

Christine wrestles with her sleeping bag. "Chrissie!" cries Violet, "Chrissie, don't be impulsive!"

"I'm the impulsive type, Violet! What the hell can I be?! What time is it?! What time is it?!"

"Two-thirty-six A.M."

"Two-thirty-six?! Two-thirty-six?! If we fail this time, my lying love, I'll have your arse for wallpaper!"

Christine scrambles from her sleeping bag and roots through her soggy backpack. "Stuff the sperm count! Stuff the hormones!

It must be now! Where's my Nana's sodding demitasse?!"

Violet crawls to her backpack, fumbles through it, flicking away an occasional tear. Christine finds the demitasse in her own backpack, thrusts it triumphantly in the air towards Dennis and Lars's upstairs bedroom. "Ah! Now, where's our turkey-baster? What have you done with our expensive Norwegian turkey-baster?!"

Violet reluctantly drags a sodden, woolen sock from the bottom of her backpack, and from the sock, the huge turkey-baster. Wiping away yet another tear and overcome with grief for her serial duplicity, she hands it to Christine who snatches it away, thrusts the demitasse at her and climbs back into her sleeping bag and closes her eyes. "I've got to lie here now, Violet, prepare myself mentally so all this nocturnal messing about won't come as a rude shock to wee Isabella's abandoned ovum."

Violet rises from her knees, slumps there pathetically twisting the ornate yet despised demitasse from hand to hand. After a moment, during which great rumbles of thunder roll ever nearer as the Hell Storm renews itself, Christine squints open one eye. "Violet! Are you still there?! Get the sodding spunk! It take him hours!"

"Oh, Chrissie, they're sleeping and...and...Dennis doesn't want to ejaculate for you! He simply doesn't want to! And... and..." Violet sobs, "And I'm afraid of thunder!"

A great, very near crash of thunder causes Violet to lurch pitifully towards Christine but is waved away. "I don't care! You lied to me! This is all your fault!, Violet! We must now go where no woman has gone before! Once more into his breach! Wake Dennis up! Scare it out of him! Activate those pheromones, girl! Flap your sodding armpits! Use a cheese press on him if you must! But get the jizzum!"

41

Violet, shivering in her damp tank-top and heavy cotton underpants, creeps to the staircase, slumps there whimpering. Christine ignores her, snaps her eyes shut, attempts to calm down.

"You can be very cruel, Christine," mutters Violet from the first stair and repeats it from the second, then, "You may know everything, Christine. But you don't know everything."

But Violet obeys, and creeps slowly up the stairs, pausing and cowering with each new flash of lightning, each terrifying burst of thunder. Why has she come here? Why is she climbing these stairs in her underwear in a thunderstorm with an antique demitasse in her trembling fingers, a pathetic clown in a storm? Then it all comes to her in a conveniently inspirational, though paralysing flash of lightning. Because she loves Chrissie! And Chrissie loves her! And little tiny Isabella Victoria Gloria will love them both in equal measure -- in due course, of course, when the original plan, Earls Court, is put into play! This is Love with a capital 'L'. True love!

True love will, as it must and always does, eventually conquer all. Besides, Violet's got something else up her sleeve besides that deliberately inaccurate little Fertile Windows notebook back in her damp shirt pocket. She simply can't take another chance with maverick spunk. But she must still go through the motions of acquiring this post-midnight specimen simply as a cover. She grins pathetically, is jaggedly comforted by her morally dubious but necessary deceit as she notes, in passing, a small pantry entrance to the kitchen.

Though theirs may be love with a capital 'L' it can also be labelled, of necessity, Devoted Duplicity when the situation so demands. "A foolish consistency is the hob-goblin of small minds" whispers Violet to herself, quoting directly from some evening-course or other. But she must at least appear to do

Chrissie's bidding in this terrible time of "The Gadfly Frenzy", this never-ending Oestrus, this period of chaotic logic and fantastical meta-biology that has inflicted such suffering on them all. Even the boys.

So Violet carries on. Her way lighted not only by the terrifying storm-split sky but by her belief that she and only she knows what's best for her recalcitrant lover. She is comforted that Christine's true fecund window had passed deliberately unscribbled into the little notebook. But when was it really, exactly when...? It's all so confusing! But it doesn't matter now, does it? Not really, in view of...!

"Lars? Lars?" whispers Violet as she taps lightly on the upstairs bedroom door, "Lars?"

The door at last creaks open and sleep-shrivelled Lars, not surprised at anything either of these vimmen would attempt, squints out. "Ja?"

"Lars," whispers Violet -- a completely new Violet, a Violet lit by luminous love, a deeper understanding of life, and the overpowering necessity to do, for a change, what all right-thinking people do -- what pleases her. She raises her arm, out of a sense of duty, somewhat higher than needed to hand Lars the hated demitasse, then vigorously fans the armpit of said raised arm, as previously instructed, directly towards him with her other hand. "Lars, be an angel and get us some spunk from Dennis. We seem to have miscalculated."

"Is something wrong with your arm, Violet?" calls Lars, sniffing the air, after her. He is concerned, as he likes the woman -- has no idea why, but he does. Oddly, now even more.

Violet descends the stairs, pausing transfixed as before, with every new flash and crash of the Hell Storm and pausing again to note a certain pantry entrance to the kitchen that would later avoid a revelatory collision with Christine.

Violet finds Christine, eyes closed, breathing deep noisy breaths as she holds the turkey-baster, clutched in both hands like a knight's sword in ritual gesture, over her heaving breast. "They'll cooperate," whispers Violet, exhausted by the physical, mental, spiritual and unethical effort of it all.

166

"I knew they would," replies Christine without opening her eyes, "pheromones."

"I flapped my armpit, Chrissie," says Violet ingenuously, "Like you told me to."

"I knew I could count on you, my darling."

"Promise me," says Violet bending close, "Promise me you don't...need him -- in any way."

"Me?! Need a man?!" cries Christine, still eyes-closed, "I need only his effluent! Darling girl, do get real!"

"You've been known to discuss books with men. At evening-class -- that oaf who insists that all literature is born of the urge to reproduce."

"Well isn't it?"

"Yes, of course it is but you needn't have squandered a whole coffee break discussing Jane Austen with him. Jane Austen has nothing to do with reproduction. Jane Austen cares only about money."

"Do not upset me, Violet, I might shake something loose."

"I wish you would."

"What was that?!"

"Nothing."

Pouting, Violet installs herself into her sleeping bag, lies there sullen and silent reprising her deeply underhanded staircase/pantry entrance contemplations while Christine continues her breathing exercises. Violet has seen a side of Chrissie that in their entire five years together she'd only glimpsed. Chrissie was always a very determined woman but this...! Why, Violet almost admires it!

"I'm the one who should be jealous, Vi-Vi," soothes Christine, "You and Jamie. You were married. To a man. You must have felt something for him? Did you?"

Violet is suddenly angry at the very thought of Jamie.

"Well?" says Christine, "What did you feel?"

"I felt I had been born with a sodding saucepan at the end of one arm and a scrub brush on the other and both my sodding feet were little round floor-polishers that went whirrrr whenever I saw a stain."

"Oh, darling! How unutterably tragic!"

"All the washing, ironing, cooking and cleaning done, I actually sat around the house...sat around the house in harem trousers and little silk slippers with curly, upturned toes like some brainless bimbo waiting..."

"Oh, my poor neglected Scheherazade!"

"...waiting for Sultan Jamie's return. When he felt like returning. Which wasn't often!"

"Count that a blessing, Vi, darling."

"I did. But I have been in denial ever since," sniffs Violet.

"Poor baby. Your marriage was simply a cosmic mistake, Fluffy, and no one's to blame. Not even him. Poor sod. Well... maybe him."

"It was a nasty trick of fate."

"That's the way the world turns, Fluffy, dear. The cruel gods play with us, seduce us, then toss us away like toys. One hardly knows whether one is coming or going."

"I've found that too, Chrissie. I've found that too! Often!"

"I know you have, darling. So have I. But now we have found each other. To have and to hold. From this day forward. To comfort one another in our mutual times of need." Christine turns, sighs, opens her eyes and takes Violet's head in her arms, pulls her close then suddenly drops her head which falls with a thud to the semi-inflated mattress. "Violet! What if they cheat?! Dennis and Lars! How will we know that the sodding effluent is Dennis's sodding effluent?!"

Violet sits up, "what difference does it make? Lars is thinner."

"But his English is terrible! Go upstairs! Go! Spy on them! Make sure!"

Violet is about to tap on the bedroom door when Lars opens and thrusts out the demitasse. "Are you certain this is Dennis's?" asks Violet, who flaps her armpit once more as it's the least she can do for Chrissie, considering her, Violet the rat's, next treacherous act.

"In all likelihood," replies sleepy Lars, referring to the pedigree of the ejaculation in question, then, "Violet? Is there something wrong with your arm?"

Lars, sniffing the air and smiling, gazes after her as she starts down the stairs. What a personable woman, he thinks, how congenial. We must invite them again one day.

Violet creeps down the stairs, silently enters the kitchen through that pantry door. Opens a cupboard, pulls out a few drawers. Violet, too, is a wizard in the kitchen.

"That was brisk," says Christine, taking the demitasse from Violet, "Are you quite certain this is Dennis's effluent?"

"Positive," replies Violet, biting her lip.

"If it isn't," smiles Christine, "then let you be struck by lightning."

The demitasse and the turkey-baster disappear into her sleeping bag just as the lights go out in a deafening crash of thunder. "There!" cries Christine into the darkness, "There! It's done! Our noble deed is done! So be it!"

Violet's hastily substituted kitchen confection has found a cosy nest. At least for tonight. But she must be sure to thoroughly wash the turkey-baster and Nana's petite demitasse before the cornstarch-gruel dries to powder again.

The lights come on. Christine lays down the turkey-baster and claps her hands, "Well and truly done! Little tiny Isabella is now an irrefutable fact of Nature! Let's ring London and tell your mum!"

"She won't like it."

"Ring her anyhow, darling! Let's gloat!"

Violet reluctantly picks up the telephone and in a blinding flash the receiver explodes in her hand and Violet with a terrible thud drops heavily to the floor. "Vi-Vi! Vi-Vi!" screams Christine and struggles from her sleeping bag just as the lights go out once more.

42

Lars is always up at an ungodly hour, usually in his immaculate kitchen -- where he is at the moment -- preparing luscious breakfasts for Dennis who, at this same ungodly hour, snoozes fitfully until Lars, on a lovely hand-carved (by Lars) wooden tray brings Dennis his 'pre-breakfast' or 'wake-up breakfast' -- as Lars affectionately calls it -- of a freshly baked hot buttered scone and super-aromatic, espresso coffee.

Dennis is daily moved to tears by this singular act of devotion, is perpetually grateful and often actualizes -- his own words in his own head -- his gratitude in intimate, and ostensibly Lars-pleasing ways. For instance, muses Dennis, somewhat later, lying here semi-comatose but still waiting for this inexpressibly divine pre-breakfast, I'll nuzzle his neck this morning, and as he bends to place the tray on our foldable table, steal a kiss. Or, muses Dennis, I'll pat his butt as he pours that lovely espresso or I'll hug him when he least expects it or...

Dennis yawns, smacks his lips, dozes dreamily off.

Of course Lars would, though he's presently uncharacteristically sullen and sifting flour in the kitchen, appreciate it all the more if Dennis just skipped one or two of those neck-nuzzles, or even a butt-pat. Not that Lars doesn't deeply appreciate Dennis's endearingly intimate efforts on his behalf. But if Dennis simply remembered to empty the kitchen rubbish or throw the daily garbage onto Lars's specially-electrically-heated-ecologically-fermented mulch-pile just behind the greenhouse Lars would consider himself more than amply rewarded. But, and Lars is the first to admit it, these chores do lack that certain 'aesthetic something'. How can he put it? Well. There it is, isn't it? The precise words themselves stymie him. But Dennis knows all about 'aesthetic somethings' and can effortlessly label them by the dozens!

So Lars had better just leave Dennis to his DVD editing, his epic novel (if only he could find it), various creative dreams and other aesthetic pursuits whilst he, Lars, tends to the cooking, and laundry, and bloomless tomato plants and chickens and eggs and gardening and wood carving and his second Ph.D seminar work via Internet. But all this busywork pales beside that always appropriate, satisfying turn of phrase effortlessly uttered by his genius lover and best friend, Dennis. His very own renaissance man.

However, this morning Lars is banging about his immaculate kitchen in a most uncharacteristic way, clanging pans, slamming pots, deliberately ignoring his morning 'veeding' duties in the strawberry patch and jettisoning tender thoughts of the hothouse with its pathetic bloomless tomatoes -- serves them right! The snoozing Dennis has not even entered his head. Lars is angry, and as Christine or Violet might readily say without coaching, 'Angry with a capital 'A'!'

Dennis dozes right through this mercilessly early, ungodly hour and awakes with a terrible start to find no wake-up-pre-breakfast on the foldable bedside table -- no steaming, perfectly brewed coffee, no freshly baked scone and butter, no strawberry jam from last year's harvest. No nothin'! Something is excruciatingly wrong. Dennis's heart flutters. He is giddy with worry. Lars is always so punctual, so ritually responsible.

So Dennis springs from his cosy, dozy bed, throws on his bathrobe, descends the stairs with uneasy notions of The Mob battering at the splintering perimeter of his sleep-fogged imagination. Had they already spirited away his darling?!

Dennis enters the living-room and stumbles over Brad's MP3 player wire, yanking the simple, slumbering Yank's head sharply from its pillow. This, of course, fails to wake Brad who lies beside the similarly sprawled Dexter. They snooze on those two semi-inflated air-mattresses only last night, occupied by discontent Christine and her disconsolate but apparently destructible Violet, martyrs of the Hell Storm.

Dennis knows little of this. He is a heavy sleeper, dreaming his dreams and hatching his schemes towards a better, disease-free but still fun, world. At the moment he is in near panic over the non-appearance of Lars plus scone plus coffee, butter and jam. His domestic paradigm is vibrating badly. He enters the kitchen, exclaims with relief as he sees his unharmed, labouring Lars, "God! You're safe! Good morning, love!"

But Lars ignores him, continues to clang pans and slam pots into his perfectly soapy, highly polished, stainless steel kitchen sink.

"Good Morning!" says Dennis with his heartiest smile.

"Ja," says Lars, "Ja, it is morning."

"Why so glum?" asks Dennis moving in close, "Why so glum, dear boy?"

"Why do you English always state the obvious? Of course it is morning. Any bloomin' fool can see it is bloomin' morning. But it is not, by no means of nobody's imagination-stretching, a good morning!"

"How's Violet?" asks Dennis, dipping a daring finger into an unknown substance in a bowl.

"She is sleeping. All is sleeping. At last."

Lars slams the flour-sifter into the precisely heated dishwater. "Will she live?" asks Dennis, licking a bit of that unknown substance from his finger -- ugh, raw *unsugared*, dough!

"Ja. She vill live. But vill ve?"

"Goodo!" replies Dennis, that hearty smile intact, those blue eyes beaming, those pink cheeks aglow even sans pinching, that touseled golden hair in there pitching too. But all to no avail. Lars ignores him, slams a breadboard on a sideboard and jaw firmly set begins to knead an enormous, menacing wad of dough.

"My, my," says Dennis, "My, my, my! Aren't we the grumpy one?"

"I do not luxuriate in being knocked up at two-fifty-nine of the morning and requested of for spermatozoa," says Lars, not realizing that he might, to some small extent, also be suffering from a little-known, brochure-touted malady known as 'P.I.S.S.' -- Pheromone Induced Stress Syndrome.

"Really? Who knocked you up?"

Lars glowers and continues kneading, he's sleepy, mentally

172

exhausted and PISSED.

"Never mind," says Dennis, "I'm remembering it all -- well most of it. Love, whatever you did I'm certain it was the right thing. I'm bone-tired of sparring with these harridans. One can't win. It's a metaphysical nightmare -- my nerves are shattered, my creative life is unravelling round my knees like one of Mum's jumpers. God! Lars, are such things possible in Nature?"

"No they are not!"

Lars beats at the dough with his fists, Dennis jumps.

"No! Nej! Nej! Nej! Nej! Nej! Djävla fruntimmer! Djävla, galna, fruktansvärda fruntimmer!"

"Hey, love! English please, or not so fast! It's far too early."

"Them vimmin is monsters! First the Christine voman is pregnant and then she ain't and then she is and then she ain't! How does she know?! Screamin' all the time 'I am pregnant!' or 'My egg has flew that coop!' How does she know?! Then she has fell into South Croydon Sewer Cleansing Pond number Seven! Screaming all the time about her bloomin' fallopian tube! Now she is pregnant again! Djävla fruntimmer! Djävla, galna, fruktansvärda fruntimmer! She is crazy! They are both crazy! How does she know?!"

"Female Instinct, I believe, love. Yes, it was instinct, wasn't it?"

"They should read many, many books about replication!" fumes Lars.

"I'm afraid they have."

"They read only brochures! Thousands of brainless brochures!" cries Lars who suddenly calms down and stares unblinking at the enormous hunk of dough smashed between his fists. Then, to further relax, he allows his eyes to wander comfortingly over his meticulously warmed dishwater and thinks: Is good. One thing is good this morning. Perfect dishwater. And perhaps that nice, red dish brush.

43

Dennis catches his breath, pastes that lovely smile right back on, kisses Lars on his neck, pats him, in vain, on his butt and opens the fridge. He takes out a great pot of strawberry jam, pauses, sticks his head deep into the fridge. "Hey, love, where's the butter? With guests we got to have plen-ty butter. Where's it got to, love? We had three whole shelves of the stuff just yesterday."

"Ve got no butter!" screeches Lars and hurls the massive hunk of dough at the breadboard.

"Larsy! Take it easy!"

"Yesterday," continues Lars, his voice crumbling with terrible emotion, "Yesterday ve got a veritable Mount Everest of butter in all likelihood! Yesterday ve got a whole bloomin' moraine of butter!

"And it wasn't hollow," peeps Dennis.

"What?!" cries Lars.

"Errr...nothing."

"Today ve got bloomin' nothin'!"

"What happened to the butter, love?"

Dennis moves close, drops his arm around Lars's shoulder, Lars pulls away, takes a deep breath, hisses through his teeth, "The Christine voman rubbed all our butter on to the Violet voman's vound!"

"On Violet's wound, her lightning burn?"

"Ja! But I am real sure they eat most of it."

"Oh my, pretty pickle this."

"Vhat shall ve have on our scones?!"

"Strawberry jam?"

"It is not enough! IT IS NOT ENOUGH! Vith scones you got to have plen-ty butter! Vith everything you got to have plen-ty butter!"

"That dairy at Weaseltorp's got plen-ty butter. You could have got up at five, like you always do, and driven to Weaseltorp and you would have been back by now."

Lars attacks the dough with a rolling-pin, "I did not go to bed until five of the morning! Them bloomin' vimmin shrieked for hours whilst they ran forth and back over every single square meter of our living-room!"

"Sorry, love. I didn't know," says Dennis wishing he were anywhere else. Stress definitely detracts from ones aesthetic contemplation of the commonplace -- Hi-ho! thinks Dennis, What an excellent observation. Must make a note, 'aesthetic contemplation of the commonplace'. Perfect for his epic oeuvre-to-be (if only he could find it!) (and complete it!)! Then he repeats, for good measure, just in case Lars, over the clang and slam, hadn't heard, "Sorry, love. I didn't know."

"How could you know?! You vas bloomin' sleepin'! Get cream!"

"Cream?" replies Dennis, his sweet smile nervously reasserting itself, again to no effect.

"Cream!" hollers Lars, "K-R-E-E-M! Cream!"

Dennis winces -- this is so unlike Lars! -- but Dennis obediently takes a large pitcher of cream from the fridge as Lars sets a baking sheet of newly cut scones in the oven, says "Ve will make butter of cream."

"Oh?" says Dennis, "Can you just do that?"

"Butter is cream! Mixed hard!"

"But of course," replies Dennis, "Churned. How unconscionably foolish of me."

"As you vish."

Lars, grim-faced, knuckles straining on the electric mixer, proceeds with the cream-whipping while Dennis, bemused, watches, tries to think of anything else. Anything else.

"A slap-happy good mornin', folks!"

Here is Dexter, his fake alligator kit under his arm, an initialled towel over the magnificently scalloped, gold-brocaded cuff of his purple satin dressing gown, chicly en route to the bathroom.

"Ja," says Lars, "It is bloomin' morning. A indisputable fact."

Dennis shoots a 'tread carefully' look at Dexter, following it with a covert gesture in the direction of the guestroom. Dexter smiles, nods. Dennis grins wildly, claps his hands, "We're making butter, of all things!"

Scowling Lars, buzzing mixer sloshing through a behemoth bowl of cream, gives Dennis a smoldering frown, like boiled fish-eyes, thinks poor Dennis. But he determines to make the most of this, rare, singularly bizarre situation -- he'll humour Lars the way the dear, dear boy humours him when he is jumpy and over-imaginative -- a fulltime job. Besides, it isn't often Lars is like this. Oh why must I verbalize everything in my rattled head? thinks Dennis, Am I really that simple-minded?

"Makin' moah buttah!" exclaims Dexter ala his southern-belle party trick, "Why, I declare! Why, we had a perfect moun-tain of buttah yestahday! Why, when I was a-pokin' about in the refrigeratah, Ah saw..."

Another urgent gesture from Dennis stops Dexter mid-party-trick -- not the first time, thinks Dexter. Even in his homeland, Sunny California, he was afloat -- perpetually at sea -- even in that land of hype his jokes often fell like rotten potatoes in mud. After forty, so many friends seem to lose their sense of humour. But I must play the fool because I am the fool. I wouldn't be here worshipping a boy half my age if I weren't a fool.

Dexter deftly but sadly removes Brad from his thoughts lest he be overpowered at this vulnerable moment of the morning and continues with "Uhhhh... how's Violet?"

"The Violet voman vill live!"

Lars's cream is far from butter and he peers grimly into it, shaking it, hoping for the best, a clot or two perhaps...something 'Cornish', clotted and spreadable perhaps...

"Really?" asks Dexter, "She'll live? I was certain we were just this side of a Viking funeral last night and Vi-Vi was being hoist on her own petard."

"In Hell Storms vun must not stick vun's fingers into tele-phones," mutters Lars, sulkily poking his finger into cream that is decidedly not butter.

"Apparently not," says Dexter, "Or on them either. Hell Storms can be a dratted nuisance."

Where did he get that word?! Ah! From 'drat!' As in 'drat that little dog!' from 'The Wizard of Oz' -- Miss Gulch?" Oh, shut up Dexter! thinks Dexter, you'll do yourself an injury!

Why must almost everything he says date him? Of course, one can always get off the hook with 'Where did I get that word? Why, from that movie they showed yet again on television. I forget the name...'The Wizard of something or other.'

The perils of an aging gay man are divers. Oh God!, there I go again!

44

Brad snoozes on his air mattress, his eyelids flickering with distant music, his earphones being now entangled about his neck. Staring down at him is a grossly pregnant Christine who titters and pats naughtily at the huge pillow tied under her robe. She gives Brad's MP3 player wire a satisfying kick that jerks his head sideways. He, of course, does not waken. It takes, she knows, more than one jerk to wake this jerk. She almost wags that little finger in the air to celebrate her early morning jest. But doesn't. She's got a better jest at hand. And here it is!

"Good morning, gentlemen!" she cries and leaps into the kitchen, presenting her bogus belly from several angles simultaneously, or so it seems to Dennis and Dexter -- Lars isn't watching. Christine giggles, licks her little finger, thrusts it into the air, sings falsetto: "Joke!" as she simultaneously yanks the pillow from under her bathrobe, flings it in the air, catches it, giggles again. Louder.

No one laughs. But Christine is not discouraged because, well, because she is just so fucking happy -- pardon me, Mummy! "Do I smell scones?" she sings, "Goodness! Are we having scones?! There is nothing, but nothing nicer of a fine summer morning than a giant dish of hot, buttered scones! Isabella loves scones!"

"How do you know that?" asks Dennis.

"Because her maternal-aunt-to-be is a Scot! That's how I know!"

"Well, when you put it that way..." says Dennis.

"Scones with butter!" sings Christine, "I can hardly wait!"

Lars continues mixing cream. The very air around him seems suddenly several degrees *celsius* colder.

"How's Violet?" asks Dennis, determined to keep this situation from descending into...

"She's super-fic-ial!" trills Christine.

"How appro-pri-ate!" trills Dexter, suitably sorry for Violet's little electrical accident but well and truly weary of Violet's irascible, nay, hostile demeanour. Though he's perfectly delighted, just now, that she has survived.

Lars looks up from cream that will not become butter no matter how abused, says in a strained, choking voice directed with dark precision at Christine, "You...devoured ...all...my... butter."

"What?!" sings Christine, still obstinately light-hearted because she, nay, *they*! She and Isabella feel perfectly marvellous! What might have been a tragedy last night was only a sheep in wolf's clothing. Her Violet survived an onslaught of Nature at her electrically rudest!

"You devoured all my butter in the night," repeats Lars in exactly the same timbre and decibel, with precisely the same unpleasant, so-unlike-him, look.

"We most certainly did not!" sings Christine, "What wasn't used for medicinal purposes, dear one, was not fit for human consumption."

"Hence," says Dexter, "You super-humans devoured it."

Christine, who will simply will not be brought down, chirps: "Violet is just fine and so, my dears, are we! Je suis preggers! Voila! Je suis beau coup preggers! (or something like that)."

"Voulez vous coucher avec moi, ce soir?" asks Dexter.

"But. darling, how jejune, I needn't," exults Christine, "Can't you tell by my rosy cheeks? Je suis enceinte already!"

"Mon Dieu!" cries Dexter.

Christine happily pats her tummy, receives another dark

look from labouring Lars who mutters "You said that before, a whole alots of times. And you bloomin' vasn't."

"Bloomin' *veren't*, my churlish darling. A woman has a right to change her mind, hasn't she? From our loins flows the future of the world!"

"Or something like that," adds Dexter, "Terrifying, isn't it?"

Christine twirls happily, pats her tummy again and zeroes in on Lars who has stubbornly retired to a far corner with his bowl of intransigent cream.

"Lars, dearie-darling, could you do something about the sodding telephone? You're the handy man around here, aren't you, love? It's certainly not Dennis! I and Violet have important calls to make this morning. Violet tried last night to ring her mum, silly girl, and you know what happened then!"

Christine throws her head back, laughs gaily. Lars, with his bowl of cream does not answer, does not even look at her.

"Lars?" says Christine. Then, to the others: "His name is 'Lars'?"

Dennis and Dexter nod.

"Lars, love? Did you hear me, dearie-darling? What are you doing over there?" Then, to the others: "What on earth is he doing over there?"

"Don't ask, Christine," whispers Dennis.

"Whyever not, Dennis?! Why are you whispering? Lars?! Lars?! Yoo-hoo, is anybody home?! Whatever is he doing?"

"He's making butter," replies Dennis sotto voce.

"Butter?!" says Christine, "Cows make butter!"

"I...make...butter" says Lars, doggedly, from his corner.

"Can you just do that?"

No answer.

"Lars, dear, speak to me. Did you hear me about the telephone? I and Violet have important calls to..."

"Telephones is not to be used in Hell Storms."

"*Are* not, dear. Telephones *are* not to be used in Hell Storms. But the Hell Storm is over, passed! And we're all none the worse for it. Lars, we've got to get that telephone repaired, honeybuns, and pronto. Anyone in the loo?"

Christine spins past Dexter who is about to open the bathroom door, slams it in his face, begins, inside, to whistle merrily.

"La," peeps Dexter, "I do declare."

Dennis smiles understandingly, Lars scowls malevolently, and designer-briefed, earphoned Brad saunters in and goes directly to the bread box, cuts two slices of home-baked bread, drops them in the toaster, saunters to the fridge, opens it and squats before it and peers in tapping his MP3 rhythm into the exquisitely polished wooden floor.

Dennis holds his breath, hopes Brad is not going to say what he is certain he is going to say -- but he does: "Hey, you guys, where has all the butter went to?"

Dennis and Dexter remain poker-faced, Lars, sullen. The toilet flushes and out springs Christine who chirps "I'd be happy to do any washing up but I see it's all been done."

Christine bounds out of the kitchen while Brad, fingers on the floor, tapping to his eternal beat, seems to have forgotten why he is squatting before the fridge. Sleepily remembering, he mutters: "There was lotsa butter yesterday. I seen it."

Then here's Violet! -- beaming, her hugely bandaged hand, a sacred talisman, thrust before her, "Good Morning!" she calls with a generous wave of that talisman, "Good Morning everybody! Not to worry, I'm superficial! I hear there's scones! Nothing like scones and butter! I just love scones and butter! I just love butter! Masses of the glorious stuff!"

"Lightning becomes her. Or perhaps one should say Morning Becomes Electric," says Dexter and turns to enter the bathroom. But Violet swoops past him and, crying "Ladies first!", plunges in, slamming the door. Dexter slumps against the wall. "La," he says.

Great splashings of water and soapings of soap are heard just beneath the rapturous humming of frenetically happy Violet -- the new Violet! The no longer threatened Violet. The victorious Violet. The no need to be duplicitous dirty-rat Violet. Yes! They're finally leaving, she and Chrissie! Finally! Isn't it super?! It was difficult to do, to lie to Chrissie like that. Even more difficult to wash, with one good hand only, the dried powdery cornstarch out of the turkey-baster and demitasse. But so much is at stake and she mustn't feel guilty! Now they've got that nice Icelandic sperm technician, Gunilla, and her duly certified spunk to fall back on. Not Dennis's foppish, fly-by-night funny-fluid that could engender God-knows-what, particularly after years in this maddening wilderness! A 'Throwback' even! Yes! A Throwback! Whatever that is. "Ah!" exults the new Violet amidst the bubbles, the soap, the tangled strands of gauze and discarded, dairy-saturated poultices, the troweled-on layers of melting butter, "Oh, joy! Oh wooded bliss!"

Violet fancies herself a happy heroine on holiday in a jolly turn-of-the-century teenager's novel, rose-tinted lenses and all. The first genuine relief in days! The future, Violet is absolutely certain, lies ahead.

"Lars?" mumbles Brad from the floor in front of the fridge, "Lars?"

"Ja?" replies Lars, still mixing, from his star-crossed, cream-spattered corner.

"Lars, where has all the butter went to?"

A crash echoes from the bathroom followed by a great thud against the bathroom door, "Whoops!" calls Violet through the door, the genial Violet, the carefree, even allergy-free, though manipulating but only minutely ashamed for it, Violet, "Don't worry everyone, I just slipped on some butter!"

"Who's worrying?" mutters Dexter, "Worry? I'm about to wet myself but worry? What's that?"

"I heard that, Dexter," says Violet, cheerfully, behind the bathroom door.

"Then vacate the loo, Vi-Vi, and soon!"

"Lars?" repeats Brad, still squatting, still tapping aimlessly, now with both thumbs, on Lars's spotless floor, "Lars? Butter? Where has it all went to, anyways?"

More soaping, splashing, and humming from the bathroom.

"The Violet-voman vashes our butter from her vound to our sewer."

"Huh?" says Brad.

"Ach. Forget it, laddie," says Dexter.

Brad shrugs, un-squats, bumps out of the kitchen muttering over his shoulder: "Hey you guys, toast without no butter sucks anyways."

Tiny puffs of smoke slither from the edges of the oven door. "Lars?" asks Dennis, deeply deferential even reverential, "Lars, love? The scones?" then, softly to Dexter, "It annoys him when I interfere in his kitchen. I daren't touch a thing. Lars, love? The scones? They seem, in their own little way, to be perishing."

The bathroom door slams open and Violet, warbling maniacally, bursts out as Dexter, desperate for a pee, bursts in. Violet sticks up her newly bandaged hand, crows, "Nothing like butter for a burn, is there? I saved four whole sticks for my morning dressing -- just enough too!"

She thrusts her nose in the air, sniffs, "What's burning?"

"Je smell burning," calls Christine at the kitchen door in her comfy tartan hunting vest newly dried on the hearth, eager for another Hunt Breakfast, "What's burning? I hope it's not breakfast!"

Dexter, pleasantly relieved, appears in the bathroom door -- he'd dreaded the possibility of using that outdoor loo, bugs, don't you know, or a viper. "Do I smell something burning?!"

Then Brad reappears, scratching his hidden treasure, "Hey you guys, what's happening? I smell fires or something a heck of a lot like those."

Dennis dreads this inevitable moment, wipes his furrowed brow, motions for all to be silent. Sullen Lars slowly turns, sets down his bowl of non-butter, puts on two brightly coloured, elbow-length oven gloves, opens the oven door, removes the baking sheet of burnt-black scones, hurls them into the sink. He fetches his tragically non-butter, empties it over the carbonized scones and tosses the bowl into the air to be handily and fortunately caught by Dennis, who is by his own admission a lousy catcher but somehow...today, he must step in, be the...man of the house.

As the others stare, Lars removes the oven gloves, pulls on his gardening gloves, takes up his gardening basket and exits with an enormous door-slam into his impeccably pruned and, until now, peaceful garden.

"He'll be veeding the strawberries," says Dennis with a disjointed, though youthful smile.

"They von't vait," reply the others almost in unison. Minus Brad, of course, who ain't heard nothin'.

Anyways.

45

The two women wave goodbye as the four men climb into the mini-bus -- Lars making one last thorough inspection of the ropes guying their sleek, aluminium canoe to the mini-bus's roof. The "vimmen" said Lars, who is now completely recovered from this morning's butter snit, were welcome to come too. But Christine and Violet felt that three men in a boat were quite enough -- Dexter was only going along to sunbathe and read.

"Little tiny Isabella has indubitably been exposed to enough water already," Violet had said, ex-rat tongue in cheek. She was totally convinced that her own covert juxtaposition of Christine's serendipitous cycles as well as her, Violet's, malfeasance with cornstarch gruel, had finally put 'paid' to this particularly unsavoury version of little tiny Isabella.

There was a taut moment though, early this morning, when Christine, bless her heart, noted a powdery, intimate residue, and had, though casually, remarked that Dennis's spunk seemed to 'dry funny' and wondered if it was some peculiar Nordic junk-food he was gorging on.

So, amidst the exhilarated waves of a newly irrepressibly gay Christine and a seminally victorious Violet, the mini-bus grinds off in a noisy cloud of dust, and the women, humming and happy, as usual for very different reasons, ready themselves for a relaxing sunbath in the garden before their own departure later in the day -- they're taking the rental car, hurrah, hurrah!

But Violet has never been so cheerful which is cause for some suspicion.

"Violet," says Christine, left eyebrow raised, right eye narrowed.

"Yes, Chrissie, love?" replies Violet as Christine vigorously rubs tanning lotion over Violet's already reddening shoulders.

"Violet, why are you so totally cheerful? In our five astounding years together you have never been so cheerful so early in the morning. This is cause for un petit peu of innocent suspicion. I'm not complaining, Vi, as it's a nice change. But why, love?"

"The future is before us," chirps Violet.

"Yes, darling," agrees Christine, still puzzled, "that is a definite possibility. Now you slather some lotion on me. I'm so glad the boy's telephone line is up again. The telephone company just came along, checking the line for storm damage. Can you imagine that ever happening in Earls Court? So soon? The telephone man was rather dishy too. You don't suppose Dennis has ever dallied with him and become a mite septic?"

"Of course not," smiles Violet as she rubs tanning lotion vigorously across Christine's shoulders and doesn't feel even un petit peu guilty and grins innocently and bats her eyes as she delicately hands the tanning lotion back to Christine.

They curl into their canvas recliners toasting pleasantly in the warm sun, reprising yet again their two immediate but disparate futures, each inclusive of little tiny Isabella -- wherever she might be at the moment. Though the other half of Isabella, Violet is convinced, still resides in a sterile glass tube some miles south.

Grandmother-hood does not come cheap -- nor easily. Delayed departure, missed buses, and a horrific storm! Poor Mum. Here she sits in a taxi that is costing her the earth. Every recent mile she's travelled is etched on her crumpled face. She'd begun so full of hope, dressed to the nines, her face professionally cleaned with expensive astringents, scrubbed, defoliated and day-creamed, her makeup perfect, her hair a phenomenon by Miss Polly of Pimlico, actually Deborah Cramer, sufficiently recovered enough from the thrill of her daughter's recent child-birth to expertly trim and set Mum's hair. Mum's smart white pumps were positively glowing, her Laura Ashley print a marvel of perfectly pressed pleats, her white summer gloves, spotless. But wind and rain (and lightning!), hours without sleep, and an impudent, chocolate-smeared brat have transmogrified her into a wrinkled ruin surrounded by small moist piles of pink and blue infant's wear, much of it knitted by her own, now flagging, fingers with knitting needles nearly appropriated by Airport Security. But to be on the safe side, a strip search was necessary. They were extremely polite about it but seemed a bit suspicious, even as she boarded the plane. She secretly hoped the departure delay wasn't her fault.

So here sits Mum, in that extravagantly expensive taxi, hope dying under her once glorious, now flat coiffure, as billions of pine trees, the next looking precisely like the previous, fly by. She cannot help wondering why so many Swedes bothered to kill themselves when they could be so easily bored to death by their own scenery.

46

Violet has gone off for a brief jog and Christine snores in her canvas chair, an open book over her face against the now too eager sun. She sleeps a jerking, tetchy sleep born of exhaustion, frustration, and a surfeit of static electricity generated by her over-galvanized imagination. The animals of the forest, Brad's old friends or others suspiciously like them: an acorn scavenging squirrel, two grazing deer, a hare standing tall on its hind-legs, gather at the edge of Lar's lovely lawn, curious, friendly, open to new experience. Until Christine suddenly swallows a shriek, bolts upright, the book on her face, Fianulla Smythe's hot new novel 'Fear of Fucking', toppling to the lawn with a great, grassy plop causing these startled new animal friends to flee back to their pine-needled safety.

Brad has finally lured book-reading, landlubber Dexter into

the sleek aluminium canoe and they frolic happily, rocking the boat crazily at the centre of a small, picturesque lake. Dexter, Brad-animated, has never been more energetic. Dennis and Lars lie reading at the lake's edge, grateful to relax after the women's recent mental, spiritual and finally, even physical assaults and Lars's precarious and so uncharacteristic butter calamity.

But Dennis and Lars, according to Lars, have learned so very much from Christine and Violet, and all experience, Lars has adroitly, if too painstakingly, pointed out to Dennis, is grist for an artist's mill. Lars's own lesson, well learnt, is that one cannot whip butter from thin, coffee cream. Dennis, for his part, has swiftly accepted Lars's 'grist' theory partly because he hasn't the mental energy left to reject it but mostly because he quite fancies Lars's description of him as A Complete Artist, though at the moment a seriously dispirited one in search of an appropriate metier.

"Violetttttttt! Violetttttt! Violetttttttttttt!" rings from the cabin loo, sailing out its open window on clear summer air and thence into tall pines; a wail of abject misery, a plaint of nearly unutterable sorrow, an ineffably sad and continuous bellow that might have shaken the birds from the trees had they stuck around for more; a cry from the very soul and centre of a deeply disappointed, desperately disillusioned, darkly distraught female human being. The wail seems in an uncanny way to gather strength from Nordic Nature and bounces with renewed force between granite outcrop and tight-woven woods up the road towards Mum's speeding taxi, at least a mile from the cabin.

"What was that?!" asks Mum of her driver, "What was that?! An animal?!"

"Our God only knows, kind Mrs," replies the driver who is a deeply religious man with but a smattering of English.

At the lake, Lars, on his stomach in the sun lazily looks up from his cookbook, tugs his bathing suit down a mite over a reddening buttock-edge, says "Those two will fall out and drown in a minute."

After precisely one minute, Dexter and Brad, grappling and giggling, overturn their canoe and Dexter, just prior to disappearing immediately beneath the surface of that charming little lake gurgles:

"Help! Help! I can't swim!"

Mum knocks on the cabin door. Where is everyone? She sets down her suitcase and the two soggy Babykins bags and waves goodbye to her apprehensive taxi driver. He's still wondering where that mystifying ululation came from. Then Mum realises with a start, cries "God! What if no one's here? What if they've all gone on vacation together?!" But what an odd thing to do, thinks Mum, to go on vacation when one is attempting to artificially conceive a child.

Since her sixtieth birthday things had been getting odder and odder and Mum fully expected them to become more so. But having a grandchild was definitely a dazzling way, notwithstanding that rude, pubescent, punkish giantess on her plane, or the horrid chocolate guzzling babe on the bus, to find comfort in old age. As well as, of course, to endow a lucky grandchild with half a longing lifetime's grandmotherly love.

Mum wipes a tear from her eye, knocks again, much louder, then hears just behind the door "Violettttttttt?!"

Mum knocks yet again, louder.

"Violettttttttt?!"

The door is flung open and, her eyes rumpled slits of pain, Christine wails to the Nordic world: "I'M MEN-STRU-AAAAA-TINGGGGGG!"

On the lake shore Brad very expertly administers the kiss of life to the wet and prostrate Dexter whom he has recently very expertly flipped on his side and pumped till Dexter's lungs were clear. Dennis and Lars stand close by with a blanket and pillow at the ready, aghast with surprise at Brad's sudden, extreme competence in this mortal emergency. "Precisely how much vater," quizzes Lars of Brad, "must Dexter expel from the lungs before the required mouth-to-mouth procedure is administered?"

"Huh?" replies Brad, looking up from Dexter's slippery, quivering upper torso.

And all is once again quite right with the world.

"You're not Violet!" screams Christine, tearful eyes now wide open and staring into Mum's equal surprise.

"Christine?!" hollers Violet, rushing up, "Baby! Are you all right?!"

"I'm menstruating!" chokes Christine.

Violet's eyes light up, "Surely not!" she says and turns away to conceal her nearly helpless delight, only then notices Mum and adds "Who is this woman?"

"I am Dennis's mother," says Mum who draws herself up to her not inconsiderable height, thrusts one battered Babykins bag of pink infant's wear at Christine and the other, of blue, at Violet, "You must be Denny's Lesbians" says Mum moving directly to the bar and pouring a little drink, "Now how can I help you?!"

"A chaste kiss," murmurs Dexter, giddy and wet and still reeling from Brad's recent expert mouth-to-mouth. Dexter has never been so resuscitated. He is blooming with resuscitation as he nestles -- feigning a bit more fatigue and shock than he is experiencing -- into the strong, bare arms of his beauteous, so surprisingly, so unnervingly capable Brad. Their mini-bus -- Lars at the wheel, Dennis beside him, rattling canoe and oars tied to its roof -- rapidly approaches the cabin wherein waits, for Dennis, the mother of all surprises.

"MUM!" cries Dennis, for here is Mum, drink in hand, flanked by a militant Christine and a newly rat-like Violet steadfastly barring entrance to the cabin.

"Mum!" cries Dennis again, "How did you get here?"

"Dennis!" thunders Mum, as resolutely as Lady Bracknell ever admonished her daughter, Gwendolen, "DENNIS! THE SPERM BANK!"

47

"I ham Juanita but ju may call me 'Juan'. Now wheech of ju weel produce thee specimeen?"

"I'm the culprit," replies Dennis to the tiny, Spanish-Swedish, immaculately uniformed young woman.

"What ees 'thee culpreet'"?

"Forget it, Juan," replies Dennis, Lars at his side, gazing in awe around this gleaming white-tiled-stainless-steel-state-of-the-art Swedish sperm bank.

"Wash jour hands first. Do not allow thee water upon jour disease-test jab wounds else they can infected be," says Juanita, authoritatively from under her black, severely cut, fringe.

"My arm hurts," whines Dennis, "I hate jabs. Even of any kind."

"Don't be a baby, Denny," coaches Lars, "Tests are necessary for everything these days."

"Here ees thee jar for jour specimen. Ju weel find suitable arousing magazines in thee drawer hunder thee washing basin een jour cubicle. Here ees jour Chlameedia test packet."

Juanita thrusts a small plastic envelope at Dennis.

"My what?"

"Jour Chlameedia test! Read thee instructions carefully. A hlot may depend upon eet."

Dennis opens the packet, reads aloud: "Insert long wire cotton-wool swab as far as possible into the limp penis using a sharp, twisting motion..."

"Not now, por favor! Read eet in thee privacy of jour cubicle. As ju know," says Juanita, "we are processing jour See-phee-less, Honorrhea and HIV tests. We must insure that jour specimen, she ees not tainted. Si, Si?

"Yes, of course! God yes! But could you make that 'jour specimen, he ees not tainted'?" says Dennis.

"Si, si. We weel have jour results before ju leave. We Swedes are muy efficiento."

Dennis and Lars shoot a pained glance at one another and continue to rub their sore, jabbed upper arms. "Pardon me, Juanita," says Dennis, "but what ees...Sorry I mean what is 'Chlameedia'?"

"Eet ees disgusting! I ham not pree-pared to speak of eet! Leave jour Chlameedia test packet on thee washing basin after ju have completed eet and leave jour specimen in thee leetle jar I hov provided for ju." A dark look. "A hlot may depend upon eet."

Then, with a frown so determined, it shoots a shiver through both Dennis and Lars, she glares at Dennis: "Ju must screw thee lid of jour leetle specimeen jar hon tight. We do not wheesh to smear jour specimeen hon hour feengers. Do ju hear me? Screw eet hon tight!"

"A hlot may depend upon eet?" asks Dennis.

"Si," says Juanita as she opens a cubicle door, irritably waves Dennis into his cubicle, "Go now."

Dennis enters the cubicle, Juanita casually kicks its door shut and turns to Lars, reads from her papers: "Chlameedia for ju too I see?"

"I hope not," replies Lars.

"What are ju?! Meester Wise-Guy?"

"Not at all. I only..."

"Standard safety procedure for thee sperm deposeets always tests thee genitalia partners whatever their gender."

"I only meant ..."

"Jes, Meester Wise-Guy?"

"We had our HIV tests last year. They wasn't even necessary. We never have extra-marital...err sex."

"Nevair?" replies Juanita arching her one continuous eyebrow at both ends simultaneously.

"Nevair," says Lars. "What is 'Chlameedia'?"

"I ham not pree-pared to speak of eet. Here ees jour Chlameedia test packet. Read thee instructions carefully and perform them ahs ree-quired. A hlot may depend upon eet. Jour other tests are being pro-cessed. No ejaculation for ju, I see."

"Not just now, Thanks."

190

Juanita kicks open the next cubicle door for Lars, briskly motions him in. "Go now, Meester Wise-Guy, Tweest that Clameedia swab!"

Juanita returns to the front desk, smartly slaps her papers down, sits, straightens her thick, black fringe and flings a wild grin over the reception desk at an exulting Christine, the even now scheming anew Violet, and anxious Mum who sit in the waiting room.

"She's every bit as nice as that Earls Court Gunilla," says Christine, grinning back at Juanita. You don't have to come from Iceland to be a qualified spunk technician! Everything, just now, seems to be flowing her way -- thinks Christine, including specimen! And she and Vi have found another understanding and possibly very useful, friend -- Dennis's Mum, who seems completely promising. And Violet is behaving so much better! I must ask Vi what was wrong with her for those three miserable days, it was so unlike her, she is usually such a congenial girl, thinks Christine, unaware of newly minted treachery clinging like a spider in that deceitful web behind her lover's pained smile.

Juanita suddenly gives the women a thumbs up, cries "Seesters!"

"Indubitably!" shouts Christine, returning Juan's thumbs-up with gusto. Mum just stares at them all and continues perusing her magazine. Where does Dennis find these raucous people? she thinks, adding, But a bit of social inconvenience is a small price to pay for an authentic grandchild.

Mum chuckles to herself. The impossible is about to come true. If only Dennis does not let her down. If he could produce just the tiniest fraction of the semen she had laundered out of his adolescent underwear they could found a regiment!

Dennis fumbles ineffectually in his stark, aseptic little cubicle. He suddenly remembers Juanita's promise of 'suitable reading material in a drawer hunder thee washing basin' and jerks open this drawer to find a large poster which he immediately unfolds. It is of an enormous-breasted woman slathered with heavy, makeup, flat on her back, legs akimbo and sporting a lubricious smile. He gasps, staggers backward, recovers, refolds the poster, crams it back in the drawer and slams the drawer shut. He sits with a sigh and even longs for his own DVD of Biff and Bart, 'wi-brator' et al. Perhaps his DVD wasn't so bad? Perhaps he had found his true calling at last? But what about that epic novel of his...if only...he...could...find it?!

"We'll be late for the funfair. It takes Dennis ages. Dexter and Brad will wonder what happened to us," says Christine, "and Dexter has enough on his hands just looking after himself."

"And Brad," adds Violet.

"Dennis was always such an active little boy," says Mum from behind her magazine, "I do not know what's got into him."

"Lars," say Christine and Violet in unison, "And vice versa."

"Some men are fast. Some men are slow," says Mum, not getting it, "That's all that can be said about men."

"My ex-husband, Jamie, was on and off before I knew what hit me. I felt nothing," says Violet, "Absolutely nothing. He thought only of himself."

"That's par for the course," adds Christine, "The heterosexual inter-course." She licks her little finger, wags it in the air, cries "Joke!"

"Never the twain shall meet," murmurs Mum with a sad though resonant sigh.

"Except for replication purposes," adds Christine.

"I'll take a test tube any day of the year," says Vi.

"And a vibrator," whoops Christine with a large, askew grin, "For those hard-to-reach crevices. And there you have it. All any woman could ever ask for! A petite demitasse and a turkey-baster for spawning and a vibrator for an extra spasmodic bounce. Who could ask for anything more?"

"I could," sighs Mum, softly recalling holding hands by the electric fire with Dennis's disappeared Daddy, "I could."

"I'd never even heard of climax," mutters Violet thumbing impatiently through her magazine, "Neither had my mum. Or her mum before her. I lived a cloistered life." She browses a few pages, "We'd never even had an orgasm! Three generations of super-randy females and not a single, sodding orgasm between us! And we'd never heard of the multiple sodding orgasm!"

"Well you have now, Vi-Vi. Or if you haven't, you do an excellent imitation!" says Christine, with a happy grin.

Violet looks up, takes Christine's hand, squeezes it. They gaze fondly at one another.

Mum looks on affectionately. What good friends these ladies are! So frank. So spirited. Would that she had had more spirit in the old days. Would that she had sussed the coming storm in her marriage and run for cover in time or at least bought a sturdier umbrella. And had not, perhaps, blamed her husband quite so virulently for his completely -- in retrospect -- understandable departure. They were so young. They'd made a terrible mistake. Both of them. But it might have been more cordially rectified. She liked the man. Still does. He was so amusing. She'd even have him back! For the companionship alone -- he was a witty fellow. Companionship. That's what counts in the twilight years. Mum sighs. We were so young. She sighs again. Dexter and Brad, such nice boys. She must speak to young Brad at least once before she leaves. Although it could be difficult -- how will she gain his attention? But one must attempt to acquaint oneself with this new world evolving under ones very feet lest one be toppled and trampled. The future seems so ripe and full of hope just now. The women have promised her the role of doting grandmother and impossible dreams are about to begin to come true. 'Next month at fertile window time,' Christine has assured her. Violet, however, squinted and said nothing. Christine does lead poor Violet a merry chase. Mum sighs again. How glad she is to have invited everyone to the funfair for a celebratory farewell treat before their various departures. Especially when there is something so, well, momentous, to celebrate!

Trapped in his sterile cubicle, flagging Dennis has given up on spunk procurement for the moment. A diversion, even of any kind, is required. So he now grips the long, savage-looking wire and cotton wool swab in one hand reads the 'Chlameedia' instructions in his other hand, makes a sharp twisting practise-motion in the air, gulps, feels faint, drops his naked buttocks to the WC's clammy though spotless, tissue covered lid.

"What in God's name can be keeping him?" says Christine, "Doesn't he know we're waiting for him?"

"I believe he does, dear," replies Mum.

"Do you think if I stood outside his cubicle and flapped my pheromones through his door vent it would help? asks a helpful though increasingly impatient Christine.

"To be perfectly honest, no." says Violet from behind her magazine.

A loud crash from Dennis's cubicle causes Christine to sit up smartly, peer anxiously down the cubicled hallway.

"The natives are restless," chuckles Violet.

"God!" cries Christine, "Has Dennis hurt himself?!"

"Probably," says Violet, "Intentionally, of course."

Mum looks up, concerned for her genetic future.

"Oh, my God!" cries Christine and jumps from her chair and followed by a concerned Juan is pounding at Dennis's cubicle door in an instant. "Denny! Denny! Are you all right in there, honeybuns?!"

"I...suppose so," replies Dennis through the door after a very, very long distressed moment.

"What happened, honeybuns?!"

Another very, very long moment.

"The errr...the toilet seat fell off."

"Oh, is that all," says Christine and returns to the waiting room, "The toilet seat fell off," she tells Violet and Mum.

"Is that all," says Violet.

"Need help, Denny?" whispers Lars through a wall vent in the next door cubicle.

"Uh-huh," moans Dennis, "Uh-huh!"

48

Everyone crowds round the reception desk as Juanita goes over the test results. She looks up, smiles at the women, "I ham hoppy to say that everytheeng she ees een order. Ju are very lucky."

With great reverence and a toothy grin she hands to Christine a largish parcel tied with a heavy string. "All ees well. Thee specimeen she ees deep-frozen and sealed and packed for thee journey to London -- the very latest technique. When ju arrive in jour home ju must put eet into thee freezer at minus twenty degrees Celsius until thee day you insert eet. A hlot may depend on eet. Ju have a freezer?"

"Yes," says Violet, "We use it for gentlemen-callers."

"Thee specimeen she ees mucho high quality seee-meen with mucho, mucho motility!"

"There," says Dennis, "Whatever that is, it sounds super. I wasn't so bad after all, was I?"

Lars hugs Dennis, grins shiftily, says, "Not bad at all, Dennis."

"Congratulations, darling," says Mum, "For heroism under fire. Your efforts are all in a most excellent cause."

Everyone hugs everyone all around and Juan sings several lively verses of La Cucaracha for the insistent Violet who remembers her evening-class Assorted Languages instructor, Rosa Flores's, rendition of that very song.

Christine lofts her parcel of deep-frozen treasure, her inchoate Isabella, high above her head, exclaims "To the victor go the spoils!" Follows it quickly with a wetted little-finger wag and "Joke, everyone! Joke!"

All laugh, more or less, Violet rather less. Her eyes are full on that alien packet, that bungled bundle; her mind, buzzing already with rapidly thickening plots and alternate schemes should those rapidly thickening plots fail. Her body is tensed for just the right moment. Sabotage is, as always, the name of her thoroughly reopened, serial dirty-rat games.

They meet Dexter and Brad at the funfair gate and Christine immediately buys everyone a one-size-fits-all plastic helmet sprouting fierce foam rubber Viking horns. She gaily distributes them, insisting they wear them in celebration of what has come, and is to come...Joke! And hoots happily and crams on her horns. Violet only reluctantly dons hers, her mind racing. Mum -- her hair's a mess anyway -- sticks on her horns and grins. She'll have fun too, just like the youngsters! It's never too late.

Brad is delighted with his horns and if Brad is delighted, Dexter, still vibrating with that recent mouth-to-mouth monumental resurrection err... resuscitation, is ditto. Dennis, to avoid a sparring match with Christine and thankful that his lady guests, are soon to depart, dons his Viking horns under duress but Lars complains that the Vikings never had horns on their helmets, never, and this vulgar motif is merely a romantic remnant of some dreary nineteenth century opera. He and Dennis have the definitive opera book, haven't they, and they've never cared for Wagner anyhow. Lars has read every word, measured in his clockwork mind every over-decorous set, every outrageous costume. Those eminent Victorians! He acquiesces however, when Dennis pleads "Let's just get it over with, love." Lars could never deny Dennis anything. And vice versa, he blissfully concludes to himself and sticks the silly horns on his head.

So the little group, this small herd of one-size-fits-all horns, forges ahead into the hurly-burly of Fortune wheels, Ferris wheels, dizzying skyrides, a loop-the-loop roller coaster the size of Godzilla (and not hollow!), beautifully kept trees and blooming flowers and very, very noisy surging crowds populated with more tots than Mum has seen in a lifetime of gut-wrenching grandchildren-watching.

Mum buys everyone Swedish cream-waffles and a juniper-wood handled cheese cutter, for good luck they're assured by the vendor, and they sit gorging on their waffles and planning their various rides. But Violet, of course, has something else on her mind.

Oh my, thinks Christine, Violet's got that inscrutable look again. We must discuss it but my God, these Swedish cream waffles are excellent! Almost as yummy as Lars's!

"Oh wowwwwwwww!" yells Brad, as the loop-the-loop careens far above his head. Love child Brad parrots his adored hippie grandparents who just couldn't resist sticking long-stemmed carnations down gun barrels, just couldn't allow the seventies to slip away and continued, puffing weed, to live the happy lie. Which suited Brad to a tee. And Dexter, too. Life is a waking dream and we make of it what we will.

Dexter pats Brad's shoulder adoringly, exulting in Brad's archaic oh-so-seventies demeanour. "The world just left my boy and me behind," whispers Dexter who pledges to forever respect and protect this vulnerable, though frighteningly effective when called for, simply gorgeous creature. Everyone sooner or later settles into their own time-warp, thinks Dexter, and it comforts him. Isn't he lucky? It's lovely to have such young and lovable company. But he adds, with a longing look at earphoned, waffle-wielding Brad, will it last? And sighs, then sighs again, much like Mum. Not nearly so optimistically but certainly as resonantly.

Mum adores the Swedish cream waffles. They're almost as good as Lars's. She munches and gazes longingly at the many very young children having the time of their lives. "Enjoy it, dears," she whispers, "You'll find soon enough that life is a barrel of worms," not realising, of course, that children love to play with worms.

But Mum knows now, that life is also full of impossible dreams that do come true and sweep you off your feet and hand you a future you never dreamed of in your wildest, well, dreams. She, like Dexter, and perhaps everyone -- certainly including her son -- survives on dreams with a lot of help from their friends. In Dennis's case, Lars, and Christine has Violet and Dexter, well, has Dexter and said dreams. These Swedish cream waffles really are wonderful! thinks Mum, though not quite as good as Lars's.

Dexter is a real nice man, thinks Brad, bumping to his

internal beat and wiping strawberry waffle jam from the corners of his perfect lips while he contemplates his juniper-wood cheese cutter, A real nice man. So is Dennis's mom, for buying me this good-luck-wood-handled cheese-cutter stuff. He enjoys people buying him stuff. And things.

As for Violet, who chomps her waffles contemplatively, not caring a hoot who made them, Lars or the man in the moon, she's in Earls Court, her winged feet presently pointed towards that authorized sperm bank. One might almost think she was infatuated with Gunilla, its Icelandic sperm-technician. But one would be desperately wrong.

Violet looks up from her contemplations and Swedish cream waffle just in time to see Christine leading Dennis by his plump arm to a lovely white filligreed bench near the hammer and bell concession where an excessively handsome young man -- watched by another excessively handsome young man and two downright gorgeous young women -- attempts to slam the hammer on a peg and ring the bell at the top of a brightly painted pole.

My God! Christine could have used the spunk of either of those two handsome young gods, thinks Violet. Either of them! Both are preferable to middle-aged Dennis. Her attention strays back to Christine and...and her, VIOLET'S WALLET! Stuffed with sterling from her, Violet's own mother's, recent winning lottery ticket and given to Christine and Violet as a special, vacation shopping present. What on God's green earth is Christine doing with their money!?

49

Violet throws down her waffle fork and bounds towards Dennis and Christine but instantly realises a quick purge in the loo is more urgent and disappears round the decoratively painted corner of the North Star Wonderful Waffle House.

"I and Violet have given most serious thought to this, Dennis, and we would like to present you with..."

"Oh, no, please, Christine," protests Dennis, colouring more extravagantly than usual as the wad of bank notes emerges from Violet's inscribed wallet.

"Please accept this five hundred pounds as a token of our deep and abiding appreciation..." says Christine.

"No, please, I can't," replies Dennis, his resistance diminishing as much as his colour rises. Even a good man, he thinks, can't hold out forever. But I have suffered. Spunk doesn't grow on trees. It's only fair. Isn't it?

"Did you say five hundred pounds?" he whispers, the final "s" catching in his throat.

"Little tiny Isabella would want this..."

"But," protests Dennis, "But..." Then, from the corner of his eye he sees...not thirty feet away... Oh, God! Is nothing in this absurd world as it seems?! he thinks, his face now aflame before Christine's ever growing admiration.

Crikey! We're certainly getting our money's worth! thinks Christine watching with helpless joy as the pink roses of Dennis's always blooming cheeks become a luminous, spreading scarlet. She exclaims, "You Men! Can't live with you, can't live without you!" immediately licks her little finger, wags it in the wind and cries "Joke!"

Grinning merrily, Christine counts five one hundred pound notes into Dennis's trembling though still outstretched hand -- this wonderfully complected Dennis who hunches fearfully beside her on that white filigreed bench, one eye furtively peeled on the stupefying antics of Biff and Bart, the other on the loot.

A conversation in Swedish -- roughly translated:

"God! Biff! Do you see who's over there?!"

"Where, Bart?"

These two muscular men, recent hyper-hunky participants in Dennis's Safe-Sex DVD film, have adopted their DVD names as they, as well as their two ravishing girlfriends, their beauteous equals in every possible way, quite like their boyfriend's new, Americanesque monikers.

"Over there!" continues broad shouldered Bart, slamming the huge hammer on the peg and effortlessly clanging that bell at the top. "on that bench with that brawny little woman in a man's hunting vest! Dennis hasn't seen us yet!"

But of course, unfortunately, Dennis has. He had witnessed, in fact, one burning kiss per couple immediately prior.

"Where is this Dennis person?!" asks Inga, Bart's ravishing counterpart.

"Where?!" asks Annika, Biff's ditto.

Bart gestures with one gleaming, robustly muscled arm towards Dennis who crouches there with wallet-wielding, precious parcel clutching Christine.

"You must hide!" says Bart to Inga.

"You must hide too," says Biff to Annika.

"Why?!" replies Inga, not amused.

"Why?!" replies Annika, irritated.

"Because Dennis thinks we're gay."

"We would not wish to misillusion him," adds Bart, "He travels through delicate journey on this life."

(Still roughly translated)

"And," adds Biff, "if he knew we was not gay he might not pay us our five hundred pounds!"

"And if he does not pay you, our five hundred pounds," adds Inga, her ravishing Botticelli hair streaming in a bracing breeze, "we cannot venture to fetching Sicily next month."

"Which would be very sad," adds Annika, her skin, luminous, her thick golden eyelashes aflame in the low, still setting Nordic sun, "Very, very sad for all of us."

"And you promised us," adds Inga through pouting pink lips that have never known lipstick.

Dennis, his eyes still on the fabulous Biff and Bart is wondering who those two superb female beauties whom the boys were passionately kissing just before could possibly be. Their sisters or their cousins or their aunts?! But of course, and sadly, he knows the answer. One never deep-kisses ones sisters. And one deep-kisses ones cousins and aunts only if said cousins or aunts are exceptional or perhaps uncles instead of aunts.

"Dennis?" says Christine, grinning at him through her recent joy, "Dennis, what are you staring at? Hadn't we better get back to the others at the loop the loop? Lars must be wondering where you are."

Christine kisses her precious parcel and tucks it close beside her on the bench, pockets Violet's wallet and begins to zip up a few of the storage flaps on her hunting vest. But Violet, lurking covertly nearby, seizes this moment she's been waiting for. Quicker than a mongoose she rockets in and snatches the contentious parcel and is away, seeming able to leap tall buildings at a single bound!

Christine stares speechless after her leaping lover for a split-second only and streaks off in frantic, screaming pursuit.

Dennis, hardly aware of Christine's screaming departure, contemplates the five hundred pounds in his hand, considers his debt of honour, considers Bart's prime arse as said bends to take up the hammer. The two ravishing women have disappeared and Biff, after making sure he's got Dennis's eye, gives Bart's butt a friendly pat and grins over at Dennis, nodding lasciviously. Dennis nods back, rises reluctantly and, zombie-like, knowing what he must now do, makes his way slowly, reluctantly towards Biff and Bart. Five hundred pounds, thinks Dennis, borrowing a favourite phrase of Dexter's from their younger days, is a lot of moolaroony.

But should he part with it so abruptly? Wouldn't it be awfully nice to just carry it around for a while, feel it in his pocket? Perhaps bring it out on the spur of the moment in the presence of Lars's generous Mum who might think it's an advance payment for his sociologically significant safe-sex film? Or even his miraculously recovered epic novel? No! This is fate. It must be fate! This precise amount needed to get him off the hook. Placed in his trembling fingers only thirty point seven feet -- Lars might have said -- from where Biff and Bart, in all their animal glory but sinister Sicilian connections stand. But Dennis is an honourable man. His choice is clear.

"Are we alone?" whispers Dennis, arriving at last between hyper-hunk Biff, and meta-muscular Bart.

"Oh ja!" replies Biff, sparkling clear eyes darting guiltily aside to check if Inga and Annika have made it safely to cover, "Bart and me is here together real intimate having good time amongst we!"

Biff is elated to have at last properly pronounced an English "W" and he pats Bart on his arse again, "Is correct, Bart?"

"Oh ja! Sincerely surely correct," replies Bart, making a desultory grab at Biff's substantial crotch. Biff, surprised, jumps away. So does Dennis.

"Good," says Dennis. "If I pay you 500 pounds then our contract is null and void, right?"

"Null and Woid?" asks Biff, backsliding language-wise.

"What means 'null'?" asks Bart.

"What means 'woid'?" asks Biff.

"Forget it," says Dennis, handing Biff the moolaroony, "Just give me a receipt."

"Receipt?" asks Biff.

"Receipt?" asks Bart.

But should I have parted with the money so abruptly? thinks Dennis stumbling away in a daze with their scribbled receipt. Five hundred pounds. The precise amount needed to get me off the hook with Biff and Bart who had stood not thirty point seven feet away nuzzling, embracing and kissing two simply gorgeous women!

Ah! The treachery! Biff and Bart were not what they seemed! But is anyone? *Anything*, what it seems? Five hundred pounds... There they stood, hunky heterosexual Biff and hunky heterosexual Bart, in all their bogusness and...oh, my, animal magnetism! And here I stand, a man of honour, deceived, all my vulnerable homosexual regalia displayed and betrayed. Hath not a gay, eyes? Hath not a gay hands, organs, dimensions, senses, affections, passions?...Fed with the same food, hurt with the same weapons, subject to the same diseases, healed by the same means, warmed and cooled by the same winter and summer as a heterosexual is? If you prick us, do we not bleed?! If you tickle us do we not laugh?! If you poison us, do we not die?! If you wrong us shall we not revenge?! But...I digress...

50

"Fluffy, come back!" screams Christine. Violet, like a speeding bullet and, in this case, more powerful than a locomotive, that pernicious parcel clutched close, zips behind The Wheel of Fortune, and thence, unknown to Christine, into the Hall of Mirrors where she drops herself into a deserted glassy corner and reflects. She tucks the parcel securely between her knees, wipes her running eyes. "Yet again!" she thinks, "I am blubbing yet again! What has my dearest Chrissie brought me to? Why have I allowed myself to become so...unlike my true jovial self?"

"My poor Violet," thinks Christine, "Why is she so irritable and unpleasant and so... unlike my own dearest Vi? She was such a jolly woman. God! Jolly, up to that very moment in Trondheim when Dexter showed me Dennis's photo. Surely she cannot believe that Dennis means anything more to me than a dollop of warm, fertile spunk? As a person, he is fine. But other than his fabulous colouring he is simply not my erotical type even if he were the right gender. He's not got Violet's purply eyes or dark wavy hair. My God, he's not even got great firm, heaving breasts! What does one do with a person sans breasts? He's a bit jumpy as well and worries too much about imaginary things. Always going on about the Mob. What Mob?! My God! And I would much rather discuss books with Vi than anybody else. Can't Vi see this?"

Christine drops herself on a bench in front of the Hall of Mirrors, faintly recalls the hall of mirrors shoot-out scene in Orson Wells's 'Lady from Shanghai' seen recently in their Assorted Classic Films class. But Christine is not, nor would she care to be, Rita Hayworth, that pitiful, though spectacularly and luminously gorgeous 1940's martyr to men. She, Christine, is nobody's female St Sebastian! Though her own arrows had often enough found their mark in those closest to her. Like, gulp! her beloved Violet. But completely innocently of course. Christine instantly erases this unpleasant surmise, she'll think about it tomorrow.

She sighs. "Oh Vi, darling, where are you? And what are you doing with our spunk? Don't you know, darling, how important it is to me?!"

Violet takes from between her knees and dangles the purloined parcel by its string, swings it, an evil pendulum, before her eyes, squints at it, says aloud, "What shall I do with you? What? Shall I cast you out upon this barren ground? Shall I..."

"Vi-Vi! There you are, you naughty girl!"

Violet looks up, sees Chrissie's happy face in a kaleidescope of mirrored reflections! She's surrounded from every angle by Chrissie's loving concern! And loving concern it is -- for the briefest moment...

"Violet! You treacherous traitor! You Delilah! You Jezebel! How could you?!"

Violet snatches up Dennis's spunk, darts down a multi-mirrored corridor, her own miserable face squinting at her from a thousand places at once. Then suddenly it is Chrissie's frowning face and her crushing condemnation above, below and beside! Wherever Violet looks, there is Chrissie! But where is Chrissie?! Above? In front or behind her?! And Chrissie's terrible cries!

"Violet! Stop! Stop! This is criminal, Vi! Criminal! This is sabotage! Treason!"

Chrissie's shouts! The-mirrors-the-shouts-the-mirrors-the-shouts! Here is Violet, blubbing again! Blubbing her miserable heart out! Now she's a criminal, fleeing in The Hall of Mirrors! What next?! Will Oestrus sodding Sunday never end?!

Then, crash! Crunch! Smash! Directly into Chrissie! No it isn't Chrissie! It is unyielding glass into which she's crashed and

Chrissie's multi-faceted censure shatters in a mirror of such size that seven year's bad luck is only a beginning.

Violet knows nothing now, she's sprawled on the glass-spattered floor, dazed, that spermatic parcel locked stubbornly between her knees as a thousand more Chrissie's bear down on her from all sides. A thousand very shame-faced Chrissies.

51

"She was lucky," whispers Mum wringing her hands and thankful that it was Violet who had demolished that mirror and not Christine who will ultimately, after a painstakingly, assisted-by-Mum, gestation, decant a shining little bundle of joy, the delight of any stork worth its feathers. Mum is sorry her concern for Violet couldn't be deeper. But the overriding issue here is genetic survival. Although -- Mum adds in her tailor-made interior dialogue -- love of ones fellow man or woman always runs an excessively close second.

Anyhow, poor Violet had only put her nose out of joint -- easily seen-to when one got back to civilization, namely, Earls Court. Her own nose, recalled Mum with a chuckle, was often out of joint. Particularly these days. Noses out of joint couldn't always be solved with a tipple or a toffee though God knows she'd tried. And by the way, what on earth has happened to Dexter's nose?! I hardly recognised him!

The funfair management, and in particular a certain, distinguished gentleman in charge -- well noted by Mum who had fancied she'd seen a distinct glint in his eye for her -- had agreeably promised to pay for cosmetic surgery. They were assured by Christine, as she signed their affidavit, that this would not be necessary though she did accept their generous offer of dinner for all in the luxurious Sky Tower restaurant to which everyone was looking forward.

"Oh, Vi, darling," mists Christine, beside the hastily prepared bed at the sperm bank, compliments of amenable Juan, "I was so worried when you collided with that mirrored wall."

"Worried about Dennis's sodding frozen jizzum?" replies still dazed Violet, feeling for the packet of frozen sperm safely under her pillow.

"My dearest girl, you must look upon it as our frozen jizzum. Not his frozen jizzum. And you needn't have held on to it so unflinchingly between your knees either. I was afraid I might injure your spine by even attempting to remove it from your vise-like grip!"

"Oh, Chrissie!" moans Violet miserably from her immaculate, white pillow, "Will your awful Oestrus never end?! You've become a procreating monster. You've driven everyone mad with your selfish pursuit of spunk. You've thought of nothing -- nothing but your raving, writhing womb!"

"Violet, darling. I've thought of nothing but wee Isabella. Our Isabella Victoria Gloria."

"Isabella doesn't exist, Chrissie. Not yet. But I do! And you're driving me away! You've made me a monster too. I've become so excruciatingly unpleasant. You know I'm not this way at all! You've hung our dirty underwear on a clothes-line for all the world to see!

"But we haven't any dirty underwear, darling. We're immaculate!" protests Christine.

"In everything but conception! There you've made a mess of it. I've tried to be understanding to a point, says Violet, whose double-dealing now flies like a barbed dart to the very center of her self esteem. "But you've just plowed on, breaking all your promises. You've become a fertile farce!"

"Darling," cries Christine, "I'd do anything to keep from hurting you."

"You've done everything, it seems, to hurt me!"

"Vi, I feel so guilty, so horribly, perplexingly, gut-wrenchingly guilty!"

"That's because you've finally got a proper guilt-complex. Well-deserved it is too. And more power to it!"

"I've got a 'Guilt-Complex' and you've got a 'Crisis of

Confidence'! Oh, Violet, baby!"

"I hope, upon our return, Christine, to discuss this thoroughly in front of our Domestic Psychoanalytical evening-class seminar. We can also print and disseminate the relevant brochures."

"Violet, darling, there'll be no need for that. I admit it. I have brought all of this upon us by my stubborn refusal to recognize that others, namely you, have human needs and certain expectations. Needs and expectations that must be ministered to post-haste and not allowed to play second fiddle to the importance of having spunk!"

"Oh, Chrissie, you make me so happy!"

"Now just hand me Dennis's spunk, Vi, darling, and we'll say no more about it."

52

"Motherhood will become me, make me an excellent person all round. And pronto!" Christine nods appreciatively at Juan for the timely use of her native language, then continues well within earshot of Lars and Dennis and Dexter who have gathered nearby. Brad, in his fetching new lederhosen shorts compliments of Dexter, had run into some German 'uncle' and could not, at the moment be found.

"I'm sure motherhood will make you excellent, dear," says Mum, "Parenthood builds character."

Christine considers this last with a tiny though perfectly hidden frown, "Yes, so I've read."

"You've got a guilt-complex, baby," says Violet, lying there prostrate and pathetic, "Like me."

"Possibly, Vi," says Christine, "possibly, darling."

"We'll learn to rationalise it together, Chrissie," mutters Violet through a sleepy snort. She's in shock, been through such a lot, nerve-wise.

"Yes, darling, we shall."

"I thought you already knew how to rationalise, Christine," says Dennis at his drollest.

"Leave her alone," wheezes Violet, now semi-conscious but coming delicately to Christine's defence, "She's got a guilt-complex. Like me."

Christine, Lars, Dennis, Dexter, Mum and Juan crowd protectively round Violet's bedside.

"Is it not wondrous to be loved as Vi is loved by one and all?" murmurs Christine to herself. "We are so lucky."

"Where in God's name is Brad?" murmurs Dexter.

"Heading for The Black Forest with his Kraut," mutters Violet who now falls completely asleep, gently lulled by Christine and ever-faithful Juan.

Christine pats that perfidious parcel now safely installed under her arm. Violet will come round to the idea, she's sure. Violet will, when she fully realizes how much this means to me, come round. Comforted by her own soothing partiality, Christine squeezes the sleeping Violet's hand, nods happily to Juan who nods back thinking it's high time for me to find a 'significant muchacha' to sing me 'La Cucaracha'.

Dennis, Lars and Mum have decided to take in more funfair before dinner in the Sky Tower while Violet rests. And Dexter is extremely anxious to meet Brad's German 'uncle' upon whose lap Brad was last seen skidding down a waterfall in the popular 'Flume Water Ride'.

Dennis and Lars immediately head for the Flume Water Ride, their favourite -- Lars always sits on Dennis's lap too at this satisfying venue. Mum prefers the 'Voyage Through the Universe' in the Super-Widescreen theatre with the jerky, mechanised seats. Distraught Dexter has gone off somewhere looking for Brad who it seemed was no longer skidding down water falls with 'uncle'. But Violet, whether she knew it or not, was correct. Brad intended to abscond with the German -- coincidentally the same German motorist who'd several days before given him that ride and all those euros and pine needles. Destination: The Black Forest. What goes round, like, comes round. Or something, like, real close to something like that, thinks Brad as he pencils a farewell note to Dexter whom he'll meet, well, like, somewheres in Europe in like a few days. Anyways.

He'll drop a note, like, at American Express in, like, London where they'll, like, catch their charter flight home. Like. He hesitantly erases the last 'like' and signs his name followed by a huge "X".

The view from the luxurious Sky Tower Restaurant is superb and their table exquisitely, bounteously set. They all love the very expensive champagne and the red-leather dining chairs with arms on them, which poor moping Dexter has yet to notice. "I wonder where Brad is?" he moans, having not yet read Brad's parting note which is presumably tucked under the windscreen wiper of the mini-van.

"What a totally fantastic view! It looks like Earls Court!" exclaims Christine in a fit of happiness that she will soon be home and turkey-basting again. Violet, close beside her, rested, reasonably nasally recovered and stoically resigned to Dennis's frozen spunk, has just apologised to Dennis and Lars and poor deserted Dexter. Her irritability was, she assured them, entirely Christine's fault and Christine, bless her, concurred and would make 'every attempt to be a better girl in future,' and might even make a public apology to Violet in Domestic Psychology. Which suited Violet immensely.

Perhaps there was something to be said for the pokeless pig. And the pokeless pig Christine had chosen wasn't -- though he was a bit past it -- all that bad. Bright pink cheeks and golden, curly hair could be, well, totally gorgeous, on a girl.

"That is not Earls Court, Christine," says Dennis, correcting Christine, and referring to the view from the spectacular Sky Tower restaurant, "that is Gothenburg."

This immediately forces Violet to reassess her recently revised and more favourable opinion of Dennis. She hated people correcting Chrissie! That was her domain! "Whatever city it is, it is not worth being rude about!" -- decorum being one of the centrepieces of Vi's spanking new simpatico. And, anyway, Christine had said it *looks* like Earls Court, not that it *was* Earls Court.

"I wonder where Brad is," whines Dexter.

"In The Black Forest," repeats Violet, "where the bears come from."

Dexter had found Brad's note on the minibus and caused a suitably tearful scene. But climbing in he'd immediately discovered Brad curled up in his new lederhosen shorts close beside him on the back seat and sleeping like, thought Dexter, that recumbent statue of the naked Shelly to whom he often pantingly compared Brad. Dexter's joy is of course immense if not complete.

Then, everyone in their places and speeding down the highway to the airport, Christine says "I must apologise, Dennis, I was in a reproductive frenzy when first we met."

"And somewhat after," adds Dennis.

"I'll vouch for that," says Violet.

"It was only my oestrus, and of course, your spunk that caused our world to... tilt a bit."

"And *your* spunk, Christine. *Your* spunk," repeats Dennis, "I have never experienced such shockingly kinetic energy," with the major exception of Lars's, he adds in his head. "The Ice Age itself wouldn't have held a candle," he says, fully aware he's miserably mixing metaphors, "against your irresistible onslaught."

Christine glows. "I am rather a force of Nature, aren't I?"

"Every woman is. Or potentially is," replies Dennis.

"D'accord!" sings Violet.

"Oh, Vi, darling, you've been pecking at your phrase book again, my little Tom-tit."

"Merci beau coup!" chirps Violet.

"But Dennis, I do hope I didn't permanently alienate you," says Christine, "I wouldn't want that. Particularly now that you are to be the father.."

"In due course, of course," adds Violet, gently rubbing her swollen nose.

"The father, of course, in due course, of course, of little tiny Isabella Victoria Gloria..."

"What a lovely name!" cries Mum, "Let us hope she's a girl."

"She will be," says Dennis.

"Twas beauty, killed the beast," reprises Dexter, nestling against sleeping Brad's comforting haunches in the back of the expertly vacuumed, tidy, compliments of he knows who, car seat. Rejection, thinks Dexter, more seriously than ever before, rejection is his cuppa. He might even have smiled if he'd been even a bit more sure of himself. Never mind, we'll see back in California, he thinks -- paraphrasing one of Christine's more sane serial pronouncements -- whether 'the longest journey does indeed begin with a single step'.

"It must have been hell for you, Dennis," continues Christine.

"Hell for me too," says Violet, studying her purpling nose in Christine's hand mirror.

"We know about you, dear," says Christine, "you've never been one to hide your moods under a bushel basket."

"Or my nose," sniffs Violet at her reflection.

"It was hell for me too," says Lars.

"Please!" says Christine, "I am attempting to sodding apologise! It was hell for us all!"

"It's been heaven for me!" says Mum.

Dennis smiles a perfect, accepting smile at them all; acceptance, even of his own miserable shortcomings, his myriad mini-failures. For he knows he has at least one great success. He has caused Lars to love him. If one consciously causes such things. Or is love self-starting? One has nothing to do with where it finds its mark? The lover simply is. The 'lovee' simply is. If this is the case, thinks Dennis, snared yet again in his own much-imagined inadequacy, then it is lucky for me because I probably would have botched that too.

"Hey, you guys," says Brad, sleepily pulling himself up from the car-seat. "We all love each other. Ain't that what counts? Love?"

Everyone turns towards Brad and nods a ho-hum, but puzzled nod.

"Ain't it love what counts? Ain't it, Dexter?"

"You are so right, dear boy," says Dexter, his utterly innocent hand just below the lederhosen on Brad's utterly desirable bare knee.

"Ain't it, Dennis? Ain't love what counts?"

"Of course it is," says Dennis. "No doubt about it. None whatever."

"Ain't it, Lars, love what counts?"

"Why not? Is a fact. Is good."

Bending over the seat and uncomfortably close to the back of Violet's neck: "Love is what counts, ain't it, Violet?"

"I suppose so," says Violet, not turning, "but you do act an idiot. And stop breathing down my neck."

"Ain't love what counts, Christine? Ain't it?"

"*Isn't* it. *Isn't* it love that counts." replies Christine, with a happy smile. "Of course, it is, honeybuns, love always counts."

"Yes, Brad, dear, It is love that counts," says Mum without even being asked.

"Yeah, it sure as heck is. You know what else? You guys know what else?"

"No!" they all call out united in boredom. "What else?"

"It is said that we are all of us God's creatures, ain't we?"

"So it is said, say all of us!" reply all.

"It is said that God, anyways, made us all in his own image, didn't he?"

"So it is said," say all, in increasing awe at this complete, nearly grammatically correct sentence.

"If there is such a thing as sin, it lies in our suppressing, not expressing, God's many-faceted nature, don't it?"

"Oh-My-God!" whispers Dexter, glowing with the purest, untainted, even divine love, "So life is, after all, a tale told by an idiot?"

"And we all know that..." Prompts Dennis, "We all know that 'A HLOT...' "

"A HLOT MAY DEPEND UPON EET!" cry all and break into gales of laughter, knowing in their various good hearts, compliments of a certain Miss Prism, that the good always ends happily and the bad unhappily. That is what fiction means.

"LISTEN EVERYONE! I'M NOT FINISHED!" cries Christine, as their mini-bus careens on towards the airport, "I was apologising, for God's sake! I was saying it must have been hell for us all, particularly you, Dennis."

"All's well that ends hell," says Dennis, "Anyways."

"He's right," says Lars, at the wheel, "He's right." His Dennis is a genius, soon to be recognised, and his epic novel might be published even sooner than we think -- if Dennis could just remember where he'd left it.

"D'accord!" says Violet about nothing in particular, and who wishes she'd taken another term of night-school French and more than two aspirins for her throbbing, ever more purpling nose.

"I know motherhood will agree with me," adds Christine, only now beginning to droop ever so slightly with the delayed fatigue of her fearsome Frenzy -- she plans to sleep on the plane back -- "But..." She pauses, smiles naughtily at all. "And it's a very big 'but'!"

"But?" says Violet.

"But?" says Dennis.

"But?" says Dexter.

"But?" says Lars.

"But?" says Brad -- who is listening.

"BUT?!" say all in unison.

"But there must be an EASIER way!" chimes Christine.

Then, after the briefest of pauses, Christine grins her very best, persuasive grin, mentally thanks her wisest of Mums, licks her little finger, wags it spunkily in the air, cries "Joke, everyone, joke!"

53

"I'm so happy!" says Dennis, watching the post-person's van disappear down their newly snow-plowed little road through an excellent snowstorm.

"Me too," says Lars who smiles and sets against a wall the special delivery, gargantuan, posterized photo they have just unwrapped. Duly depicted here are happy Christine and ecstatic Violet holding their tiny infant twins, a coffee-coloured boy, Lars Viktor, cunningly attired in Dennis's Mum's gift of pink infant-wear. And a tiny golden Isabella Viktoria (new spelling!) Gloria in a delightful blue ensemble, from the very same shop. Both infants wear Mum's hand-knitted booties and this same exulting Mum crowds close beside, displaying the empty 'Babykins' carry-bag in front of her, the very first trophy of her prescient grandmother-odyssey. Also, and importantly, Mum had recently received a proposal of marriage from the Swedish funfair manager who had arranged that last sumptuous dinner in Sweden and manages successful funfairs Europe-wide. They had met several times later, during his business trips to London. She is joyously considering his proposal.

Violet's mum would have been in the photo too but she e-mailed congratulations (a hefty bank deposit was also credited towards Isabella's education in Paris and Lars Viktor's tuition at a school of his choice). But this grandmother is still enjoying the Lottery's complimentary round the world cruise. Grandmother three, Lars's mum, will include a visit to Christine and Violet et al when she is next in London to design the décor for three luxury hotels.

Grandmother four, Christine's mum, recently remarried and on her fifth honeymoon at an undisclosed location, promises to return in time for the twins' first birthday party.

"But what will it all mean?" says Dennis.

Lars takes Dennis's hand. "What will it all mean, Denny? The children? All this? It will mean," says Lars with a grin, warmly remembering coming to Dennis's aid in that little sperm bank cubicle in Gothenburg, "It will mean whatever it will mean."

But there is yet more good news to happily digest. Lars's Ph.D has been granted and he and Dennis will soon attend the presentations at the University of Gothenburg. Also, Dexter seems to have at last located his other half, his somewhat older but distingué and terribly well-preserved plastic surgeon, he of Dexter's splendidly constructed new nose. As a wedding present -- since they are to dwell in the enlightened U.S.A. state of Massachusetts where such marriages are possible -- his fully licensed groom-to-be has promised totally free, eternal facial improvement (or as long as they both shall live).

It seems too, that the beautiful Brad has found a suitable metier as well. He is the hunky chief spokesperson for a new self-realization organization and travels from city to city, like, poetically describing his epiphany in a Swedish pine forest, like, particularly the part where that tiny voice, in answer to Brad's "I am so insignificant!" had very emphatically affirmed -- according to Dexter -- Brad's 'cri de cœur'.

Dennis twinkles, unusual for him as he hates the very sound of the word. He gazes out over drifting snow and the half-buried greenhouse that he, the usually late-riser, had inspected this very morning at that ungodly hour in a snowstorm, just before he served Lars his morning coffee and buttered (lots of it) toast in bed.
"I forgot to tell you, love, that the new tomatoes are finally blooming," says Dennis, turning towards his new office addition to continue his nearly completed epic novel, which incidentally, has already found a publisher, a generous advance payment, and does after all, seem epic indeed. How fortuitous it was to accidentally drop Mum's knitting basket at the airport and find the long lost floppy disk of his epic novel which had been used

as a spindle around which Mum had been winding her yarn for more years than she can remember.

To repeat, with absolutely no risk of redundancy, as Oscar Wilde's 'Miss Prism', in 'The Importance of Being Earnest' says: "The good ended happily and the bad, unhappily. That is what fiction means."

This is indeed good news. Particularly for Dennis's up and coming jolly epic novel where there is no 'bad' in sight -- not even of any kind, not even for ready money.